HEAVEN SENT?

"Joshua? Oh my lord, Joshua!" Abigail blinked. It was all so completely impossible. "But . . . but . . . you're dead!"

"Yeah? I had noticed that, Abbie."

A body would think that everything he'd been through—dying and all—would have changed him more.

But he still looked just like himself, all rangy and handsome and cocky. With dark, dark hair, and those eyes that were always so startlingly bright against his deeply tanned skin.

"What do you think?" He'd caught her looking, and he grinned at her, just like he had after the first time he kissed her. A gratified smile that said he knew exactly what wicked thoughts were popping around in her head—and liked them.

She refused to tell him that he looked pretty darned alive to her.

"Go away, Joshua. Just go away and leave me alone. And this time, stay away for good."

Books by Susan Kay Law

Journey Home
Traitorous Hearts
Reckless Angels
Home Fires
Heaven in West Texas

Published by HarperPaperbacks

Heaven in West Texas

 SUSAN KAY LAW

HarperPaperbacks
A Division of HarperCollinsPublishers

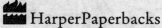HarperPaperbacks
A Division of HarperCollins*Publishers*
10 East 53rd Street, New York, N.Y. 10022-5299

This is a work of fiction. The characters, incidents, and
dialogues are products of the author's imagination and are not to
be construed as real. Any resemblance to actual events or
persons, living or dead, is entirely coincidental.

ISBN 0-06-108474-3

Cover illustration by Jon Paul

First HarperPaperbacks printing: January 1997

Printed in the United States of America

Visit HarperPaperbacks on the World Wide Web at
http://www.harpercollins.com/paperbacks

❖ 10 9 8 7 6 5 4 3 2 1

To Connie Brockway:

*Because she's an even better friend than
she is a writer, and that's going some;
because I no longer feel like I really missed
out on having a sister;
and because this whole darn book is
entirely her fault.*

Heaven in West Texas

Prologue

"*Aw, shit.* I'm dead, ain't I?"

"You are indeed."

The voice was smooth and compelling, and it sounded like it was coming from right inside his head. Joshua West couldn't locate the source any more than he was able to decide whether it was male or female.

He was enveloped in some sort of dense fog, so thick he could barely see his hand when he waved it in front of his face. But it wasn't the dreary gray of a regular fog; this was white and shimmery, like being inside a pearl. It glowed with a soft, pure light that seemed to come from all directions at once. He looked around, trying to get his bearings.

"Oh Lord." He quickly cupped his hands over his privates. "I'm naked!"

"You are at that."

"But. . . But . . ." Joshua tried to jump up in protest, but there was nothing for his feet to land on. He had no sense of up or down, and found himself spinning slowly in space, like a dandelion puff blown on a lazy breeze. Whirling around like that, it was too hard to keep his hands safely over his crotch, so he gave up. If they—whoever they were—were going to be offended, they should have let him keep his britches.

"There are no clothes here, Joshua."

"No clothes?"

"Joshua." The voice was warmer now; it sounded amused. "We have no *bodies.*"

"Oh." Weird; he wasn't getting dizzy at all. He tucked, delighted to find himself tumbling faster. "Is this. . . heaven?"

"Of course."

"Well, what do you know about that." He grinned. "Always thought I'd go the other way."

"That can still be arranged."

Joshua winced and quit spinning. "Now see here," he began, then stopped, thinking frantically. What could he say now that would help him? He'd never given much thought to the afterlife, but he was pretty darn sure he didn't want to go the other way.

The laughter bubbled from right out of the fog, loud and joyous and musical as a thousand magnificent bells pealing out at once. "Don't worry, Joshua. We save that other place for the truly irredeemable souls. The rest of you get to go back until you get it right." The voice paused, as if mulling it over. "I believe you are on your thirty-fifth or thirty-sixth try."

"Oh." Joshua tried to swallow, only to find he had no sense of his body at all—he didn't feel the bob of his Adam's apple up and down his throat, and, come to think of it, he couldn't feel himself breathing, either. "Are you. . . *Him?*"

"Him?"

"You know." He couldn't have said why he lowered

his voice to a whisper; it just seemed like the thing to do.
"The Big Boss?"

"Oh, you mean the Lord. No, I'm not 'Him.' I simply
assist wherever I can."

"Do you know what happens to me next? I mean, do
I go back right away? Who do I get to be this time?"
This could be tricky. He didn't much cotton to the idea
of going back as a jailbird or traveling preacher or some
other poor sap.

"Not quite yet."

"What, then?"

"Joshua," the voice boomed, taking on a distinct tone
of command, "we have need of your assistance."

"Uh, sure, sure." What choice did he have? This was
not exactly his home territory. Best to keep his head
down and go along with everything. "Anythin' you say."

"We are a bit shorthanded at the moment. The war
took quite a bit out of us, you know."

"You ain't the only one."

"Yes. And so, we have a bit of an assignment for
you."

"An assignment?" They'd selected him for an
important assignment? Hey, maybe he hadn't made
nearly as much of a mess of his life as he'd thought, if
they were asking for his help. "What do you want me
to do?"

"There's someone on earth who's in quite a bit of
danger. She needs someone to help her out and keep her
safe. Your job will simply be to watch over her."

She? He'd thought he was going to burn in hell, and
instead he was going to get to watch over a beautiful
damsel in distress? At this rate, being dead might not be
bad at all. "You mean like a guardian angel?"

"Let's not get carried away." The light around Joshua
intensified. "Angels have a few responsibilities that

you're not quite ready for. Think of it more like a pinch hitter."

"A pinch hitter?"

"Oh yes, that term hasn't come into use yet, has it? In any case, you'll be sort of a substitute. . . helping spirit."

"Yeah, okay." Angel, spirit, whatever. How tough could it be? "Who is she?"

The white fog swirled. Then slowly it separated like a stage curtain, and there she was, silhouetted in the shimmery light.

"God damn it!" He ducked as soon as the words burst out, expecting lightning to strike him instantly for his blasphemy.

"It's all right," the voice said soothingly. "On the rather lengthy list of your sins, that's a fairly minor one."

She was tall and skinny and bony—though she'd always insisted she was "willowy." Her nose was too long, her mouth was too wide, and her face was too narrow. He knew all that—always had—and, despite it all, she was still the sexiest thing he had ever laid eyes on.

Considering the fact that he was pretty sure his heart wasn't beating, he didn't have any idea how his body could be doing what it was doing right now, but it was having the same reaction it always had to Abigail Grier.

"Uh-uh. No way."

"Joshua," the voice chided, "she needs your help."

"She didn't need me when I was alive. She sure as he— heck don't need me when I'm dead!"

"She does."

"Abigail don't need anybody's help. She never has, and she's made it pretty darn clear."

"She needs help this time. She really is in danger."

"Can't you just. . . wave your hand and fix everything?"

"It doesn't quite work like that."

"Well, you're just gonna have to get someone else." This probably wasn't the best time for him to get stubborn, but he just could not go back there. The woman had kicked him in the gut once, and he wasn't getting anywhere near her ever again.

"There's no one else suitable, Joshua. You know the area, you know her, and you care about her."

"I do not care about her!"

The vision of Abigail tilted her head and smiled, a sad, brave little smile, and his chest started to hurt. That was exactly why he couldn't go back: he was a zillion miles away, and dead to boot, and she could *still* make him hurt. "I ain't going back there!" he shouted.

Abigail disappeared in a blinding instant of silver light. With a violent, rolling *boom* the pearly fog went black and closed around him.

"Joshua, you have no choice."

1

She'd started dreaming about Joshua again.

Not that it was all that unusual. But Abigail thought she'd rid herself of that stupid, useless habit six months ago. And even then, her dreams had never before been quite so. . . well, *naked*.

She was *not* going to think about Joshua anymore, darn it. She was at a party. She was going to have fun. The sneaky little thought at the back of her mind that she hadn't had fun since the day Joshua left was just plain wrong.

Around her swirled nearly every person who lived within three days' ride of B.J. Hallenbeck's ranch, maybe all of forty or fifty people. She knew why they were all there. Everyone had been dying of curiosity to see Hallenbeck's house ever since he swept into the area more than three years ago, just after the war, and bought every last one of old Harold Biederman's twenty-one thousand acres.

He'd then toppled Biederman's perfectly good stone

house and carted in enough wood from Lord-only-knew-where to build himself the biggest ranch house anybody in the vicinity of Barrens, Texas had ever seen. Wood, for heaven's sake. The whole region had been abuzz with the extravagance of it ever since, and the buzzing just kept getting louder when hardly anyone ever got invited to the place.

Abigail wondered just what made ol' B.J. suddenly decide to get so neighborly.

She had to admit that he put on a pretty good show, though. The sprawling ranch house shone brand-spanking white in the afternoon sun. A porch ran the full length of the front, providing welcome shade for the men who stood, gulping tumblers of whiskey, and watched their more unfortunate friends who'd been dragged out to dance by their wives.

If she didn't know better, she'd have thought everyone was having one whale of a good time. They sure had wide grins plastered all over their faces. But their laughter was just a little too loud, the timing a shade off, and Abigail knew they were all just as anxious as she was.

She waved a hand in front of her face, trying without much success to stir up a bit of breeze. Though she'd tightly braided and pinned her hair right before she'd ridden over, some had escaped and frizzled around the edges of her hairline, just like it always did.

If only it wasn't so hot, she thought. But she had a lot better things to fret over than the heat.

"A bit warm today, ain't it?"

"B.J." Abigail acknowledged her host as he stepped to her side. Immediately, she stopped flapping at the air and let her arm drop. "Do you think so? I thought it was rather pleasant."

"Whatever you say." He grinned down at her, his big, let's-humor-the-little-lady smile, made all the worse by the fact that Abigail wasn't used to having to look up to anybody. Especially when it was so obvious that person was looking down on her.

B.J. Hallenbeck, richest man around. Nobody knew for sure what the initials stood for, and speculation—especially among the women—was rampant. Bold, big, beautiful, blond—B.J. was all those things. Because it was perfectly clear he was aware of all his finer qualities, and made sure everyone else was too, and because the man didn't know how to take *no* for an answer, Abigail privately added a few more *b* words to describe B.J.: he was not only a bore, he was one heck of a bother.

"Enjoying the party?"

"Of course. Kind of you to invite me."

"Good. I'd hoped you would. Considering the trouble everyone's having."

Abigail warily eyed his beaming face. Surely he hadn't orchestrated this entire party just to show how well he was doing when the rest of them weren't.

Still, it was possible. There wasn't much B.J. Hallenbeck could do that would surprise her.

"So, how are things going over there on the Rolling G?" he asked, friendly as a gambler trying to sneak up on a new mark.

"Fine. Just fine." Abigail forced a cheerful grin, wondering why they were even trying to pretend. B.J. knew as well as she did just how things were going over at the Rolling G: lousy. Just like every other ranch in the region. The drought didn't pick and choose its victims. It hit all of them the same.

"Glad to hear it." He gave a hearty laugh. "Of course, it would be going fine, you having such a good waterhole and all. A piece o' luck, that."

Here it comes, she thought. Now B.J. would ask the same questions he always did, she'd give the same answers, and they'd both go on their way. "My father's a smart man. He chose his land carefully."

"Sure thing." B.J. tucked his thumbs into the wide, brown leather belt that whipped tightly around his waist. "I didn't see him here today, though. Time was, Davis hardly ever missed a party."

"He's just busy on the ranch. Lots to do. You know how it is."

"You sure that's all it is?" B.J. narrowed his eyes a bit. "He's not feeling under the weather or anythin', is he?"

For a moment, she wondered if he suspected anything. Surely not. B.J. was a lot of things, but perceptive wasn't one of them.

"Oh no," she said airily, "I just couldn't drag him away. You know how he is about that ranch."

"Sure. Too bad he couldn't take a little break, though."

So her father's absences were starting to be noticed. She wondered how much longer she could keep it a secret.

It had been several months since he'd been well enough to leave their own land. Her father was a fiercely proud man. She couldn't risk him having a bad spell in public and seeing the pity in one person's eyes. It would hurt him far too much.

"It's a nice little place." B.J. pronounced the words "nice" and "little" in about the same tones Mrs. Mallery would have said "dog dung."

Abigail wished he'd just get it over with. Pretending everything was fine and dandy was starting to make her stomach hurt.

But then, just about everything did these days. Thinking about the drought made her stomach hurt. Trying to take care of her father, worrying about the price of three-year-old steers falling all the way down to nine dollars a head, fighting with her brother—they all made her belly ache.

About the only thing that didn't hurt was working, so she tried to keep herself busy until she pitched into bed at night. Heck, she wished she was working right now, but it would have looked too suspicious if she'd turned Hallenbeck's invitation down completely. That, and her brother, Marcus, really needed a chance to get off the ranch and be with other children once in a while.

Marcus! Why hadn't she thought of this excuse sooner? "I'm truly sorry, Mr. Hallenbeck, but I really must go and find my brother. I haven't seen him for quite some time, and—"

"Now, now." He patted her shoulder. "I thought that was all settled. It's B.J. to my friends, remember? And I don't think Marcus really needs your help right about now."

He pointed to the far side of the house, where Marcus was pitching rocks with his best friend, Billy Mallery. Not more than ten feet away, near a clump of gnarled, near-dead scrub oak, stood a cluster of girls, giggling and whispering behind their hands. At twelve, Marcus looked like he wasn't quite sure if he wanted to run toward the girls or away from them. Either way, she was pretty sure that in this, at least, B.J. was right. Marcus wouldn't welcome her company right now.

"Let's dance," B.J. suggested.

"Dance?" They weren't supposed to dance. B.J. was supposed to badger her about selling her water rights, tell her that the work was too much for her, and make her an outrageous offer "for her own good." Then she was supposed to turn him down, he was supposed to get all angry and make a few comments about women who think they know something about ranching, and it was supposed to be all over—until the next time.

Nowhere in there was there anything about dancing.

"Uh . . . no, thank you. I'm not all that fond of dancing."

"All women like to dance." He waved at the musicians, who slowed their pace into something that she thought was supposed to be a waltz, though it was kind of hard to tell. "Evelina," maybe. Then he grabbed on to her elbow and towed her out to the dance floor like a reluctant yearling.

She really hated dancing. She knew she looked gawky and tall and out of place on the dance floor, and no matter what she did she never seemed to get the rhythm quite right. The only person she'd ever been able to dance with was Joshua. He moved so smoothly he somehow covered up all her awkwardness. His timing was perfect, and being held in his arms always distracted her enough that she forgot how stupid she felt bobbing along, trying to follow the music.

Too bad he'd turned out to be such a rat—even before he'd gone and gotten himself killed.

"Ouch!" B.J. winced and stutter-stepped his feet away from hers. "You really don't know how to dance, do you?"

"I warned you."

"Shoulda known. Don't know why I keep expectin' you to be like other women." He smiled down at her, and she almost started counting his big white teeth. Certainly he had more than other people. "Now then, did you pass that last offer on to your daddy?"

Abigail nearly sighed in relief. Finally he'd gotten to the point. "Yes. The answer is still the same, B.J. It doesn't really matter how much you offer us. I'm really sorry, but we simply don't have enough water at the spring to share. If the drought keeps up, we'll barely have enough for our own stock."

"Well, I'll just buy the whole damn thing then! Double what I offered you before."

B.J. Hallenbeck would never know that half of her almost wished she could take him up on his offer. That kind of money would keep them all for some time, and maybe even put Marcus through school, to boot. But if there was one thing she knew for certain, it was that losing the Rolling G would be the death of her father. His family and his ranch were all he ever cared about, and he'd never really separated the two. His ranch *was* his family, and his family was his ranch.

"No. You might as well just stop asking, B.J. We're not gonna change our minds."

B.J.'s face started turning red as a fresh-cooked beet. She knew he was working up a good head of steam, and wondered just how long he was going to holler at her this time.

Then he threw back his head and burst out laughing. "I'll give you one thing, girl. You sure do drive a hard bargain."

"Excuse me?"

"I gotta have that water. So it's all right, I give in. I'll marry you."

2

Abigail leaned against a post that supported the porch and gratefully gulped sugary lemonade, a slurry of undissolved crystals lurking in the bottom of the glass.

It had taken her a full five minutes to escape from B.J., and she still wasn't sure she convinced him that she'd said "no." He was absolutely positive that old maid Abigail Grier had finally found herself a way to catch a husband, and that way was owning the only spring-fed waterhole within hundreds of miles.

"Thanks for the lemonade, Horace. I needed that." She'd run headlong into Horace as soon as she'd sprinted away from B.J., and she was happy to see him as always. The Knicker family had settled on the land just to the east of the Rolling G years ago, and they'd been friends ever since.

"B.J. looked none too happy out there while the two of you were dancing. At least, not at the end there."

"Is B.J. ever any too happy when he's talking to me?"

"Guess not." Horace shuffled his feet and jerked a thumb over his shoulder. "You wanna go for a walk? I can't listen to this music any longer."

"Yes, thanks." At least if she weren't there, B.J. wouldn't take it into his head to suddenly announce their engagement. Well, probably not. She wouldn't put it past him to try.

They walked until the music faded to a distant echo. The afternoon sun had lowered, throwing their shadows long and distorted ahead of them. Dry buffalo grass crunched under their feet.

"So," Horace said quietly, "things going okay?"

"'Bout as good as could be expected."

"Yeah." He nodded his head sadly, his shoulders hunched. "Our creek's almost dry."

"I'm real sorry to hear that, Horace." She was. If there'd been any way she could think of to spare some water, she would have. She was desperately afraid there wasn't even going to be enough for her family's ranch. "How's the water in the cistern holding out?"

"There's enough, for the moment."

"If you get low on drinking water, you know you can come to me right away." Along with the pond, the Rolling G also had a drinking well, an almost unimaginable luxury in this part of Texas. And though she was having to go down farther and farther every time she fetched water, if her neighbors were out of drinking water, she'd open the well to them, too. There was nothing else to be done.

"I do know that, Abigail. Thanks."

The brittle grass crackled behind her, a sharp, unnatural sound, and Abigail started. "Did—did you hear that?"

"What?"

"I thought I heard something."

"Nope." Horace craned his neck. "Nothing.

There's no place out here for anyone to hide, is there?"

"I guess not." She usually wasn't the nervous type. All her worrying must be catching up with her, if she was starting to hear things.

"What's the matter? You afraid Hallenbeck's gonna follow you and start hollering at you again?"

"Something like that."

"Abigail." His smile faded and his voice grew serious. "I really need to talk to you."

"Go ahead, Horace."

"You know we made pretty good money last spring when we drove the cattle north to sell."

That was the newest thing, moving Texas cattle north in search of a better price. Abigail had heard that steers were going for as much as five or six times what they did down here. It was too bad she hadn't had enough hands to send some of her herd along, or enough money to pay to get them moved. Maybe next year.

"I don't have the kind of money Hallenbeck has. You know that. But I'd sure like it if you'd give me at least the chance to make you a decent offer."

"Oh, Horace. I really wish I could." Horace was handsome enough in his own way, his face boyish if a little round, and he looked so crestfallen he reminded her of Marcus. "If I could sell to anyone, you know I would sell to you."

"I thought it was worth a shot." Horace shoved his fists in his pockets and kicked at a stand of brown grass. "Well, if that's the way it is, Abbie. . . maybe we could—" he gulped "—maybe we could get married," he said in a rush, making it sound as if it was all one word.

"Married?" What had gotten into everyone today? In all of her twenty-five years, she'd never had even one proposal, and now she'd received two in one day? She couldn't quite decide whether to be insulted or amused. Of course, at least she'd gotten a few hundred propositions in her time. Even if they were all from the same man, she figured that still counted.

"Horace," she said carefully, trying to find the right words. She needed this refusal to be a bit more gentle than the last one. "I—"

"Wait, before you answer. . . I know you were kinda hung up on that West fellow, but he never was good enough for you, even though you never listened to me when I told you, and he's long gone now, anyway, and—"

Joshua again. Why could she never get free of him? She'd spent six months torn between heartbroken and furious when he'd left her, and another six months mourning his death. She was *not* going to let him upset her life again.

"Stop right there. Joshua West was a no-account, worthless scoundrel and even if he *was* still alive I'd have nothing to do with him ever again."

"Really?" Horace looked shocked and pleased. "I'm glad to hear you finally came to your senses. I always knew what a—pardon me, but there's no other word for him— bastard he was, of course, but—"

"Oh, no!" she cried as her arm flew forward. The remaining lemonade spewed right out of her glass and onto Horace, soaking right down the front of his pants, darkening the walnut-brown wool. It looked like he'd just wet himself.

"I'm so sorry, I don't know what happened, it felt like something just knocked my elbow, I just—"

"It's okay, Abigail." Horace stared down at himself glumly. He shook one leg, and pale yellow lemonade dripped into the dust. "I just hope that's not your answer."

"Horace, I—" She stopped, listening carefully. "Do you hear someone laughing?"

He tilted his head. "I don't hear a thing."

"Hmm. I could have sworn I heard someone laughing."

If Abigail Grier was in trouble, he'd eat his hat. If he still had a hat.

Joshua had gotten there only a few hours ago. They'd rushed him down here as if Abigail's life were in immediate danger. He'd kind of hoped for more instruction than "you'll soon discover your powers" and "help her."

After all that fuss and hurry, what did he find when he got here? Abbie in the middle of a party, having a grand old time. She'd been dancing, for Christ's sake, when he used to practically have to beg her to go out dancing with him. And the whole time she'd looked so damn good it was all he could do not to find out exactly what his nonexistent body was capable of.

And then, to top it all off, he'd had to listen to not one but two men propose to her! Hell! He'd knocked that lemonade all over Knicker before he even realized what he was doing. Knicker always did hang around Abbie too much for Joshua's taste; the only thing that surprised him was that Horace had taken this long to swoop down and move in.

What did they expect him to do? Act as a "helping spirit"? Crap. Abbie didn't need his help any more than she ever did. And it still hurt, damn it. Wasn't a body supposed to stop hurting when it was dead?

Well, then, so he wasn't exactly a body. A spirit, a ghost—what was the difference, anyway?

If Joshua was going to have to hang around that woman's pitiful, dusty ranch, he was darn well going to *haunt* her.

3

The slamming of her bedroom door jerked her awake.

Abigail bolted from her bed and dashed through the house to the front door. Even in the pitch-dark she managed to dart around the table and chairs without so much as a bump. She'd made this fast, panicked nighttime trip often enough that she no longer needed to see where she was going.

She skidded to a stop at the front door. Closed? It was still shut?

Dropping to her knees, she groped for the leather straps nailed to the door and frame six inches from the floor. They were still securely knotted. Good.

She rocked back and sucked in hot, dry air. Every time this happened, she always felt like she stopped breathing until she knew everything was okay.

Moving slower now, she stood and made her way to the other bedroom. The door was wide open to catch any stray breeze, and she stepped in quietly, trying not to wake them if everything was as calm as it appeared.

The single window was thrown open. A tiny bit of sickly yellow moonlight leaked in and revealed the two beds within.

Her father still slept in the spooled bed that he'd shared with her mother. He was tucked far against the right side, leaving a wide, empty space. He'd always said his wife had claimed more than her fair share of the bed, and, even after all this time, he'd never gotten in the habit of using more room.

The bed hugged the far wall, and her brother's mattress lay on the floor, wedged in the only space left in the small room. Marcus slept sprawled on his back, his mouth slack and wide, and he looked impossibly young and relaxed in a way he seldom did any longer when he was awake. His boyhood was disappearing right before her eyes.

A good night, both of them peacefully settled and asleep. A night rare enough that she stood there for a moment and savored the sight of both of her men, safe and comfortable.

So her father had not slammed her door, after all. But what, then? The house was quiet.

Too quiet; all her life, the constant soughing of the wind had been her companion. Sometimes fierce and wild, sometimes gentle and sweet. But always there, its song a harmony line accompanying her day. For the last few days, though, it had been eerily still.

She returned to the front room, which served as parlor and kitchen for the family as well as a mess hall for all the hands. Her father had built the house, a simple rectangle built of local stone plastered together, soon after he'd married her mother and claimed the land.

She leaned out a window, the plaster rough and

slightly cool beneath her forearms. The slice of moon hung low, almost obscured by the haze of dust that clung to the horizon. She never thought that she would have missed the wind, but she would have welcomed it now. Anything to cool her off a bit.

What had closed her door, then? It had to be the wind. Just her luck; she must have missed the only breath of breeze in days.

She eyed the sky again. The Big Dipper had dropped below the north star. Must be coming up on three thirty. Time to get to work. The hands—all three of them, though she could remember when the Rolling G had boasted a full dozen year-round—would be here, expecting breakfast, at four. She had no more time for gazing at the night. She had men to feed.

The scratch of the match echoed strangely in the hushed room. The coal oil lantern burst to life, throwing undulating shadows on the dim, cream-white walls. She set the lamp on the pine plank table, battered and scarred from years of feeding hungry cowboys with more appetite than manners, its flaws hidden by a red-and-white checked oilcloth.

"If only I could cook without heating the stove," she mumbled, then clamped her jaw shut. Talking to herself was a habit she seemed to have developed of late. If one of the hands had come in right that moment, he'd probably wonder if her father's illness was rubbing off and she was starting to get a little touched herself.

A small strip of bacon rind served for kindling. She added a few cowchips and the fire caught easily. One good thing about living on a ranch—they wasted little money on fuel. Plenty of "prairie coal" at hand.

She filled a tin two-thirds of the way with flour, pushing a shallow well into the center. The pale sourdough starter had risen high overnight, threatening to puff out of its crock. She dumped half into the flour and replenished the rest before returning it to its shelf.

As soon as she'd added a little soda dissolved in warm water and a sprinkle of salt, she began to work in the flour. She'd made sourdough biscuits every morning for as long as she could remember. The work required no more thought than counting to ten. Which was a good thing; she was too tired to think this morning.

She hadn't gotten much rest. She always slept lightly, ready to awaken at the slightest warning sound. But last night had been worse than usual.

It was that damned Joshua West again. Talking about him with Horace yesterday had stirred up too many memories. She'd dreamt about dancing with Joshua, him moving with that lanky, cowboy, loose-hipped grace that was always so much a part of him. He could walk across a room and make a woman start to sweat. Worse, he'd always known it.

In the dream, he hadn't stopped dancing, even as he'd stripped her right out of her clothes. Just swayed, back and forth, as his body brushed hers and his hands started playing their own rhythm on her skin. She'd awakened with a start, her heart beating too fast, half certain she could hear him whispering "Abbie."

Oh, it simply had to be the heat and drought that had her thinking silly things. She'd gotten over Joshua long ago.

She tilted the pan, scraping out the sticky dough.

The low moan came from nowhere and everywhere at once, keening inside her head, soft, low-pitched, eerie. She jumped, and the dough plopped out onto the floured table, landing with a splat. Flour flew up on a whiff of air, dusting her arms.

What was *that*?

From the open door of her father's bedroom came a

long, rumbling snore, choked off with a hoarse snort like an annoyed boar.

Her heartbeat slowed. How ridiculous of her to be so jumpy. It just went to show—she'd just *thought* about Joshua, and all of a sudden she was as skittish as a wild filly. It would simply never do.

At least she'd never be tempted to anything more than think about him ever again. His dying had relieved her of that burden—the rotten scoundrel.

She attacked the dough with a vengeance.

Once she'd finished kneading, she went back to her bedroom to dress. It always seemed silly to her to cover herself up with stifling layers of petticoats when it was hot enough to wither a fence post, but she wasn't taking any chances on the hands catching her in her nightdress. She'd lost enough ground on being ladylike as it was. Under no circumstances was she giving up any more.

The oven was heated by the time she returned to the kitchen. She pinched off lumps of sourdough and plopped them in a pan slicked with melted grease, turning each one so the surface was shiny and smooth with fat.

There. That should be enough, though it never failed to surprise her the number of biscuits they put away.

"Abigail!" The bellow was followed by loud thumping on the door. "Abigail!"

Sledge was early this morning, she mused. And, from the sound of his shouting, hungrier than an old bear coming out of hibernation.

"Coming," she called, rushing to unlatch the door and tug it open. "Sledge, you don't have to shout. *My* hearing's—"

"The remuda's gone," he interrupted as soon as the door opened.

"Wh . . . what?"

"Horses are gone."

Sledge had been her father's lead hand since before she was born. He really did remind her of a bear: he was grizzled, gray, tougher than old leather, and just as mean as a wounded grizzly if the situation called for it. She loved him like an uncle.

His dusty, woolen black hat was crushed on his head, and he puffed from the exertion of running to the house. That alone told her just how serious the situation must be. Sledge rode. He never walked if he could help it, and for him to run from the bunkhouse to the house for breakfast was absolutely unheard of.

"Okay, Sledge, back up. What happened?"

"Went down early to pick out a mount for today. Thought I'd scout north for some fresh fodder—y'know it's getting grazed down in all the places close to the waterhole. And they were all gone."

More trouble. They'd had more close calls, near disasters, and small crises this summer than they'd had in the previous five put together. She wasn't sure how much more she could take.

"Could you tell what happened?" she asked.

Sledge shrugged. "Fence is down."

"Yeah." Not surprising, really. Their corral wasn't exactly the sturdiest thing.

"Are they *all* gone, Sledge?"

"Nope." The faint thinning of his mouth was as close as Sledge ever got to a smile. "Buttercup's there."

Abigail gave a deep sigh. "She would be."

Buttercup was a tough little dun mare. They'd bought her five years ago with the intention of breeding her, for, though she was a bit mule-hipped, she was as bright and tireless as any horse in the entire state.

She was also mean, and she hated males. Enough so that, after the first two stallions who'd tried to cover her had limped away, bleeding and battered, they'd quickly abandoned the idea of breeding her.

Buttercup didn't like human men any better, but they learned slower than the stallions. She'd thrown a full half-dozen hands before they'd finally given up. Women, however, she would tolerate—barely—on her back.

They kept Buttercup at the Rolling G only because, with her disposition, she was absolutely worthless on the market. Also, if she was in a good mood, and Abigail was riding, she was the best cutting horse they had.

"Guess you're ridin' today, Abigail."

"Don't you laugh at me, Sledge. If I'm riding, you're footin' it, and we both know how much you love that."

"Better that than ridin' that hell-horse."

"Okay, roust Lippy and get him started patching the fence back together. Then you and Pecos head out and start hunting for the horses. Everything else'll have to wait today."

"You comin' out?"

"Of course." She sighed deeply. This was going to be a very long day. "After I wake up Marcus to help."

"But what about—"

"Have Lippy check on him every now and then. He'll be okay by himself for a little while." He would have to be. She wouldn't think about any other possibility, and it wasn't as if she had any other choices at the moment.

Marcus woke slowly, as he always did. She had to shake his shoulder three times and whisper-shout his name into his ear twice before he mumbled and rolled over, his eyes blinking sleepy and slow. Abigail would be will-ing to bet he'd stayed up too late last night, reading by candlelight. She caught him at it now and again, and ordered him to stop, but he never did.

"Abbie?" he mumbled.

"Got to get up, Marcus."

"Huh?" His eyes flew open and he jerked upright. "Pa? Is he—"

"Shh. He's fine. The horses got out. I need you to come help round them up."

Marcus groaned and rubbed a hand over his face. "Aw, Abbie, can't you—"

"Don't start with me, Marcus," she said, more sharply than she'd intended.

His face fell, and, just like that, he looked like the boy he was instead of the young man he was always trying to be.

"But how'm I supposed to catch 'em?"

"Rope them like everyone else does, I guess."

"You know I'm a piss-poor roper. Probably get my ownself all tangled and knotted up instead, just like the last time."

"Marcus!" She softened her tone, then gently touched one of the red-brown curls that sprang around his forehead. "I don't much care how you catch them, Marcus. Use all those brains you got in there. There's some sugar and a few old carrots in the kitchen. Be sneaky—you're good at that."

A reluctant smile tipped his mouth. "Expect I can outthink a horse, huh?"

"I'm sure of it. Most of them, anyway."

He gave a put-upon sigh. "But, Abbie—"

"Marcus." She rested her hand on his shoulder. "It's time to get to work."

4

Abigail sure hadn't changed much, Joshua thought.

Her hair still gleamed in bright spirals, shiny as a new penny. Freckles still dotted her skin, like nutmeg dusted thickly over rich cream, freckles that always put him in mind of spending long, lazy, sun-bright afternoons in bed counting every single one of them.

And, as he'd watched her whip around the kitchen fixing breakfast, she moved the same way. Like a fresh-sprung foal, all joints and long bones that never seemed to quite go in the same direction at once. To an ignorant person, that foal might look none too pretty. But the eyes of an expert horseman like Joshua saw only the tantalizing promise of grace.

About the only difference he could see was that her face had the faintest beginning of a line or two, around her mouth and the corners of her eyes. Funny that wrinkles were supposed to make a woman look ugly. These just made her look like she was right on the verge of a smile.

There was no denying he was doing a truly pitiful job of haunting her.

It wasn't entirely his fault. Cripes, it had taken him half the night before he'd figured out how to slam the dad-blamed door. The first several dozen times he'd tried, his arm had gone right through it.

He should have known that something so little wouldn't frighten Abbie. The woman just didn't scare easy.

A good chunk of west-central Texas still wasn't settled, because the Comanche were making it mighty hard. This area had been filled up only because of the nearby protection of Fort Barrens. Not long after he'd met her, the Indians had been raising more than a little ruckus, and rumors blazed like wildfire that they were going to attack near the fort after all. Most of the settlers had been scared out of their boots, and more than a few had temporarily retreated into the safety of the fort.

But Abbie—Abbie had just loaded up her daddy's old carbine, propped it by the front door, and gone about her business without so much as a shiver. So what had given him the idea that slamming a door and mooing in her ear like a sick calf was going to spook her?

Still, for a moment he'd thought it had. For sure she'd bolted out of bed quick enough. But she'd soon settled down, apparently deciding nothing was wrong. He'd figured that maybe enough noise might make her rethink that a bit.

Somehow, he'd gotten the impression that, though she couldn't see him, she could hear him a little—at least, every time he'd whispered to her while she was sleeping, she stirred and flopped over. But he'd barely had enough time to work up a nice, scary moan before old Sledge came charging in and interrupted him, and she was still jawing with him in the doorway.

How was he supposed to haunt her if she was too busy to notice his attempts?

Sledge left, and she tiptoed into her pa's bedroom. Joshua followed her, watching while she woke up her brother, and he almost got right spooked himself when he got a good look at the kid. How could he have grown so much in six months?

Joshua frowned. Marcus was complaining, instead of jumping at the chance to help his sister, who'd raised him from the time he was little, and who, from what Joshua'd seen last night and this morning, had taken on more than her fair share of running the place.

Hell, what was he thinking? He was having a much harder time than he'd expected breaking old habits. Why was he worrying about Abigail, anyway? What did he care if she was looking a little worn down around the edges?

This was the woman who'd turned him down cold, he reminded himself. Who, when he'd asked her to come away with him, had said "no" so quick he had to ask her to repeat it twice before it finally sank in. And she'd said it just as fast, just as final, just as cold, every single time. Like his offer meant no more to her than a slimy chunk of rotten beef.

He trailed her back through the house, Abigail muttering under her breath the whole way.

The sun was coming up now, lightening her bedroom enough for him to see clearly. It gave him a jolt to realize, as well as he'd thought he'd known her—though he'd turned out to be really wrong about that, too—he'd never seen where she slept. He admitted to a bit of lingering curiosity.

The room was small, tidy, and simple, with bare floors, an uncurtained window thrown wide, and a thin mattress laid across a spare frame with a metal headboard. A few faded dresses hung limp on the hooks hammered into one wall.

He had to admit, whenever he'd imagined Abbie's bedroom, the picture he'd conjured up had been somewhat more. . . decadent. At least her bed was still messed up, the sheets rumpled and the colorful quilt tossed aside, hanging on to the mattress only by one tiny corner. It looked like a good tussle had taken place there and the owner hadn't gotten around to neatening it up yet. Hell, if it was his and Abbie's bedroom, like he'd once thought it was going to be, there'd be no point in making the bed up, because they'd be mussing it up again in no time.

Two flattened pillows propped against each other at the head of the bed, neatly embroidered in bright turkey-red. He read the inscriptions—I Slept and Dreamed That Life Was Beauty, on one, I Woke and Found That Life Is Duty, on the other—and burst out laughing. If those were Abigail's sentiments, maybe he'd had a lucky escape after all.

Abigail stopped pawing through the trunk at the foot of the bed and cocked her head, as if listening for something. Joshua shut up. Laughter—even from a dead man—probably wasn't going to have the terrifying effect he wanted.

She yanked out some clothes and tossed them on the bed, closing the trunk with a thud.

And then she started to strip.

Joshua jumped back so quick that he sailed right through the wall and ended up back in the main room.

Leaving her alone to change would be the gentlemanly thing to do. But though he'd been a lot of things—an orphan, a cowboy, a drifter, a soldier, and now dead—he'd never even tried to be a gentleman. There'd seemed no point in it. And anyway, he reasoned, he was supposed to be watching over her. How could he do that from clear in the next room?

By the time he got back her dress was down around her bony ankles and she'd gone to work on her petticoats. As she bent, the morning sun settled on her, burnishing her hair like spun copper. Her shoulders were bare, and the pale skin glowed in the light. Spice-over-cream skin, just like he remembered.

A little twinge kicked over in his belly. He ignored it. For sure it wasn't passion. He wasn't fool enough to keep lusting after a woman who didn't want him. And it certainly wasn't guilt for watching her. After all, even if he'd never exactly *seen* all the skin she was baring, he sure as heck had felt nearly every inch of it at one time or another.

Abigail was down to her chemise and drawers now. The shirt she threw on, saggy blue cotton that hung well past her hips, looked like might once have belonged to her father. She hopped on one leg and stuck the other one into a stiff pair of blue denims.

Tugging the pants up to her hips made the loose legs of her drawers bunch up around her thighs.

"Damn it!" she said. "I hate wearing britches."

This time Joshua clamped down hard on his tongue to keep from laughing, a tactic he figured would have been a whole lot more effective if it actually hurt when he bit himself.

Damn it, she'd said. He could hardly believe it. So *this* was what she did when there was no one around to hear. All the time he'd known her, he'd never heard her swear, not even when she'd had every reason to. He used to tease her about it, and she'd always maintained that no lady ever let one of "those" words pass her lips. He'd never been able to figure out how she managed to avoid the habit, spending most of her time with cowmen whose every third word was a cuss. And here she'd probably been turning the air blue the whole time in private!

"She-et." She wiggled her little butt, shaking down the legs more comfortably, and looked down at herself with disgust. "Some lady I look to be." She knotted a scrap of printed red cotton around her neck and headed out for the range.

Lord, he'd missed Texas.

The tiny rise he sat on was the remnant of an old wash, long surrendered to the prairie. He checked once to see that Abbie was still in sight—she was, galloping madly after the spirited little horse she'd been chasing for the last twenty minutes—and he settled back comfortably, propping himself on his elbows.

He'd followed her out to the corral, thinking that would be a prime time to haunt Abbie; he'd just make sure she had one heck of a time saddling up. But Buttercup was the only horse available, and it seemed like it would have been downright, well, mean-spirited to try anything then. That thrice-damned mare probably did a more thorough job of haunting everyone on this ranch than he ever could. She'd broken three of his ribs when he'd tried to show off for Abbie by riding the mangy beast, and he could swear his butt still hurt from the last time she'd thrown him.

He'd figured he would think of something better out on the range. But then he'd gotten out here, and caught sight of all those miles and miles of seared brown grass, and that great big sky, where a man could see as far as he cared to dream, and decided he'd just look at it all for a little while instead. It had been such an awfully long time.

The sky was almost perfectly clear, a blue so bright

that there really was nothing to compare it to except itself. Only a few high clouds, like milk dribbled across the sky, marred its smooth sweep. The sun was huge, white-hot, and he tipped his head back, waiting to feel that warmth on his face.

Nothing. He felt nothing.

The wind that had been absent kicked in suddenly. He could hear it, rustling and whispering through the dry grass. He could see it, bending the stalks in a quick ripple and whipping stray curls around Abbie's head as she chased the loose horse. But, when he turned northwest, into the wind, no rush of air brushed his skin. The wind had no more effect on his body than the heat the last few days had—and he knew it must be blisteringly hot, for, when Abigail had bridled her horse that morning, she'd dunked the bit in water first to keep from burning Buttercup's mouth.

A tiny, worried little ache started at the back of his throat.

He sucked in, grabbing as big a gulp of air as he could manage. He'd missed the smell of Texas almost more than anything. He'd remembered the sights and the sounds so well, but he'd never quite been able to recapture the smell.

He waited for that rush of scent, sun-warmed dirt and scorched buffalo grass, faded wildflowers and the faint musk of livestock.

Nothing was there.

He could see just fine. His hearing seemed perfect, maybe even better than before. Had that been all the senses they'd given him, just those basic two that would allow him to complete his task? It seemed brutally unfair for them to send him here unable to appreciate the place, with only enough perception to recognize what he'd lost.

Don't panic, he told himself. Perhaps it was just like closing the door. Maybe he only needed to concentrate fully on what he was doing.

He screwed his eyes shut and stuck his fingers in his ears, trying to close out the two senses he knew worked all right. Then, thinking only of smell, forcing from his mind anything else, he took a good whiff.

Almost. . . It was almost there, so faint, the remembered echo of a scent more than the actuality of it. A whisper of grass, an elusive trail of dust, gone before he could catch it. Not enough. Not nearly enough to satisfy him.

He tried again.

When the scent hit, it was so powerful, so unexpected, he nearly reeled. Lilacs. Heady, sweet lilacs, in the first burst of spring, mixed with a bit of soap and that layer of warmth that was pure woman.

Abbie.

His eyes snapped open. Abbie rushed past him. She'd dismounted while his eyes were closed, and now she chased after the fiery paint on foot, who still loped along in front of Abbie just out of reach.

The horse made a wide circle in the grass. Abbie staggered after him, a coil of rope in her left hand, the big loop in her right, dragging it at arm's length behind her.

She looked tired. She'd caught two horses already this morning, neither of which had wanted to be caught, and she had hours of this ahead of her yet. Dust coated her light blue shirt. Dirt and horse sweat streaked her pants. Her hair had come completely out of its braid, forming dirty tangles around her head, and her face flushed red with heat and exertion.

Much as he tried to fight it, he felt kind of sorry for her. No woman should have to be working this hard. Even though if she'd come away with him when he'd offered her the chance, she wouldn't *have* to be running around under a hot sun, courting heatstroke or worse. He would have made sure of it.

The horse swerved, and Abbie tried to make a sharp cut after it. Her feet shot right out from under her. She hit the ground hard and a short yelp of pain escaped her. She lay there for a moment, coughing from the dust, then pushed herself to her feet and took off again, this time limping a bit on her left ankle and hollering her fool head off for the horse to stop.

Damn it, this was getting ridiculous.

Joshua shot to his feet and planted himself right in front of the paint. He had no idea if the animal could see or hear him, but figured this was as good a time as any to find out. He waited until the horse was only a few feet away before he jumped up into the air, right in front of his face, waving his arms wildly and shouting a sharp "Whoa!"

The horse reared, its hooves flailing the air inches from his nose, and Joshua hoped—a little belatedly—that those hooves had no effect on a dead man.

The horse came down with a thud and went still, its wild brown eyes focused squarely on Joshua, its ears plastered back against its head. It quivered as if it was facing a demon.

Too bad Joshua couldn't have done that when he was alive. Would have come in mighty handy.

Abbie side-armed the rope over the paint's head and pulled the noose snug. The horse didn't fight it, only trembled a bit more, clearly more concerned with the apparition before it than with her.

"Well, well," Abbie said softly. "Decided to stop finally, did you? There's a good horse."

She slipped up alongside, stroking a calming hand over the sweat-slicked neck. "Wonder what got you to stop finally. See a snake, maybe? It's all right. There's nothing there now."

She gave a tired sigh and huffed at a curl sticking to her forehead. Joshua's hand was nearly there before he caught himself. He'd almost smoothed the bright strand of hair away, just as he had dozens of times before. The first time he'd ever touched her, it had been to do just that, and he remembered it perfectly, the way that soft, shiny tendril had curled right around his finger.

The paint followed docilely as she led it back to her mare and mounted up. They turned for the ranch house; she would take this horse home before going in search of another.

But Joshua stayed, alone on the land with the wind and the sun that he could see but not feel, and wondered that he didn't seem to be doing nearly as good a job of haunting Abigail as she was of haunting him.

5

The thick, heavy trace chain made a satisfying *clank* when Joshua dumped it in a pile right beneath Abigail's window. He nudged it with his toe and, with just that small prodding, it made a nice metallic squeak. Perfect.

Once he'd gotten good and bored wandering around out on the range by himself, he'd come back to the ranch. He sure as heck wasn't going to spend the rest of the day tagging after Abigail. He might help her again before he was able to get a hold of himself and control his pesky urges.

So he'd spent the afternoon poking around the ranch, which was looking more than a little frayed around the edges. If the Rolling G had been his, he'd never have let it get in that sorrowful condition, and he was happy— yes, happy, damn it—that they were doing so badly by themselves.

The rusty chain, stuck under a wad of dusty blankets in the old lean-to, was too good to pass up. Yeah, maybe he could have thought of something a little more original, but he hadn't had a couple of hundred years to practice yet. And anyway, classics were classics for a reason. He could hardly wait to send Abigail scurrying out of bed when he started rattling the thing at midnight.

He whisked around to the front porch and settled into an old, lopsided chair, kicked his feet up on the porch rail, and waited for Abigail to get home.

He was going to do it for sure this time. He didn't care if she looked sad or bedraggled or exhausted or cute. So what? She was still in better shape than he was. First he'd been heartbroken, and then he'd been dead, and, depending upon how you looked at it, both things were her fault. He wouldn't have been running around Colorado for that freak mountain flood to drown him if she hadn't rejected him.

Yup, this time he was going to haunt her but good.

They caught all the horses, finally. As the day wore on, and the sun beat down, their need for water had called the animals to the spring. All Abigail and the hands had to do was wait, drag the animals home, and shut them up in the repaired corral, finishing just as the sun edged below the horizon.

Her arm looped around her weary brother, Abigail slowly scuffled back to the ranch house. The area between the house and the corral was worn bare of grass. The ground, gray as cinders, had cracked open in its thirst, split with deep, crooked fissures like a strike of lightning.

She was exhausted; dirty, sticky, hungry, and quite probably smelly as an old sock. She should have been in a hurry to get back home. And yet, here she was, dragging along, wishing that she could put it off just a little bit longer.

Chasing down horses was easier than what was probably waiting for her inside, though she felt guilty even at the thought. He was her father, and she owed him every bit of care and respect he was due.

So why had she stopped cold, no more than twenty steps from the house?

"Abbie?"

"Hmm?"

"Do you think he's okay?"

"I'm sure he's fine." She rubbed Marcus' shoulder soothingly and hoped she was telling him the truth. "I told Lippy to check on him now and again, make sure he got something to eat. Lippy would have come and gotten one of us if there was any real trouble."

"He don't like being left alone."

"I know." She pressed her free hand to her roiling stomach. Hungry. She was just hungry. "But he'd hate it even more if we didn't take care of the ranch properly."

"He'd never know."

It was a question that had kept her up more than one night: was she honor bound to follow her father's wishes, even though he'd lost the capability to even notice what she did? She believed so. She'd spent a great deal of energy trying to live up to what she knew Davis would have wanted.

"We'd know."

Marcus nodded, staring at the closed front door. "I guess."

"Thank you for all your hard work today, Marcus."

His mouth curled down in disgust. "I wasn't very much help and you know it."

"Yes, you were." When he started to protest, she

shook her head. "Your being here helps me, always, more than you know. Remember that."

"Yeah, right."

Abigail had no idea what to do to convince him. He was growing more uncertain, more bitter, with every day that passed, with every failure. It wasn't that Marcus had no talents. It was just that so few of them were of use on a ranch, and ranching was all they had. She was terribly afraid that he was going to lose faith in himself so completely that he'd no longer attempt even the things he did well. And she had no idea how to help him.

But then, she had very little idea about anything anymore.

"We'd better go in," she said.

The first thing she heard as she stepped through the door was the creak of her mother's rocker. The steady squeak of wood, the rhythm so even as to be eerie. No human sound could be that perfectly spaced.

The rocker had stood silent for so many years. After her mother's death, no one else could bring themselves to use it for, in their minds, it still belonged to Margaret. But none of them could bear the thought of getting rid of it, either, so it had stayed, unused and gathering dust in the far corner of the room, until her father's health had declined.

The steady motion and sound seemed to soothe him, and he spent hours there, pushing himself back and forth, staring blankly into space. Abbie tried to be happy that he'd found something that calmed him, but so often—too often—she thought if she had to listen to that sound one more second she would surely go mad herself.

She glanced around the room quickly. With relief she noted everything seemed to be in its place. "Hello, Papa," she said. "We're back. Did you have a good day?"

He still wore his nightshirt, his gray hair standing out stiffly. He blinked twice, his bleary brown eyes roaming the room before he focused on her. "Yes."

She let out a breath she hadn't even realized she'd been holding. Perhaps this evening would be a good one after all.

"Did Lippy tell you where we'd gone? We caught all the horses, finally."

"Hungry." His bare toes curled against the rough plaster floor as he pushed harder, rocking the chair more forcefully.

"I am, too. I'll see how fast I can get something together."

She sent Marcus to the well while she moved to the kitchen.

"Hungry," Davis said again. "Haven't eaten for three days, you know."

"But Papa—" she said before she stopped herself. There was no point in arguing with him.

The kitchen was a mess. Dried beans crusted the pot on the stove, its lid side-tipped beside it, the handle of a spoon sticking out at an angle. Dirty dishes piled on the cluttered table. When she crossed the floor to begin clearing the worst of it, her heel stuck on a gummy spot.

She closed her eyes, just for a moment, so she didn't have to look at it. It had been such a long day. But at least Lippy had remembered to heat up some food for himself and her father. He couldn't be expected to clean as well.

There wasn't time to make more than a simple dinner. She cleared what she could do quickly and rummaged in her supplies. It would have to be beans, again, heated with a tin of stewed tomatoes. She had it all on the freshly scrubbed table, accompanied by some leftover biscuits and a tin of sorghum syrup, by the time Marcus returned from the well.

"What took you so long?" she asked, scooping steaming piles of beans onto heavy, white ironstone plates.

He kicked out the bench by the table and plopped onto it. "Didn't take me long," he said flatly.

"Supper's all ready. Shouldn't have taken you that long to go to the well. What were you doing?"

He shot her a look that she was becoming all too familiar with. "Stopped at the bunkhouse, if you gotta know my every move. The hands aren't coming in for dinner. Said they grabbed something while you were out bringing in that last gelding and wanted to hit the sack early." His lip curled up when she slid a filled plate in front of him. "Looks like they made the right choice."

"Don't get surly with me, Marcus. I'm tired of beans, too." She whacked the spoon on the edge of a plate to get off the last of the sticky beans. "Running around in the heat all afternoon was hardly my favorite way to spend the day, either."

"The horses should never have gotten out."

"Well, they did now, didn't they?" Abigail winced at the sharpness of her tone. She had never been the most patient woman in the world, but she used to be better than this. "Why don't you get Papa to the table while I fetch the coffee, please?"

He grunted in assent.

Once the three of them were seated around the table, they bowed their heads for a brief prayer of thanks. As Marcus and her father mumbled the familiar words, she sneaked a quick look up at them.

With the daylight gone, the dim lamplight muted the harsh, aged lines of her father's features and her brother's scowl. She added her own silent thanks to the prayer. They had made it through another day intact.

Most days, that was all she dared ask for.

Davis shoveled in a heaping spoonful of food. "Ahh!" he shouted, spewing it out as quickly as he'd taken it in, spraying the tablecloth with bits of chewed beans. "Poison!"

"What?" Perhaps the tin of tomatoes had gone bad. She tasted a bit of her own supper. It seemed fine to her.

She met Marcus' eyes. He cautiously took a bite, then shrugged. "Tastes okay to me."

"Papa," she said. "It's all right. There's no poison in the food. You said you were hungry, didn't you? Why don't you just go ahead and eat your supper."

"Bad food."

"It's all right, Papa. I promise."

He glared at her, his dark eyes narrowed and wary as he dipped his tongue in a spoonful of beans. "Poison!" He slashed at his plate and it shot off the table. Gloppy red-brown drops spattered the walls and floor. "Bad!"

DearGodno. The prayer was said in one breath, one word, in her head and her heart. She jumped from her chair to go to him, to try to pacify him, but he backed away from her, shaking, his head lowered in fear.

"Why poison? Hate me so much?" He stumbled back, nearly falling in his haste to scramble away from her. "Kill me?"

She froze. "Papa—"

"Hate you too!" he shouted. "Hate you too!"

She knew he didn't mean it, knew she shouldn't blame him for things he couldn't control. That knowledge didn't make it hurt any less. It burned in her eyes and the back of her throat, lumping coldly in her stomach.

Marcus jumped to his feet and gained his father's side in a second. "It's all right, Papa," he said quietly, evenly. "No one's going to hurt you, I promise."

Davis glared at him, and, for a moment, Abigail thought that he would lash out at Marcus, too. But then there was a faint glimmer of recognition, and his tension eased, his shoulders slumping tiredly. He looked old, so very old.

"You must be sleepy, Papa," Marcus said, resting his palm on his father's back, as one might calm a distraught child. "I'll put you to bed."

Davis jerked his head up and down. "Yes. I'm tired."

"Come on then." Marcus took Davis's arm to lead him to their bedroom.

"Marcus, I'll help—"

"It's okay, Abbie. I'll take care of it." He stopped and glanced back at her, shifting back and forth a bit as if debating something. "Abbie, I'm sorry."

"There wasn't anything you could do."

"No, not that, though I'm sorry about that, too." He shook his head. "I mean about earlier."

"It's okay."

"It's *not* okay." He ducked his chin and, just for a moment, he reminded her so much of her father, the way Davis used to look when her mother had caught him at something he'd promised not to do, like green-breaking a dangerous new horse. "I just . . . I couldn't *help* out there today. I just keep messing everything up. And it makes me so mad, so mad sometimes I think I'm gonna bust." He rocked back on heels. "Don't know why I get mad at *you*, though."

She did. She understood what it was like, to feel so useless, to be so angry, and have nothing and no one to take it out on. It would be easier to have someone to blame, something to focus and release all the fury on.

"It's okay," she repeated. "You'd better get Papa to bed."

He stared at her for a moment, as if he had more to

say but couldn't quite figure out how to say it, then shrugged. "Come on with me, Papa."

Their progress across the narrow room was slow, Marcus's steps short and deliberate to match her father's stooped, shuffling gait.

Why?

How many times had she asked that question, how many endless, useless times? Why had this happened to her father, her proud, strong, vital father?

And why couldn't she ever get it right? Why couldn't she say whatever it would take to keep him calm, why couldn't she do and be whatever he needed? Why couldn't she *help* him, damn it?

Long after Marcus had closed the door softly behind him and his father, Abigail turned and wearily began to clean up the kitchen, scraping away the uneaten food.

She wasn't hungry any longer.

6

Something tickled Abigail's nose. "Go away," she mumbled, brushing at it clumsily, and snuggled back into bed. She didn't want to wake up. The bed felt too good, and her dreams were too tempting, dreams filled with color and light and softness. And scent, a burst of spring and sweetness she could almost taste.

Funny. She didn't remember ever being able to smell her dreams before.

More tickles on her cheek, like a tiny butterfly fluttering its wings against her skin. The distinct sensation of light behind her closed lids.

Light? Oh no!

She sprang up in bed, certain she'd horribly overslept. She never, ever slept past sunrise. Why had no one woken her up?

And then she stopped breathing. "What—?"

Flowers. Her bedroom was awash in them. Wildflowers everywhere, piles of them, heaps of them. Separated petals and whole blooms layered inches thick, resting in fragrant, color-splotched blankets over the floor, burying the furniture, tumbling over her bed. Over her.

"Impossible," she whispered.

There must be hundreds—thousands—of them. From other parts of Texas, wildly out of season . . . how could it be?

The white-streaked, deep pink petals of shaggy tuft; delicate yellow clusters of rain lilies; masses of tiny orange butterfly weed; wheels of Indian blanket, the intense shade of a Texas sunset; pure blue pasqueflowers; all of them, and dozens more she couldn't identify.

I must be going crazy, she thought. As crazy as her father. Tentatively, half certain they would disappear at her touch, she scooped up a handful. They were soft in her palm, delicate and velvety.

The flowers felt real, more real than anything else in her world. She brought the handful to her nose and grew giddy with the fragrance. She was drunk with it, reeling, astounded.

Magic. She'd never believed in it, never found a place or use for it in her life. But what else could it be?

Laughing, she knelt on the bed, catching great armfuls of flowers, and tossed them up in the air. They spun lazily down, fluttering bits of vibrant color and life.

It had been a long time since she'd laughed like this. Far too long, long enough that if this was madness, she wasn't at all certain she cared.

The harsh shout came as a shock, so out of place in her sun-and-flower-filled room that at first it didn't register. But it was followed by Marcus hollering her name, his voice tinged with urgent concern.

"Damn it!" She threw on a wrapper and rushed out, slamming the door shut behind her. "Marcus? Where are you?"

"We're out here, Abbie!" he yelled. "On the porch!"

She was halfway there before she realized her fists were still filled with petals. In too much of a hurry to go back to her room, she stuffed them into her pockets.

Marcus bent over Sledge, who lay sprawled in the dirt at the base of the stairs clutching his ankle, his weather-beaten face twisted with pain.

"What is it?"

"Careful, Abbie. Bottom stair's out."

The step had snapped completely in two, the damaged halves resting on the ground beneath in a ruptured V. Mean-looking splinters stuck out of the broken edges.

She leaped over it, wincing as her bare foot came down on a sharp stone, and knelt at Sledge's side.

"Easy now," she said. "Just let me take a look at this."

His boot was tight-fitting, and it took a hard yank before his foot finally slipped free. Sledge let out a low moan.

"Sorry," she said quickly. Lord, it must really be bad. Sledge was as tough as they came, and had gone through a whole roundup two years ago with a broken finger without uttering a single word of complaint.

"Don't know what happened." Sledge grimaced as she peeled off his sock. "I was comin' to breakfast. Soon as I hit the bottom step, it just gave way."

"I thought we just built those steps a year or so ago." Carefully, she probed his left ankle. There was no swelling yet, and no discoloration that she could see, so perhaps it wasn't anything too serious.

"I did," Marcus said, anxiety cracking his voice.

"Does this hurt?" She gently bent his foot up, testing.

"Not much," Sledge said, but his face twisted up, his teeth bared, and she knew it must be far more painful than he was willing to let on.

"Well, I don't think anything's broken." She looked

over at Marcus, who was kneeling opposite her, frowning. "Probably just a sprain."

"I'm . . . I'm sorry, Sledge. Really sorry."

"I'm sure it wasn't nothin' you did, Marcus," Sledge assured him. "Probably the wood was rotten from the beginning."

"Do you think you can get up now?" she asked. "I'd like to get you into the house."

"Naw, not the house. Just take me back to the bunkhouse."

"I'd rather have you where I could keep a closer eye on you."

"Maybe you would, but I don't much care for an eye bein' kept on me."

She sighed, knowing there was no arguing with him. "The bunkhouse it is, then. Marcus, you take his other side, all right?"

With both of them helping, Sledge managed to struggle to his feet, though the effort clearly pained him. They slowly inched their way toward the bunkhouse.

"You're going to have to keep that ankle propped up now," Abigail told him. "I'll put some Sloan's on there, but I really don't know how long it will be before it can bear much weight."

"You just slap that liniment on there and it will be fine. Remember how quick that bay healed up when you put some of that on after he tangled with Buttercup? Be back to work in a day or two at the most."

He leaned heavily on her shoulder, and she almost buckled with the weight.

She could only pray that he was right, and that he'd recover quickly. The Rolling G was already desperately shorthanded, and she had no idea how they were to manage all the work without him.

"Sledge?" Marcus said anxiously. "You sure that it was the board, and not the way I made the steps?"

"Oh yeah. Probably just jinxed."

As they neared the bunkhouse, Abigail was just grateful that no one else said what she was sure they were all thinking: jinxed.

Just like the whole damn ranch.

7

In the rush following Sledge's accident, she'd almost forgotten about the flowers filling her room. Once she'd gotten him settled in his bunk, she rushed back to the house, half afraid that she'd been dreaming after all and they'd be gone.

They were.

Her room was empty, bare and neat as always. She sagged against the doorjamb.

How? Why? And if she was losing her mind, too, then what would happen to them all?

For she was certain it hadn't been just a wondrous dream. She remembered it too vividly, the deep piles of brilliantly colored blooms, and, if she breathed deeply, she was almost certain she could catch a faint wisp of remembered scent.

Lord, what was happening on the Rolling G? So many weird accidents. So many unlucky coincidences. And now this.

She jammed her trembling hands into her pockets,

pockets that were filled with softness. Slowly, she withdrew a handful of blossoms.

Yes, it had been real. The flowers spilled over her palms. She curled a fist, crushing the tender petals, and it released their scents strongly, the luscious smell wafting to her nose on a current of warm air.

But in some ways it was no better to know the flowers hadn't been her imagination. It left too many unanswered questions. Was someone trying to woo her . . . or to drive her mad?

"Abigail?" Marcus spoke softly from the doorway.

She whirled to face him, tucking her hands behind her back. "Yes?"

"It's Mr. Hallenbeck. He's here, looking for Pa."

She groaned aloud. "What did you tell him?"

"I didn't know what to tell him. So I just said I didn't know where Pa was, that I'd come in and check with you."

"Good, good." She nodded, trying to think. It didn't take much guessing to figure out what B.J. wanted. But how was she to get rid of him—preferably for good this time? The last thing she needed was him nosing around the place. "Where's Papa?"

"He's still sleeping, last time I checked."

"Okay. You go out and tell him that Papa's out on the range checking the stock. You don't know for sure where, don't know exactly when he's due back."

"Think that'll be enough to get rid of him?"

"Not a chance," she said, her mouth twisting in a wry grin. "But I'll be out to talk to him as soon as I can throw on some clothes. Maybe I can hurry the man on his way."

Marcus grinned suddenly. "I'll bet. Can I stay and watch you chase him off?"

"Why, you—" She gave him a light swat. "Shoo. I'll be along in a minute."

She always dressed quickly, but even for her she was ready in record time. The less time B.J. had to cool his heels, the better, or he might decide to start poking into places that she simply had to keep him out of. Only problem was that quick wasn't generally good, and when Abigail stepped out onto the porch to meet B.J., she knew she was looking something less than her best. She hated meeting B.J. at even the slightest disadvantage. He was too adept at exploiting it.

He, however, was looking hale and prosperous, big as ever in the hot, blinding morning light.

"Good morning, Abigail." He hooked his thumbs in his belt and grinned down at her. "But then, from the looks of things, not such a good morning after all."

"I have no idea what you mean, B.J. I think it's a perfectly lovely morning. It's cooled off a bit, don't you think?"

"I mean that's a real, uh, interesting hairstyle you got there this morning."

"It is, isn't it?" She patted the snarled mess that had somehow become plastered down on the right side of her head while taking on the size and texture of a bird's nest on the left. "Rather becoming, don't you think? And so fashionable."

He stared down at her as if he had absolutely no clue what to make of her. A reaction she rather liked, she decided.

"You comin' to the fourth of July celebration, over to the fort?"

"Don't we always? You came all the way over here to ask me that, B.J.? I'm flattered."

"Ah, yes, well . . ." He cleared his throat and puffed out his chest. "I came to talk to Davis about the proposition I mentioned to you yesterday."

"And which proposition was that?"

"Both of them, actually."

"You don't need to speak to my father. I did. And our answer is, as always, no. Really, I wonder that you have so much difficulty understanding that word. It's only got one syllable."

His jaw bulged and he leaned over her. "Just who do you think you are? Look at you!" He sneered. "You're turning into a scrawny, ugly old hen, and you've got about the sense of one, too. Anyone with half a brain would know that this is the best offer you're ever gonna get!"

"Thank heavens I've got more than a half a brain, then, enough to know that having no offer is a good sight better than your offer."

"You're ungrateful as a cow fresh-pulled from a bog-hole. You should be on your knees thanking me!"

"Oh, but I do thank you. Just think how boring my day would be if you hadn't come to visit me."

"I can't imagine what's gotten into your father, letting you run around the place like this. Anybody could tell you this pitiful ranch's no place for a woman, and if you keep up like this much longer, ain't nobody gonna be able to tell you even *are* a woman. Davis is one sorry excuse for a father, to let you come to this."

Thank God she was too angry for his words to hurt as much as they could have. "Get off my ranch." She spoke evenly, though she had to clench her molars together to do it. "You are no longer welcome here. Not now, not ever again. The next time I see you set foot on the place, I'm getting my gun, make no mistake about it."

"Then you make no mistake about this." He leaned forward, towering over her. "I made you a right fair offer for your water. You got 'til tomorrow to accept it. If you don't, you might find that you'll lose that water, anyway, and you'd be wishing you'da at least gotten somethin' for it while you'd had the chance."

Damned if she was going to let B.J. Hallenbeck intimidate her. She narrowed her gaze and lifted to her toes so her nose was almost even with his. "Are you threatening me, Mr. Hallenbeck?"

"Who, me?" He bared his teeth in a facsimile of a genial grin, one that someone who hadn't tangled with him as often as she had might have taken to be friendly. "I don't need to threaten anyone. But you know what it's like out here, Abigail. Once a herd gets a whiff of water, there's no stopping them. And the range is a dangerous place. Accidents happen."

With that, he wheeled around and strolled over to his buckskin gelding as if he had all the time in the world. He swung into the saddle and tipped his hat at her. "Be seeing you around, Miss Grier."

"Damn you," Abigail said softly as B.J. cantered away.

Accidents happened, he'd said. And accidents *had* been happening, a lot of them. Could he have . . . No. All the little accidents that had happened around the Rolling G in the last few weeks had to be just that. Not that she had any illusions that B.J. was too upstanding for sabotage. But if he'd been trying to ruin them, she doubted that the little "accidents" he'd arrange would be nearly so benign as the ones they'd had so far.

But he'd planted a new worry in her head, a very real one. If B.J. decided to just drive his herd right onto her land and to her waterhole, how could she possibly stop him? There were dozens of hands over at the Bar B. She had only six people in defense, including a woman, a twelve-year-old boy, a man laid up with a bum ankle, and her father, who couldn't be trusted with a dull pocket knife, much less a rifle.

She was in deep trouble.

Where to go for help? Horace, perhaps? But friendship only went so far. She had nothing that she could afford to offer him in exchange.

Sighing, she stepped off the porch, carefully avoiding the broken bottom step. She must remember to fix it, before someone else fell.

The well was only a hundred feet from the house. Her father'd looked for water first, and then built his ranch around it. He'd always said he'd done only two really smart things in his life, but they were all he needed—he'd found water, and he'd found her mother.

Even the stones that formed the bulk of the well seemed cooler, as if they took their temperature from deep within the shelter of the earth and not from the sizzling air around them. She lowered the bucket, the rope creaking as she let it out. They'd planned for years to get a new, efficient pump, but her father had always had a new bull or horse that needed buying first. Improving the ranch was a much higher priority than just making the housework easier. And then he'd gotten sick, and there'd not been enough extra money for either one.

So she still cranked up water the slow way. Her lips were suddenly parched, and she licked them in anticipation. Only a bit farther.

The bucket swayed as it reached the top, water pouring over the sides and back into the well. She unhooked the pail and water sloshed out and onto her, soaking the front of her shirt.

She shivered. It was cold, delicious. She couldn't remember the last time something had felt so good.

No one wasted water in west Texas. Never. It was an unforgivable indulgence.

Abigail glanced around. The yard was empty, dust simmering right over the gray, cracked earth. Marcus was still inside the house with her father, and there was no sound from the bunkhouse twenty yards to her right. Sledge had probably taken advantage of the situation and gone back to sleep.

It was so wrong.

"Aw, what the hell." She lifted the bucket and dumped it over her head.

The cold rush of water left her gasping and invigorated. Hair clung to her neck and back in thick twists. The parched ground sucked up the water as soon as it dripped off her, and she was blessedly cool for the first time in weeks. She leaned over the well to rehook the bucket. A chilled updraft of air, scented with water, brushed her face.

She felt a quick, hard shove at her back.

"What the—"

And she hurtled headlong into the well.

8

She was falling . . . falling.

Into the pitch blackness. Her screams bounced off the rock walls, a painful echo.

And then, quick as it had begun, it was over. The swift downward plunge stopped, and she bobbed slightly, like a yo-yo reaching the end of its string. Something—it felt like arms, but that couldn't be—was wrapped tightly around her middle. Slowly, ever so slowly, still dangling upside down, limp arms flopping over her head, she rose.

She twisted from the waist, trying to get a look at what held her, but could see nothing. The darkness gradually decreased, exposing the rough, shadowed stone walls of the well, deep gray and splotched with damp moss.

Was she dead? So fast, so abrupt? This had to be her ascent into heaven; she could think of no other reasonable explanation.

But then she was lifted free of the well. The world

tilted. She gradually spun upright and settled gently on her feet. Definitely not heaven; she was still at the Rolling G. The snug hold on her waist released.

"Are you all right?" a voice asked, low in her ear.

She gasped, whirled, and found herself staring into all-too-familiar eyes.

"Joshua? Oh my lord, Joshua." She blinked, disbelieving. Impossible. It was all so completely impossible. "But . . . But . . . you're dead!"

"Yeah? I had noticed that, Abbie." When she'd pitched into that well Joshua thought he'd never been so scared in his life, not even in the middle of battle with cannons roaring overhead. He'd dived after her instantly, but he'd been terrified he wouldn't be fast enough.

Thank God he had been. Yes, he added mentally, I mean *You*. Thank you.

"I know they never found your body, but they found all your things by that stream after the flood, and no trace of you, and . . . Oh! You're not dead!"

She was babbling, her arms flapping wildly, drops of water splattering off into the air. She looked far too pale for his peace of mind. Actually, Abbie always looked pale, but not like this, a pasty, death-like color. He wondered if it was all going to be too much for her, especially since there was an awful lot more to come.

"No, Abbie, I *am* dead." He paused, wondering how he was supposed to explain things that he understood so little himself. "At least, according to the way you think of it, I'm dead for sure."

She stared at him, shocked, doubting, unable to take in the evidence before her. "Dead? But— Oh, lands!" She spun around, clapping her hands over her eyes. "Joshua West, you're naked!"

"Shoot." Bemused, he looked down at himself. He

was naked all right. He shot a glance skyward. "Ah . . . in all the rush, I think we forgot somethin' here."

"Sorry." The voice spoke right inside his head. "Minor detail."

"Minor?" Jeez, for an angel, or whatever it was, that voice sure could be a mite insulting. "Abbie never thought it was minor."

"Here you go. This is it, though, Joshua. You're on your own, starting now."

A black sateen shirt, collarless and double-buttoned, appeared on his body. The dark canvas pants and plain brown boots didn't look nearly lived-in enough, to his way of thinking, but they'd do. "Hey, thanks. But what about a hat?"

Silence.

"Gotta have a hat," he grumbled, with no effect. Heck, he'd much rather have foregone the pants than his hat. Guess when the voice had said "this is it," it had meant it this time.

He returned his attention to Abbie. Her back was still to him, and her shoulders were sort of hunched over, making her look much smaller than she really was. All he wanted was to go to her, to wrap his arms around her and make everything all right, but somehow he thought a hug from a dead guy was probably not quite the comforting she needed right now.

"You can turn around now." He waited for her to face him before he went on. "Sorry. Where I've been, I haven't had much use for clothes."

"Did you ever?" Her eyes, sharply dark in her pale face, went wide and her mouth popped into an O, as if she couldn't believe she'd just said that.

Now that sounded more like his Abbie. He grinned, delighted, and a reluctant little smile just tipped one corner of her mouth.

"Aw, Abbie, sure is good to see you smile."

In a flash, the smile vanished, replaced with a fierce scowl.

"Sorry I mentioned it," he said.

"Nope. You're not going to do that to me again. You're not going to charm me into . . ." Her voice trailed off.

"Into what?" Durned if it wasn't good to know that, at some time before she'd stomped all over his poor abused heart, he'd been able to charm her.

"No. Don't you do that. Don't you smile at me."

How many times had he heard her say that? Just about every time he'd tried to sweet-talk her into something that he just *knew* she wanted to do—even if she wouldn't admit it—she'd said that . . . right before she said "no" to him anyway.

But then, she'd turned out to be much better at saying "no" than he'd ever imagined.

"What did I charm you into, Abbie?" he asked urgently, wondering why now, after all this time, when there was so much else to deal with, this small thing seemed so damn important.

"Nothing. Nothing at all."

"Didn't think so."

She wouldn't look at him anymore, just stared down at the pattern of water dripping off her sopping clothes into the brown-gray dust. The silence was strained, raw. Too many memories. Too much lost. A hundred things to say, a thousand questions to ask, and no easy way of addressing any of it.

Finally she lifted her head. "Dead?" she repeated slowly, drawing out the word as if she was saying it for the first time.

"Dead."

She paused, thinking it over. Vivid color abruptly

burst on her cheeks. *Uh-oh*, he thought. Not that she
didn't look better now, with her eyes all snapping bright,
than she had a moment ago when he'd been scared she
might keel over in a faint. But he knew this look.

He was in for it now.

"Oh no you don't." She stabbed at the air with a stiff
forefinger. "You are not going to haunt me!"

Abigail took off for the house, her soggy brown skirts
flapping around her ankles. She jumped over the broken
step, and her heels pounded a furious rhythm across the
porch. The door slammed decisively shut behind her.

When she charged into her bedroom, Joshua was
waiting for her, propped comfortably against the far wall
like he'd been there for hours, lazing away the afternoon.

"Oh! How did you get in here? What did you—?"

He simply lifted one eyebrow. "Do you really want an
answer to that?"

"But . . . Never mind." Before, she'd been too
shocked to really take a good look at him. A body would
think, with everything he'd been through—dying and
all—it would have changed him more.

But he still just looked like Joshua, all rangy and
handsome and cocky. Dark, dark hair, long enough to
brush low on his neck and curl around his ears. Eyes
that she'd never quite decided were blue or gray but
were always so startlingly bright against his deeply
tanned skin. When she looked real hard, there might be
just a shade of translucence around the edges of his
form, a fuzziness, a shadow of the wall behind him
showing through. No other evidence of his . . . condition.

"What do you think?" He'd caught her looking, and
he grinned at her, just like he had after the first time he
kissed her, a gratified smile that said he knew exactly

what wicked thoughts were popping around in her
head—and liked them.

She refused to tell him that he looked pretty durned
lively to her.

"Go away, Joshua. Just go away and leave me alone.
And this time, stay away for good."

His smile disappeared instantly. "I can't do that."

"Don't haunt me." She hated the pleading note
that crept into her voice. "Haven't you haunted me
enough already, all those months after you left, and
all those months after I thought you were . . . when
you were . . . after you died?"

"I haunted you?" Damned if he didn't sort of like the
thought of that. Even if she didn't exactly have the right
to be haunted by his leaving, being she was the one who
sent him off with his tail between his legs, he was still
glad he hadn't been the only one suffering. He straightened. "Really? I—" He stopped abruptly. Something
she'd said. . . . "Hey, wait a second. Back up there.
What was that you said about months and months?"

"After they told me you died. I know you probably
thought I wouldn't mourn you, but I certainly never
wished you dead. Not that you didn't deserve it."

"But . . . somethin' ain't right here. How did you find
out about my death, anyway?"

"You must have still had some of the things from
when you worked for B.J. with you in Colorado. When
they found your belongings, someone sent notice to the
Bar B. Hallenbeck told me."

He frowned. "When was this, exactly?"

"I don't know, *exactly*. B.J. told me about it at the
fourth of July social." She grimaced. "You know B.J.,
always one to make sure I had a good time at a party."

It wasn't right. Something just wasn't right. "What
year is this, Abbie?"

"Now?" That was the last question she expected. "1868."

"But I died—"

"A year ago, of course."

"A year ago!" he shouted. "A whole damn year!"

"Hush. Someone will hear you."

"No they won't. No one but you." He stalked back and forth across the room. It took Abbie a moment to realize what seemed so odd about it. There was no sound to accompany his pacing, no echoing thud of boot heels against the scuffed wood floor. "Jesus, where the hell have I been for a whole year?"

"How would I know?" she said impatiently. It was all so unbelievable, so much to take in, so much she didn't know, and he was worried about the stupid date? "What does it matter?"

"What does it matter?" He whirled on her. "I thought it just happened! Hell, I haven't even been here all that long!"

"So?"

"They stuck me on ice somewhere for a whole damn year and all you can say is 'so'?"

"For heaven's sake, Joshua, you have all of eternity now! What difference does a year make?"

"Oh . . . yeah." Sheepish, he hooked his thumbs in the pockets of his pants. "Guess so. I s'pose time don't really have the same kinda meanin' to them as it does to us, does it?"

"No, I suppose not." Lordie, what was she going to do? Joshua West was in her bedroom, standing there, hips cocked, big as life and looking far too real. All those dreams she'd had over the past year and a half, all the ones she'd tried to pretend she'd never had, seemed to be coming true—though not precisely in the way she'd imagined.

She couldn't let it happen. Somehow, some way, she had to get rid of him. Now, before she started spending too much time thinking about those dreams. Before she was tempted to give in to them.

This was Joshua, she reminded herself. It didn't matter how handsome he was, how much he made her smile. When she wouldn't run off with him, he'd high-tailed it out of town without so much as a second glance, making it all too clear how much she'd meant to him—not enough.

No, she had to get rid of him right away, before she got used to having him around again. Because she knew, far too well, what it was like to have Joshua leave her. She'd fought too hard to forget him to let him back in her life now.

And she was terribly certain she'd never survive loving and losing Joshua again.

"Wait a minute, Joshua." In the back of her mind, something clicked into place. "You said you haven't been here that long. Just how long *have* you been here?"

"Not too long," he hedged.

"You didn't just get here?"

"Well . . . maybe not *just,* exactly." This was going to be a problem, he thought. Pretty soon she was going to connect him with spilled lemonade, and there was going to be hell to pay.

"How come I couldn't see you before?"

"I think . . . I think it's because you know I'm here now, after I caught you, and you didn't before."

"And you've been—you've been lurking around, invisible, for days?" Her voice pitched higher with each word.

"Well, maybe not days, exactly . . . "

"You—you *snake*!" Her hands fisted. "You've been behind all the things that have been going wrong on the Rolling G, haven't you, you low-down, rotten—"

He lifted his hands, the picture of innocence. "Abbie, no, I swear—"

She launched herself at him, aiming for that irritatingly square chin, mad enough to knock his head clear into the wall.

Except she flew right through him, as if there were nothing there but air. The force of her charge took her right into the wall herself. Hard.

Unwilling to move, hurting, she simply stayed there, plastered up against the rough wall. Her knuckles were bleeding. Her cheek burned, and she was certain she'd scraped it up but good. She took a ragged breath.

"Abbie? Abbie, are you all right?" He came up behind her, slipped his arm around her waist to support her, and she was cradled between the sun-warmed surface of the wall and the man behind her. A man who'd hurt her deeply, a dead man, but a man she could feel, the hard bulwark of his chest against her back and the gentle strength of his arms holding her safe.

"Aw, jeez, Abbie, what'ja have to go and do that for?" With his free hand, he checked her over, his fingers brushing at her cheek, her hairline, barely whispering over her temples. "Talk to me, please. Tell me where it hurts."

She should move. She knew it, and yet could not bring herself to do it. It felt too good, too familiar. She closed her eyes as his lips slid softly over her injured knuckles, soothing.

How could any of this be real? He was warm behind her, solid, almost unbearably alive. And yet he simply couldn't be.

"It wasn't me," he was going on, his voice low, edged

with desperation. "I swear to you, Abbie, all that stuff. It wasn't me. I could never hurt you like that."

And even though he'd hurt her before, even though she knew she shouldn't, a big chunk of her heart, a foolish, young, ridiculous part of her heart, believed him.

A good thing that she'd learned well not to trust her heart. Turning away from its demands shouldn't even be painful anymore. Too bad it still was.

"Get off me."

He let her go immediately, and she felt the loss as keenly as the bruises on her knuckles. She turned to face him slowly.

"How . . . I could feel you. How come I can't touch you, couldn't hit you, but I could feel you when you touched me?"

He lifted one hand, meaning to test it, wanting to touch her once again. But surely he was the last person she wanted to touch her, so he dropped his hand back to his side.

"I don't know," he said.

She scowled at him.

"Really, I don't. I'm kinda new at this, you know." He brushed his thumb over his fingertips. Nothing. He couldn't feel it. But he could still feel Abigail, as if his fingers held the memory. Could still clearly feel the spring of her curls against his fingers, the softness of her skin, the sticky wetness of the tiny bit of blood on her skinned knuckles.

What now? He'd done one hell of a job of helping her so far, hadn't he? "Abigail, I am not here to destroy the ranch. I swear it."

She stood tall, stiff, her mouth compressed into a thin line. "How long?"

"Just since B.J.'s party."

"The lemonade?"

"Well . . . yeah," he admitted.

There was not a flicker of change in her stony expression, and that bothered him. Somehow he would have felt better if she got good and riled at him. Her anger would be easier to deal with than this rigid, distant control.

"What else?" she asked, the words clipped.

"Just that old paint, out on the range. I sort of . . . stopped him so you could catch him."

"Anything else?"

He rocked back on his heels. "Only the—"

"The flowers."

He nodded.

"Why?" She stepped close to him, looking up into his face, and Abigail burst onto his senses, the scent of lilac water and the echo of her warmth. "Why did you do that for me?"

How to explain it? He could tell her that he'd felt guilty, guilty that he'd even considered haunting her, back before he'd found out that there was more going on in her life than he'd ever imagined. That he'd thought to scare her, before he'd heard her father say "I hate you" and saw the deep, anguished wound in her eyes, and he was ashamed he'd ever hatched the plan.

There was all that, yes, but the real answer, the truest one, was simple. So simple he doubted she'd believe it. "I wanted to see you smile."

"Uh-huh." Amazing how much sarcasm she could get in those two little syllables.

"No, really, that was it. I was here when . . ." His voice trailed off. She probably wouldn't appreciate knowing he'd been hanging around, watching, but— "God, Abbie, what the hell happened to your father?"

"Couldn't you tell, Joshua?" she said calmly. "He's lost his mind."

Abigail doubted he would have looked more shocked had she told him she was dead, too. In fact, the only time she'd ever seen that much surprise on his face was when she'd refused his offer to run away with him.

"What happened, Abbie?" he asked, his voice filled with gentle concern, enough to make her want to burst into tears, throw herself in his arms, and tell him the whole sad story. Darn it, why did he have to go and be *nice*? It was a lot easier when she'd forgotten he was capable of being nice.

She couldn't tell him, precisely because she wanted to so much. She'd break down; she could feel it, pushing up against the bottom of her stomach.

This was her problem, not his. What possible good could it do to tell him? Her father had always taken pride in handling everything alone, and he would want her to do the same. *Never depend on someone else, need someone else,* he'd always said. Because it was too hard when you lost them.

And it had been. God, it had been.

"Abbie?" he prompted.

"Leave me alone," she said. "The last thing I need in my life right now is a ghost."

9

She wasn't going to tell him. Joshua recognized her resolve. But there was the slightest quaver in her voice, the glimmer of moisture in her deep brown eyes. He wondered if it would be better to push the issue a bit right now, to make her spill it all and get it over with.

But he'd never been that great at heartfelt conversations. Never really wanted to dig that far below the surface—God only knew what kind of junk was hidden down there. He'd always believed that, if something was buried that well, it was probably down there for a reason and was better left alone.

There was one thing, though, he'd always been good at it where Abigail was concerned—well, two, actually, but he figured the second one was out of the question right now. He really wasn't sure how many of his parts were in full working order, plus he wasn't exactly certain if the Big Boss would consider it a damning sin.

But he'd always been able to make Abigail smile.

"A *ghost?*" he said with exaggerated effrontery. "Don't be ridiculous. I'm not a ghost."

"Oh no, of course not. You're just a walking, talking, a body-can-fly-right-through-you dead guy. Certainly not a ghost."

"Nope." He dusted his hands together. "I'm an angel, of course."

Her jaw dropped. "An angel?"

"Yup," he said, adjusting an imaginary halo. "An angel."

She hooted. Bent over at the waist, loud and long, big gulping laughs like someone who'd forgotten how, it had been so long.

Exactly as she had when he'd first fallen in love with her. He'd been drifting since the war, kicking from ranch to ranch and job to job, and had just hired on at B.J. Hallenbeck's place. He'd been out riding the perimeter, looking for strays, when he'd come upon her doing the same thing on her own land. She'd sat tall and rigid in the saddle, her expression grave. He'd introduced himself, merely for the sake of politeness, and her acknowledgment had been nothing more than a stiff little nod.

He couldn't have said why, but he'd taken her response—or near absence of it—as a challenge. Maybe it was his pride; he wasn't used to being virtually dismissed by women. Or maybe it was simply that he was bored. He'd told her some little story—he couldn't even remember what it was now. But what he did remember was how she'd gone still, like she wasn't quite sure what to do, and then burst out in the loudest, rustiest, least musical laughter he'd ever heard.

From then on, he'd spent every spare moment he could find hurrying over to the Rolling G, just to see if he could make her laugh again, because it always made this secret little warm spot in his chest expand. And he'd spent the next six months doing it, longer than he'd been in any one place since he was fifteen.

"Oh my." Finally quieting, she straightened, wiping the laugh-tears from her eyes. "That's a good one, Joshua. You, an angel."

"Whaddya mean?" He gave an injured sniff.

She rolled her eyes at him.

"Well, all right," he admitted. "Maybe not an angel, exactly. Would you believe a 'helping spirit'?"

"Oh? And just exactly who are you supposed to help?"

"Guess." He grinned wickedly.

"Oh no," she said, shaking her head emphatically and backing away. "Uh uh. Not a chance."

"Yup."

"Never. Impossible."

"Sorry. Got no choice."

"Well, what about me? Don't I get a choice?"

"Guess not. You're my assignment."

"Assignment?" Her tone grew suspicious. "What do you mean, 'assignment'?"

"Well, all the real angels were sorta busy. So guess who you got instead?"

"Lucky me."

"It's a good thing you're finally startin' to realize that."

Real help she could have used, Abigail thought. But Joshua floating around, fading through walls and conjuring up flowers, didn't seem particularly helpful. More like complicating, frustrating, and distracting. "Couldn't you have just said *no*?"

"We're dealing with a Supreme Being here, Abigail. I kinda thought it was best to do what I was told."

"I don't need your help!"

"Abigail." His voice gentled. He stepped closer to her and, just for a moment, she thought he was going to reach out to hold her. She wondered if she would have pushed him away, as she should, or if she simply would have curled right up against him and let him do it. "I would give anything if you didn't need my help. But you're in trouble, sweetheart, and we both know it."

Trouble. She had it, all right, and didn't have the faintest idea how to deal with it except keep going, hanging on day by day. To do what she could and try to ignore the rest.

There was one thing that she was pretty certain of, however. Having Joshua West around was likely to cause her a whole lot more trouble, not less.

"Someone's trying to run you out." He studied her intently, his gaze never wavering, and she wondered if she'd ever seen him look so serious. "Did you . . ." he swallowed, "did you really think I was the one doing all those things to your ranch?"

Had she? Perhaps she'd only *wanted* to blame it on him. If it had been Joshua, there'd be no real danger. It would have been easier, so much easier, to chalk it up to his bizarre sense of humor and send him on his way. And, if he'd been guilty of all the rotten things that had been threatening the ranch, perhaps she'd finally get angry enough, hurt enough, to get completely over him, once and for all.

Because she knew now that she never had.

"Not really," she admitted.

"It would be one thing if it were only letting the horses out or running off a calf here and there. But, my God, Abbie!" He touched her this time, grabbing her shoulders, his fingers digging in hard enough to make her wince. "Abbie, someone tried to kill you!"

"To . . . kill me?" So much had happened, the shock

of seeing Joshua again when she'd thought him long dead, that she'd forgotten about the well. It all rushed back to her, the dark plunge, falling, the cold panic, a terror she could not have even imagined, and she started to shake. "No . . . no," she said, trying to block it out.

"You're not going to try and tell me that you just *fell* down that well, are you?"

If only it had been just an accident. The idea that someone had actually tried to kill her was unimaginable, a hundred times worse.

But she remembered the distinct feel of hands at her back. It had only taken one strong shove.

Nausea swamped her. She swallowed heavily.

"You look a little pale. I think maybe you should sit down." Joshua guided her to the bed and sat her carefully on the edge. He knelt before her, looking up into her face. "Better?"

"Better?" Hysteria threaded the words. How could she be better? Someone had just tried to murder her!

But it would do her no good at all to fall apart. She breathed in . . . twice . . . three times, and nodded. "Better," she repeated, meaning it this time. "All right, then. Who pushed me?"

"I'm not certain."

"But you were right there. You had to be, to catch me so quickly. Didn't you see anyone?"

"Well, ah, I wasn't really looking around," he said, his expression abashed. "You'd dumped all that water over your head, you see, and got your bodice all wet, and that cold water made your, ah—" He waved his hand in the general direction of her chest. "I was sort of preoccupied, you see."

She glared at him. "You haven't changed much, Joshua."

"Yeah, I know." He tilted his head, studying her. "But

you don't look like you're going to be sick anymore, either."

"No."

"Who do you think it is? I'd be willing to lay a helluva bet on Hallenbeck."

"I suppose so." As annoying as B.J. could be, as furious as he made her, she still had a hard time believing that he could actually—Lord, she could hardly even bring herself to *think* it—try to kill her. Still, who else could it be?

"What do you want to do next?"

Unfortunately, she could hardly just ride over and dump B.J. down a well himself, which was what she really felt like doing. It was wildly frustrating, but there didn't seem to much she *could* do at the moment. And she was too exhausted to do a decent job of it, in any case. "I'll just have too be a lot more careful, I guess, now that I know that it's not just bad luck and someone actually is trying to run us off."

"Well, I think we can manage to do a little better than that. First off, you're going to take a little nap. You've had a heckuva day already. And I—" His smile was filled with sin. "I'll just have to watch you very, very closely, won't I?"

10

She slept, though she hadn't expected to. Deep, quiet sleep, without any of the dreams that had plagued her. Dreams that, she was now certain, she'd been having only because Joshua had been planting them, whispering wicked things in her ear as she drifted off.

There'd been no sign of him when she'd blinked awake, though she'd half expected to find him there, perched on the end of her bed, "watching over" her.

And she was relieved, damn it. Yes, *relieved.*

No sign of him all the time she prepared supper, either, though, twice, as she stood over the pot of sorghum boiling in bacon fat, she'd heard something behind her. She spun around, splattering thick drops of syrup, to find the room unchanged, the only movement her father rocking slowly back and forth in his chair.

She called them all to eat. By the time she'd helped her father to the table, Marcus, Lippy, and Pecos had all taken their places.

"Sledge didn't come with you?"

"No ma'am," Lippy said, dropping into his chair without taking his eyes from the steaming platter of hotcakes she slid in front of him. He was barely seventeen and a fuzz of pale blond whiskers decorated his upper lip. "He's still feelin' a mite down, I'd say. Got his foot all swaddled up like a new baby. Stole both our pillows to prop it up on, too."

"I'll run a plate down to him after supper, then." Poor man. The last time he'd been thrown, he'd been back on the horse inside of half an hour. It must be terribly lowering for him to be finally brought down by nothing more than a weak stair.

"Sure he'd appreciate it, ma'am." Lippy launched into a description of the terrible sprain he'd sustained once when he dismounted and stepped into a hole, an injury that somehow—though Abigail missed the connection completely—degenerated into pneumonia.

She could always count on Lippy to make sure there were no lags in the conversation. He was their newest hand, hired a shade over two years ago, and in all that time she'd never heard him at a loss for words. She was grateful. His babble made the meals seem more normal, covered up her father's awkward silences and equally awkward bursts of senseless speech.

Tonight, though, her father seemed calm. He hadn't touched his cakes and syrup, but had already tucked away a good-sized pile of apples fried with sugar.

Grateful he was eating at all, she reached for the bowl of apples. She worried about his eating. He was too thin, skin hanging loosely over bones that used to be layered with muscle. She spooned another generous helping onto his plate. "You always did like the sweets best, Papa. Here's some more apples."

He looked at her, his dark eyes blurry, unfocused. His expression cleared abruptly. "Thank . . . you," he said haltingly. "Abigail."

She blinked, hard. *Abigail*, he'd said.

They had bad days and good days, more bad than good lately. But even on the good, it had been so long, a month or more, since he'd looked at her with recognition and said her name.

"Papa," she whispered, sliding her hand over his paper-skinned one. He patted hers briefly, before picking up his fork and eagerly digging into the shiny-glazed apples once more.

She looked up to find Marcus watching them, smiling broadly as his eyes gleamed wet.

And, despite water and ghosts and worries, right that moment, it wasn't a bad day at all.

The moment just didn't last long.

"Oh, by the way, Abigail," Lippy was saying. "Found a coupla problems with screwworms on the head I checked today."

"You found screwworms?" Though she'd listened to his rambles with only half an ear, she picked up on the word immediately. "On how many cows?"

"Hmmm," he mumbled around a mouthful of syrup-soaked hotcakes. "Three, I think."

"Great. Blowflies." Of all the potential problems with her herd, this was her least favorite. Not that it was all that difficult to treat, although it was excruciatingly painful for the cattle, and it could even be deadly if not caught soon enough.

It was just that picking worms out of cows' wounds and smearing the sore with a smelly mixture of axle grease and carbolic acid was not exactly her favorite way to spend a day.

"Three?" They often saw it in the spring, right after

the fresh branding. But there shouldn't be so many at this time of year.

"Uh-huh. Maybe four. An' that's just what I saw. Pecos has been findin' 'em, too."

Suddenly unable to bear another bite, she shoved her plate away. Her supper sat heavy in her stomach, a hard lump that burned. She pressed a hand against her belly, trying to ease it.

The warmth started deep within, so slowly at first she barely felt it. Seeping, relaxing, soothing, a fine glow like she'd just swallowed old brandy. It smoothed away the tension, calmed the acid, blunted the pain, and she closed her eyes, letting that loose feeling work its way through the rest of her body.

Her head slumped, and she felt a gentle massage at her neck, dissipating her tension. Relaxed . . . She'd never been so relaxed. "Joshua," she murmured.

Joshua! She straightened her back with a snap and shot a glance around the room, searching. Where was he? Hiding behind a chair? Puddled in the empty sink?

"What did you just say?" Marcus asked. His head tilted, he was studying her as closely as he studied one of his books.

"I . . . ah . . ." Oh dear. She'd said Joshua, right out loud, without thinking. "I said . . . washing. Tomorrow, I was going to do the washing." She made a face. "I guess we'll be picking screwworms instead."

"There's more to it than that," Pecos said, sitting back in his chair and crossing his arms over his chest.

She was almost afraid to ask. Pecos was half-Mex, from west of here somewhere. He'd had his own place once, but gave it up when he'd lost his wife and, with her, his heart for the struggle. He'd been at the Rolling G five years and, in all that time, she'd never learned more about him than that.

Except that when he had something to say, she'd best pay attention. "What do you mean?"

He scraped a thumbnail down his jaw, rasping the gray-flecked stubble. "Them sores . . . they don't look natural."

For the cattle to become infected, there had to be open wounds on the animals first, for the flies to lay their eggs in.

"Unnatural, how?" she asked, very quietly.

"Either they all done found themselves the biggest, sharpest patch of thorns I ever seen . . . or someone's been cutting 'em up."

"What?" Marcus brought his fork to the table with a thump.

At her side, her father, oblivious to the tension that sharpened the air, continued happily spooning apples into his mouth. Everyone else looked at her expectantly, awaiting her reaction.

Stalling, she fingered her utensils, aligning them carefully as if their precise arrangement mattered. What could she say to them? Up until now, she hadn't mentioned to anyone the possibility that all the accidents at the Rolling G weren't merely accidents. She knew too little, and hadn't wanted to make assumptions. Also, she wasn't sure how the hands would react. Sledge would stay, she was certain, but what of the others? There was no way she could run the ranch without their help.

"Are you absolutely certain, Pecos?"

"Absolutely? No." He ran his tongue over his teeth as he considered. "But I'm sorry, Miss Abigail. I'm pretty sure. Those cuts looked like a knife to me."

What a sick, vicious thing to do, to purposely slice into the animals' hides, knowing the flies would find the fresh wounds. Knowing the acute pain it would cause the cattle.

But then, shoving her down a well had been a pretty vicious thing to do, too.

The initial incidents, the ones she'd dismissed as bad luck, had been annoying but harmless. A few calves lost from their mothers, a broken corral fence, a piece of equipment gone missing. Nothing like this. And the suddenly looming danger meant she no longer had a choice. They deserved to know the chances they were taking. She must tell them her suspicions.

"I suppose that settles it. You all got the right to know . . . I think someone is trying to run us off the ranch."

Marcus swore, a word she hadn't even realized he knew, and half rose from the table, as if he would rush off and track down the offender himself, immediately. She should reprimand him for cursing. Their mother never would have permitted it, she thought tiredly. Except it seemed a minor transgression at the moment.

Lippy's young face flushed dark with anger. Pecos simply tipped his chair back and nodded at her.

"I was wonderin' how long it was gonna take you to figure it out."

"You knew?"

"Nothin' else it could be. Too much bad happenin' to be just chance. How long you known?"

"Just today, for certain. I only suspected before."

"Got any ideas who?"

She wiped a hand across her forehead, pushing back the frizzles of hair that clung there. "Somebody who wants our water, I assume."

"But that's . . . that's . . ." Lippy's mouth worked, open and shut, at least three times for every word he managed to get out. She'd never thought she'd see the day.

"That could be anyone within fifty miles," she finished for him.

"Yup," Pecos agreed. "Probably ain't, though. 'Spect it's someone a lot closer'n that."

"But what are we going to do?" Marcus still hovered above his chair, his hands bunched into tight fists, his eyes blazing.

He was furious, in a way she wasn't sure she'd ever seen him. Not the temper of a child, but the anger of a man whose territory was threatened. For someone who'd claimed to dislike the ranch, who often spoke longingly of the time he could leave it, he certainly didn't want anything to happen to it. Maybe, she thought hopefully, he had a tie to the place that even he hadn't realized yet.

"There's something I have to say first." She depended on hands, all three of them: Lippy, so young; Pecos, so alone; Sledge, as much a part of the ranch as the open land. There was no way the ranch could survive without them, but she had to give them the option to leave, before someone got hurt. "This isn't merely an annoyance anymore. This is getting dangerous, fast, and more so all the time. I can't ask you to put yourself at that kind of risk for me. If you feel you can't stay here anymore, well, I'll understand. I'll tell the same thing to Sledge, when I take him his supper."

"Miss Abigail!" Lippy was clearly appalled. "How could ya even think such a thing? That we'd be low-bellied coward enough to turn tail'n run off just when ya needed us the most?"

Pecos narrowed his eyes at her. "Somethin' else happen?"

She shot a nervous glance at Marcus. Between the ranch, the drought, and their father's condition, the boy had enough to worry about. She didn't want him to know that she'd nearly died that day. And how could she possibly explain the reason she hadn't? She'd never been good at lying to him.

"What makes you say that, Pecos?"

"Just seems kinda a big jump to me, from a coupla cut-up cows to you thinkin' it's too dangerous for us to hang around."

"No. Nothing like that," she said quickly.

He considered, then nodded, accepting, and she let out a breath of relief. She didn't know if he believed her or had merely chosen to keep his peace for the moment, but, either way, she was grateful.

"We're going to have to start keeping watch at night," she said. "The drought's a lucky break for this, I guess, since the cows all stay 'round the waterhole at night. But we're going to have to take turns, so one of us is always with the herd."

Worried, she drummed her fingers against the table. It was going to be difficult, especially with Sledge laid up. They worked hard during the day. There wasn't much energy left for guarding a herd all night long. "Three-hour shifts would be best. With only the three of us—"

"Four," Marcus put in.

Surprised, she turned to him. "But—"

"Four," he repeated in a tone that brooked no argument.

He was too young to be guarding the herd at night. It was simply too dangerous, and there was no one else to look after his safety but her. And, if she was going to be honest, he wasn't good enough, either. But she didn't know how to tell him.

For sure, she couldn't embarrass him by saying anything in front of the hands, in any case. Later, she'd tell him he couldn't go.

She returned to the matter at hand. "Now, then—"

"I'll take first watch," Lippy volunteered.

"Fine." Lord, she realized, if it really were B.J.—and it

had to be—one lone cowboy out there wasn't going to make the least bit of difference if he decided to stop slinking around making trouble and go for an all-out attack. Still, it was the only thing they could do. "Lippy? Be careful. Be real careful."

His Adam's apple bobbed as he swallowed, and she remembered just how young he really was. "Yes ma'am," he said. "I will. Don't you worry none. I won't let nuthin' happen, not to me or the beeves."

There was absolutely nothing she could do but hope he was right.

11

Abigail delivered Sledge's supper—and her warning, which he'd waved off gruffly, just as she'd expected. Too restless to stay inside afterwards, she decided to fix the broken step.

It took some doing, but she finally found a board in the lean-to tacked on to one side of the shed. The old wood had long ago weathered to dull gray, but it would serve. It would have to; they were getting low, and lumber was too expensive to buy more.

After scooping up a hammer and a handful of nails, she returned to the house. The lowering sun washed the land with an angry red that suited her mood, and heat rolled up from the hard ground.

Her father rocked in the porch chair, staring unblinkingly off to the horizon. She wondered what he saw there. His land, his life? His past, his future? More likely nothing at all, though the thought wrenched her.

She knelt beside the stairway to pry off the broken wood. A rusty nail let go with a metallic shriek.

"I can do that." Marcus came up beside her, thumbs hooked in his back pockets.

Squinting against the glaring light, she looked up at him, his little-kid freckles standing over cheekbones that were rapidly honing into those of a young man. He'd worked hard that day, done everything she'd asked. A troubled frown tugged at his mouth, and she wished she hadn't had to tell him about the attempted sabotage. He'd had a childhood without a mother; he deserved to spend what little was left of it without such worries, at least. But she'd had no choice.

"No, that's okay. I'll do it." She nodded over her shoulder at the old chair that stood waiting in the center of the bare, cracked yard. "You should practice."

His mouth thinned. "Why? So I can go to the fort next weekend and make a fool of myself in front of everybody, instead of just you?"

She didn't like the sulky edge to his voice. Another of his lightning-quick changes of mood; she couldn't keep up with him.

"*Why* is because it's something you need to know how to do, and practice is how you get better at anything." She pried at a stubborn piece of the step. "I don't expect you to enter anything next weekend."

"Don't you think I can do it?" Dusky color suffused his cheeks.

"That's not what I meant—"

"You're not going to let me take a turn at watch, are you?"

"I haven't decided yet," she hedged. She'd never forgive herself if anything happened to him, but she needed to find a better reason to give him, one that wouldn't hurt his prickly adolescent pride.

He turned on his heel and stalked away, scooping up the limp coil of rope that draped over one end of the porch. He carefully measured his distance from the straight-backed chair and shook out a good-sized circle of rope. With one more angry glance in her direction, he started swinging the lasso over his head, then hurled it in the direction of the chair.

The loop came in low and too hard, with the force of his anger behind it. Instead of settling over the top, the rope whapped the side of the chair and toppled it into the dust. His movements jerky, Marcus wound in the lasso and yanked the chair upright.

Abigail sank to the ground, swiped at her damp forehead with her shirtsleeve, and wondered for the hundredth time—maybe the thousandth time—if it was all worth it. Why was she trying so hard to hold this place together?

Her father had spent a lifetime building the Rolling G for his family. It had been his work, his pride, the one thing he had to give them. But what if his family didn't want it?

Marcus didn't want the ranch, had never wanted the ranch. She'd hoped he might change his mind as he grew, that eventually he'd develop a deep connection to the land and life that had meant everything to their father.

Was she holding onto the Rolling G only for herself? She liked it well enough. The open spaces suited her, the privacy, the fact that the work didn't care if you were male or female, only that you were willing to do it.

But giving it up wouldn't break her heart. The city had its advantages, too. She'd never have to wear pants again, for one thing. Her rear end certainly wouldn't miss the hours in the saddle. The truth was, either one would probably be all right with her. She was certain she could be content wherever the people she loved were happy.

The wind blew hard from the west, rattling a loose pane in the front window. Her father started, looking over his shoulder at the source of the noise, and then returned to his study of the vast, empty spaces.

From the day her mother died, he'd spent every evening after supper right out there on that porch. It seemed as if, inside the house, a territory that had clearly belonged to Margaret, he was reminded too much of her absence. On the porch, he could think of his land instead, plan for tomorrow's work, and forget, at least a little, that he'd lost the main reason he'd worked the land in the first place.

Her father. It always came back to her father.

Some days, she wondered if he'd even notice if they left the ranch. If he hardly ever recognized his own children, what difference did it make where they lived? B.J. had offered enough for the water to keep them for a while.

But what would they do after the money ran out? She could get a job as a housekeeper, perhaps. What were the chances of finding an employer who would let her bring along not only a younger brother but an unpredictable and demanding father?

The last time she'd tried to take Davis off the ranch, months ago, he'd become confused as soon as he left his own land, so upset and furious she hadn't been able to calm him no matter what she'd done. They'd had to turn around and come right back home. It was not something she was anxious to try again any time soon. It had been too painful to see him that way.

So she would keep him in familiar surroundings as long as she could. They would muddle through as well as they could and pray for rain. For if the drought did not end soon, she was horribly afraid she would lose the ranch anyway, and not even have the money that B.J. would have paid to show for it.

She pried off the last piece of the broken step and flung the shattered board away from her, hard. She'd gather the splinters up later—any wood was too valuable to waste—but, right now, it made her feel better just to throw the busted thing as hard as she could.

"You should have let Marcus fix the step, you know," Joshua said.

She dropped the hammer, darn it, and mentally swore at herself for letting Joshua's sudden appearance startle her so much. She shouldn't be surprised at it. She'd known he had to be hanging around somewhere.

He sat on the top step, watching her. Lord, did he have to look so good? She'd rarely seen him without a hat, but she liked it, the way the early evening light threw all sorts of interesting shadows beneath his cheekbones and brushed a bit of copper in his dark hair.

It would be too easy to forget—not only what he'd been, but what he was now. To armor herself against that, she concentrated on all the signs of his current state, on the slight fuzziness that outlined his body and the faint light that seemed to glow through his extremities.

Was it her imagination, or was he somehow a bit more . . . solid . . . than he'd seemed just that afternoon? His elbows were propped on his wide-spread knees, his hands dangling loose between them. She'd always loved his hands, strong, scarred fingers and broad joints hiding that unexpected, amazing gentleness of touch that had never failed to surprise her, even as it never failed to arouse her.

And there she found clear evidence of how much he'd changed.

"Joshua! Your finger!"

"Yeah." He grinned and held up his hand. "Looks kinda weird, don't it? I'd almost forgotten what it looked like whole."

As long as she'd known him, the first joint of his left middle finger had been missing. He'd lost it when he was fifteen, he'd told her, cocky enough to be careless when he'd roped an old steer and quickly dallied his lariat around his saddle horn, catching the tip of his own finger in the rope. His horse had pulled one way, the steer the other, and the tip nipped right off.

She'd wanted to sympathize, had longed—even after all that time—to kiss the old, scarred wound and make it better. But he'd just laughed it off, maintaining it had taught him caution better than any other, less-painful lesson ever could.

"But how—" She stopped, staring. It looked so odd, to see his hand whole and unscarred. That, more than anything, seemed proof that this was not the Joshua she'd once loved—not the man who'd left her.

"Heck if I know," he said, bemused. "I guess all that stuff the preachers say about how, when it's all over, 'all will be made well' is the truth."

"Oh." Her head was spinning. If there were any more surprises in store for her, she doubted her brain would ever straighten it all out again. She'd been too busy struggling to get through each day to spare much time for philosophizing about the sorts of things that were now sitting at the top of her broken stairway.

But thinking didn't get her step fixed. She might not know much about matters of the spirit, but she did know how to work. She bent to wedge the wood into place.

"You should let Marcus do it," Joshua repeated quietly.

The warped board rocked in its spot, and she flipped it over, hoping to find a more solid fit. "He's got other things to do."

"It doesn't matter. He needs to do this."

She ignored him, squared a nail with one edge, and began to tap it in with the hammer.

"He built the step in the first place, didn't he? He'll think you don't trust him to fix it properly. He needs to know that you do."

"He knows I trust him. He just has more important things to do right now." She whacked hard at the nail and it slammed into place.

"He doesn't, Abigail."

She dug through the small pile of salvaged nails, selected the straightest one she could find, and placed it carefully.

"You know my brother so well, do you?"

"No. But I know what it's like to be a twelve-year-old boy."

The fingers that were holding the rusty nail in place wobbled slightly. Damn it, she would allow let him do this, make her question whether she was making the best choices. Who was Joshua to waft back here after a year and a half and tell her how to manage her brother?

She pounded the nail home.

"Where were you during dinner?" she snapped.

"Gone, just like you asked," Joshua said. She wasn't going to let him help her, he thought, studying the determined set of her shoulders and the stiff expression on her face.

He didn't know why it surprised him. She'd inherited that rigid pride from her father; it was one of the things he'd always admired about her. But right now she needed all the help she could get, and he would have thought the fact that he'd been sent from above might have carried a bit of weight.

"I know you were there."

The hammer slipped a bit as she tapped the next nail, nearly whamming her thumb, and he had to stop himself from grabbing it out of her hand and finishing the job himself. Abigail wouldn't appreciate his assistance and he darn well knew it.

"You told me to disappear, so I was gone. I always do what you tell me, don't I?"

She gave him a long, skeptical look.

"Well, okay," he admitted finally. "I was outside the window."

"You . . . You *sneak*." He winced when she whacked a nail with such force that he knew she was imagining bringing that hammer down over his head.

"I thought you didn't want to see me."

"If you're there, I sure as heck want to know about it!"

"Whatever you say," he agreed in his most obliging tone.

The arch of her brow was pure suspicion.

"What? You don't believe me? I don't know why not." She glared at him and he burst out laughing. "Okay, so maybe I do."

She set the hammer aside and tugged at the step, testing. Satisfied, she sat back on her heels and regarded him seriously.

"Was it you?"

"Probably. It usually is." He grinned at her. He was too much, she thought. Too handsome, too charming, too funny. Far too tempting. "Was what me?"

"My . . . belly. Did you do that?"

"You mean this?" He closed his eyes, concentrating.

The seductive warmth unfurled in her stomach, bloomed like a morning glory opening to the new sun.

"Stop it!"

He opened his eyes and the warmth disappeared immediately.

"How did you do that?" she said, hating the breathlessness that crept into her voice.

"I just . . . It's hard to explain." He leaned forward intently. "I just think of you, of heat, of what I want you to feel. I didn't really know if it would work, actually." He looked entirely too pleased with himself. "Guess it did."

"Why did you do it, Joshua?"

"I noticed that, when you get all tensed up, you rub your stomach. I figured it was hurting you. It was, wasn't it?"

Her expression must have given her away.

"Thought so," he said, faint puzzlement creeping into his voice. "I don't know why I never noticed it before this."

Perhaps because he'd never studied her so closely before, he thought. Had never just watched her, for long periods of time, without distractions or conversation or any other thoughts but what *she* was thinking and feeling. Whenever he'd been with her, he'd been too busy trying to seduce her to pay close attention to how she acted in difficult situations.

And the truth was, seduction still had one hell of an appeal.

"Anyway," he went on, "I just wanted to make you feel better. Did it?"

"Stop it," she said sharply. How was she to defend herself against him? He knew her too well, too closely, knew the pathways around any barrier she might erect against him. He'd had six months of practice at it.

The realization that he could, with only his thoughts, put warmth into her body, call forth feelings she had absolutely no control over—what else might he be able to do to her? It was terribly frightening.

And terribly, awesomely exciting, and she had to make certain he never did it again.

"Don't do it anymore," she said, forcing as much

cold anger in her voice as she could manage. "Never again."

"You didn't like it?"

"No. I didn't like it," she lied. Unable to meet his gaze—he'd always been able to read her far better than she would have liked, and she'd always been able to read him too little—she started gathering up the extra nails and bits of wood. "Stay out of my body, Joshua."

Darn it! That hadn't come out exactly how she'd meant it. If she looked at him, she knew he'd be smiling at her, ready to make some sexy little comment that would make her laugh and bring all that turbulent heat flooding right back without him even having to try. That was how he'd seduced her before, not simply with his touch but with laughter.

The laughter was even harder to resist.

"Oh, Joshua, why can't you just leave me alone?" Her voice shook. She grabbed her leftover supplies and fled toward the shed.

"Abigail!"

She ignored him.

"Abbie!" he called once more as she dashed around the corner and into the lean-to.

She sagged against the rough board wall. It was dark inside, musty with old, useless things, close and hot as an oven, but at least she had a chance to collect herself. She hooked the hammer on a nail stuck high on one wall. The handful of nails clinked against each other as she dropped them one by one into a box, taking as much time as she could before she must go back and face him.

Would he take her at her word? Would he be gone, or would he be there when she returned?

She wanted him gone. She needed him gone. He'd said he was there to help her, but what kind of help could she get from a phantom cowboy that only she could see? He could confuse her, distract her, make her wish for things that could never be. Make her cry and hurt and want, and a hundred other things that she had neither the time nor the energy to fight.

Please, she prayed, *when I get back, let him be gone*.

He wasn't, of course. He was leaning against a post that held up the porch roof, his arms crossed casually across his chest, looking for all the world as if he belonged there. And she couldn't help it if her foolish heart gave a giddy little lurch.

She shouldn't be so happy he was still there, and she knew it.

It didn't matter that she shouldn't be.

She was.

12

Still doing battle with rope and chair, Marcus beat up a choking cloud of dust on the ground as the loop fell, again and again, short of its mark.

Joshua shook his head and pushed away from the post, sauntering over to stand close to Marcus. As Marcus began, once more, to circle the rope over his head, Joshua closed his hand over the rope, too, a bare inch from where Marcus held it.

"What are you doing!" Abigail shouted.

They threw the rope together. It sailed smoothly through the darkening air, a clean arc against the dusky sky, and dropped unerringly over the chair back.

Marcus stared it, his jaw agape, as if he were afraid that, if he looked away for a moment, the rope might no longer be snugged around the chair. His grin spread slow and big over his face, the kind of smile she hadn't seen there for far too long. If only it were his own accomplishments, and not Joshua's aid, that had put it there.

"Abbie! Did you see it, Abbie? I did it!"

"Yes, I saw it." Joshua looked over at her, and she jerked her head, indicating the back of the house. She could hardly holler at him right out here in the front yard. Marcus would think she'd lost her mind. And at this rate, she very well might.

Joshua just furrowed his brow, perplexed. She made a shooing motion with her hand.

"I can't believe it," Marcus continued. "It just went right around it so easy. Almost as good as—" He broke off, wincing as he glanced her way. She'd be willing to bet that she knew what he'd almost blurted out.

Almost as good as Joshua. Joshua, who'd been widely acknowledged as the best roper around and had easily won the fourth of July contest at the fort the summer he'd worked at the Bar B.

"Gee, I wonder why?" she muttered.

"Well, anyway." Marcus cleared his throat. "I can't believe how easy it was."

Joshua stood relaxed, smiling at Marcus' excitement, looking as innocent as a new calf, as if he hadn't the faintest idea why she was glaring at him.

She gestured furiously, pointing around the back of the house.

He only shrugged.

He was doing it on purpose, she just knew it, pretending he didn't know what she wanted.

He hadn't been sent here to help her.

He'd been sent here to drive her crazy.

"I have to talk to you!" she burst out.

"Huh?" Marcus wheeled around, one end of the rope still clutched in his hand. "Go ahead. I'm listenin'."

"It's nothing," she said, flustered. "I was just thinking out loud. You should . . . stay and practice now. Okay? I'll talk to you when you get in."

"Okay." He admired his feat once more before he lifted the rope off the chair and began coiling it up again.

Abigail marched around the far side of the house. If that man didn't follow her, she was going to . . . What was she going to do? Wringing his neck sounded appealing, but it probably wasn't going to have quite the effect she was looking for on a dead man.

The shadow of the house was a long, squat rectangle against the brown grass. From here, there was no hint of the ranch buildings clustered on the other side of the house, nothing to see but a long, empty sweep of open grassland, stretching distant miles before it met the clean edge of the horizon.

She whirled to face Joshua. So he had followed her, after all. For some reason that only made her all the more angry.

"Just what did you think you were doing?"

Unconcerned, he hooked his thumbs in his pockets. "I was helping Marcus."

"Just how does you throwing the rope *for* him teach him to do it himself, hmm?"

"He needs to know he can do it, Abigail."

Her hands fisted. That was twice today that he'd questioned the way she'd dealt with her brother. What did he know of it? He hadn't been a sister for twelve years, a mother for nearly as long, a father for one. And if sometimes she couldn't quite figure out how to do all three at once, she certainly knew a whole lot more about it than Joshua did.

"Did I ever tell you about learning to swim?"

"No." Puzzled at the abrupt change of subject, but grateful that she wasn't yelling at him, at least, Joshua leaned against the house. Always a tricky thing, he nodded in relief when the wall held him up. "Tell me."

All he'd wanted to do was help her. From the

moment he realized there was something really wrong with her father, not to mention with the ranch, he'd abandoned any idea of haunting her. It didn't matter any more whether coming to her aid was his assignment. He would have wanted to stay no matter what.

But, despite his best intentions, it seemed he could do nothing but make her mad. That wasn't helping her. Even with the one thing he had done right—rescuing her when she'd fallen down the well—he couldn't help feeling that he should have been able to prevent the whole episode in the first place.

"I was six. I was out with my father, checking the waterhole, and I didn't listen to his warnings about staying back and toppled right in." A lonely gust of wind whipped around the corner of the house, tugging strands of hair free from her braid. "He pulled me out."

"And then he taught you to swim, right?"

"Right." She jammed the hair out of her way behind her ears. "I was terrified of the water. And so he took me out in it, just over my head, and let me go."

"What?" He couldn't have heard her right.

"I must have swallowed half the pond before he fished me out. He waited until I stopped coughing, then did it again."

The anger was so strong Joshua almost staggered. How *could* he? How could Davis have done that to his daughter?

"I learned to swim that day." She looked at him, direct, unsmiling. "It was never a problem again, and I was safe."

He knew she wanted him to understand, to believe that her father's actions had been necessary and efficient. But he didn't care if Davis was old and senile; Joshua wanted to shake him for what he'd done to the frightened little girl she must have been, and for that damned, unbendable, stiff-necked pride he'd instilled in his daughter.

Damn it, she wasn't going to let him help her. Accepting help from another just wasn't in her, anymore than it had been in her father.

He had no choice but to try anyway.

"Abigail," he said softly. Her hair wouldn't stay tucked away, blowing across her cheek, shiny red against palest ivory, and he gave in to temptation, reaching over to brush it back. Pure sensation washed his fingertips, so soft and sweet and intense that his hands shook and he did a bad job of his task, the hair pulling free again as soon as he released it. "Let me help you. Please."

Help her? How could Joshua possibly help her, she wondered. He could tempt her. Even as just the barest brush of his hand against her face made her want to hurl herself against his chest and plead for more.

But help her? The last time she'd needed him, he'd left her.

She knew it was unfair to resent him for that still. She'd refused him, after all. But she'd never expected that, just because she wouldn't run off with him, he'd kick up his heels and be gone before she'd realized what happened.

She should have expected it. Joshua was a drifter. A man who left, often and always. She'd known it when she met him. But, for some reason, deep, deep inside, she'd never really believed he would leave *her*.

"And just how are you going to help me?"

"Good question." One he had no decent answer for. What *could* he do? Wandering around invisible, doing the few things he'd learned how to do— It wasn't going to do her much good. He would have been much more use to her alive, when he could ride and shoot and rope, than he was like this. "I could watch over you."

Her eyes darkened, deep and unsettling as the shadows that were now on the verge of bruising into night. "Watch over the herd, then, if you must. Watch over my hands, my land." She stepped away, and the fierce wind whipped her skirts around her legs and blew her blouse tight against her lean body. "Don't watch over me, Joshua. Don't watch over me."

She took off around the corner, back to the front of the house, and he didn't even attempt to stop her.

Damn it, why had they sent him here like this, so useless, so unprepared!

Frustrated, seeking any outlet for his roiling anger, he balled his fist and threw a roundhouse punch at the stone-and-plaster wall.

His arm disappeared up to his elbow. He swore viciously, not even caring if *they* heard him.

Abigail finally needed him, and he couldn't even hit a wall.

Some help he was going to be.

13

He took her at her word. Abigail couldn't decide if she was happy about it or not. For nearly two days, she'd seen nothing of Joshua, so much so she was beginning to wonder if the entire episode had been a hallucination. She's become ill from the heat, perhaps.

Except in those two days, not a single thing had gone wrong on the Rolling G. Not one injured calf or missing cow, no broken tools or damaged fences. Over breakfast that morning Lippy had speculated that the ranch had finally seemed to acquire a much-needed guardian angel, and he'd looked at Abigail strangely when a muffled giggle escaped her.

No, Joshua was still here somewhere, she was certain. She could feel him, the same way her father had always been able to sense an approaching storm or when a cow was about to calf, long before there were physical signs that anyone else could read.

Those things were in her father's bones, and he knew them better than he knew himself. Abigail was terribly afraid that Joshua was imbedded just as deeply in her own bones, and she would never be able to completely free herself of him. Worse, in the secret, forgotten recesses of her heart, she didn't even want to.

Abigail worked on the western edge of the Rolling G, not far from where it marched along Hallenbeck's much larger spread. The cattle ranged wide during the daylight hours, searching farther and farther from the solitary waterhole for good forage, then the entire herd clustered together near the spring at night, where the hands could keep close watch.

The wind blew hard today, relentless, screaming in from the west, flattening the scorched, brittle grass nearly to the ground. Instead of cooling her, that hot, fierce wind only served to intensify the heat, scouring her skin raw.

Part of the herd—the ones that were her responsibility this afternoon—milled off to her right. The cattle wisely gave wide berth to a ground-tied Buttercup, the mare flipped her tail and munched contentedly a few yards away.

A brown, curly-haired calf lay on its side in front of Abigail, bawling piteously for its mother, who stood guard nearby lowing in protest.

"Come now," Abigail said. "This is not so bad, I promise. Much easier than the branding."

She dipped two fingers in a jar, scooping out a generous amount of the sticky, dark mixture of tar and iodine, and bent to smear the smelly stuff over the calf's belly.

"Done," she said, and released the animal. It scrambled to its feet and loped over to its mother. "Nothing to it, was there?"

"Got a sucker, do you?"

She was proud of herself. When Joshua spoke from behind her this time, she didn't jump like a rabbit who had been flushed out of its hole. Didn't even suddenly twist around and look at him. Though she was far from accustomed to his unsettling presence, much less his abrupt comings and goings, she was getting a good deal better at pretending she was.

"Yep." Attempting casualness, she checked her jar to see if plenty of salve remained. They had a calf who liked to suckle. After his mother lost patience with his continual demands, he turned to pulling on the umbilical scars of the other calves. His vigorous tugging could cause a hernia in the other animals, but the bad-tasting iodine concoction should be enough to discourage him from trying. "Haven't seen you around for a while."

"Just doing what you asked."

"Then what are you doing here now?" After steeling herself against his impact, she dared to steal a glance at Joshua. Tall and lean, boots planted wide, he squinted over the herd of cows, looking so much a part of this place and life that, if he disappeared again, this was precisely how she'd always remember him.

"Watching the cattle, just like you told me to." He slanted her a look. "Can I help it if you happen to be here, too?"

She tucked her tongue in her cheek. "Guess not."

"Didn't think so."

Joshua had assured himself that he'd no intention of talking to her. In the midst of a tour of the ranch, he'd stopped here only briefly to get a closer look at this year's crop of calves. He fully intended to leave Abigail completely alone, just as she wanted him to.

He'd paused here only to inspect the herd. If he glanced her way once or twice, so what? After all, over the last few days, he'd gotten pretty good at watching her without her noticing. She hadn't caught him at it yet, even though he'd followed her around most of yesterday.

Nor had she discovered him when he'd spent a good chunk of the night in her room, as the translucent moonlight washed across her bed and he'd attended perhaps a shade too closely when she kicked the sheet away and her nightdress rode high on her pale thighs. It only proved that, after all, he was still just a man, a man who couldn't turn away from a sight like that.

So there was no reason she would have suspected his presence today if he hadn't shown himself to her. But she'd seemed so alone, out here on the desolate land with nothing but that she-devil horse and the other animals to accompany her, and he just had to be with her. Just for a little while.

"Joshua?"

"Hmm?" Since she'd called his name, he figured he could look at her now without breaking his promise to himself.

She sat cross-legged on the ground, sharp knees poking through the thin fabric of her work pants, wearing a grubby old blouse and with her bright hair snarled by the wind. Grease smudged her cheek, dark stains splotched her fingers, and she was still the best damn thing he'd seen in his whole life.

Her lips curved up, a mystified, wondrous little smile. "I missed you," she said.

It took no more than those softly uttered honest words. Something jolted in his chest, hard and painful, in that place inside him no one else had ever touched but she always seemed to discover with unerring, effortless precision.

"Aw, Abbie—" He broke off, listening intently. "Do you hear that?"

She cocked her head, puckering her lips in concentration. "Is that—"

"Let's go!"

She sprang to her feet and scrambled for her horse.

Once mounted, she wheeled Buttercup around, then stopped and looked back at him expectantly. "You going to ride with me?"

He eyed the horse dubiously. Any other horse, and he would have jumped at the opportunity immediately. A chance to ride with Abigail, tucked up behind her, her slender form curved right against him? Sounded pretty fine.

Except this was Buttercup. He grimaced, absently rubbing his right thigh, the precise spot where her hoof had once connected.

"I don't think so."

"But—"

"You go on. I'll be right there with you, I promise."

"Okay." She tapped her heels against the horse's side, crouching low over Buttercup's neck, and galloped away.

After five minutes of hard riding on her part, him breezing effortlessly along behind her—now, *this* part of being a spirit he could find some use for—she pulled Buttercup to a stop.

"Shit," he said softly.

"Exactly."

At least a third of B.J.'s herd sprawled across the distant horizon, walking steadily east. The line shimmered in the waves of heat rolling up from the hot plains. The elusive tremor Abigail had felt before was now a perceptible rumble.

At least half a dozen men, their hands conspicuously resting on their gun butts, roamed the edges of the herd, urging them on. And, leading the way rode B.J. himself, mounted high on a huge buckskin stallion, surveying the land before him as if he owned the whole of Texas.

"Joshua, if those cows come much farther, they're going to catch scent of our water and there'll be no stopping them, no matter what."

"Yeah, I know."

Abigail tensed in the saddle, her fingers curling so tightly around the reins that her knuckles whitened. Buttercup skittered beneath her.

When B.J. caught sight of Abigail, he spurred his own horse in her direction. Abigail dismounted and walked forward to meet him halfway.

Lord, what a woman, Joshua thought. Alone on the empty plains, facing so many, and she didn't run, didn't flinch, just stood tall and proud, waiting to face the man who probably intended to destroy her.

Hallenbeck halted his horse with a showy flourish. He swung himself out of the saddle and swaggered over to Abigail.

"You're on my land, little lady. I don't recall inviting you."

She nodded at the approaching herd. "You bring those much farther, and you're *all* gonna be on mine."

He grinned broadly, unconcerned. "Can't say I didn't warn you."

Fury swamped Joshua. How dare B.J.? How *dare* he? He'd threatened Abigail, insulted her, dismissed her, and now was going to simply drive his herd right onto her land? He'd probably even tried to kill her!

He couldn't let B.J. get away with it, and no longer cared if it would damn his own soul, once and for all. He would beat that cocky grin off B.J. Hallenbeck's face, and, in the process, make sure he never bothered Abigail again. The vision of Hallenbeck, bloodied, helpless, and unable to hurt her again was rousingly satisfying.

He lowered his shoulder and got a running start, aiming for B.J.'s midsection. An arm's length away, he dove.

And hit nothing.

Next thing he knew, he was face down in the dirt. He rolled over to find a clear view of B.J.'s broad rump.

Damn it! At least he could do *this* for her.

He sprang to his feet directly behind B.J. Closing his eyes, he emptied his mind of anything but B.J.'s head and the feel of his fist slamming down on it with punishing force.

Concentrate.

Hit him, hit him. The command thundered in his brain.

He raised his hand and propelled it down. His arm swung clear, unimpeded as a hawk in free fall.

He opened his eyes again. B.J. and Abigail faced each other, not more than ten feet apart. B.J. glowered down at her, his arms jammed over his wide chest, his frown a cruel slash, clearly trying to intimidate her. Abigail, chin lifted at a sharp angle, wasn't giving an inch.

Joshua rushed to stand behind her. "I'm sorry."

"Are you all right?" she asked softly.

"Of course. I just . . . I think maybe I'm not allowed to actually *hurt* someone. Even B.J." Jesus, but he was useless. Why the hell had they sent him here for her protection if he couldn't *do* anything useful?

The tension vibrated from Abigail, her body taut as a fence wire in gale-force winds. Joshua wondered how much more she could take before she snapped.

Hesitantly, unsure whether his actions would help or hurt, he placed his hands on her shoulders. She jerked, once, and he waited for her to brush them away. She only released a long, shaky breath and swayed back, closer to him.

God, she felt good. Firm muscle under thin cotton; warmth that quickly seeped through the fabric and into his palms. He rubbed gently, stroking his thumbs along the tight cords where her neck curved into her shoulders, and he felt her tension ease, just a notch.

"Thank you," she said.

"What're you mumbling about?" B.J. hitched his thumbs in his wide belt, the polished buckle flashing silver in the sun. "Talkin' to yourself now?"

"I must be," Abigail agreed.

His eyes slitted. "You sure are a strange one, Abigail Grier."

"You got a way with courtin' words, B.J, no doubt about it. What a thing to say about the woman you wanted to marry."

"*Wanted* to marry?" He gave a hearty laugh. "I just knew you was gonna change your mind. Too late now, little lady."

Abigail clapped a hand to her chest. "I'm so heartbroken."

The herd straggled closer. Raucous bawls and the clank of horns clashing together occasionally drowned out the audible crack of their ankles as they walked. Their skin was drawn taut over sharp bones, and desperation glazed the animals' dull eyes. An eager buzzard wheeled overhead, trailing the herd, its sharp eyes searching for failing stragglers, hoping for a fresh meal.

"They're so skinny it looks like they only got one stomach apiece," Joshua said.

"Yeah," Abigail whispered. She hated the cows' condition, deeply mourned their thirst and weakness. But there wasn't a damn thing she could do about it without condemning her own herd to the same brutal fate. "You're not taking those animals on my land, B.J."

"Yeah?" he jeered. "How the hell you gonna stop me?"

Abigail carried her six-shooter high and out of the way, holstered across her body. With precise, deliberate care, she pulled her gun from its sheath and aimed it straight at B.J. Hallenbeck's swaggering chest.

14

"Well, would you look at that! The little lady's got herself a gun."

"Sure do," Abigail said agreeably. "I always carry one out on the range. Sometimes I come across snakes out here, you know."

"You ain't got it in you to shoot me, Abigail, and we both know it."

"You're right," she admitted.

"Oh, sure you do," Joshua whispered in her ear, and was rewarded by the slight, upward tilt of her mouth.

"But I could shoot your lead cattle," she suggested. "No problem at all. And your herd isn't going anywhere if they've no leads to follow."

"Guess what?" B.J. grinned, enjoying himself, clearly never doubting for a minute what today's outcome would be. "I got a gun, too." He unholstered his own revolver and aimed it in Abigail's direction.

Abigail flinched beneath Joshua's hands, and he realized he'd tightened his grip, his fingers digging into her shoulders. He forced himself to loosen his hold.

"You're not going to shoot me either, B.J.," she said.

"Probably not." His thumb slid over the hammer of the gun. "But I wouldn't mind shooting your horse." He swung the barrel around to cover Buttercup.

"Oh God, yes!" Joshua said. "I swear my butt still hurts from the last time that idiot nag threw me. Let him shoot the damn horse! Please!"

A short bark of laughter escaped her.

"You laughin'?" B.J. asked, incredulous.

"Of course not," she said gravely, but humor bubbled through her voice. "Just look at all the trouble I'm in. What could I possibly have to laugh about right now?"

He glared at her suspiciously. He'd obviously thought he'd have Abigail in a weak, whimpering puddle by now, and was more than a little rattled at her calm confidence.

Not much farther, and the cattle would be on Rolling G land. They were also nearing shooting range.

Abigail picked out an old, sway-backed bull, plodding along in front of his herd, and took careful aim.

"That's far enough, B.J."

"Go ahead, Abigail," B.J. said. "It's going to take more'n that to stop me. You're finally out of second chances."

Under Joshua's hands, Abigail's shoulders lifted and fell as she took a deep breath, tensing her arm muscles in preparation for firing.

"Wait," Joshua said. "I've got an idea that might work."

Abigail hesitated briefly, then nodded.

Joshua headed straight for the lead cattle, the old bull with one broken horn and his two deputies. A herd would follow its lead cows anywhere, even off the edge of a cliff. If Abigail shot one, however, another would only take its place, and she could only kill so many animals before running out of ammunition—or worse, B.J. ran out of patience and took steps to stop her. But if Joshua could halt the lead animal, deflect it, the herd would stop.

At ten yards from the cattle, Joshua rushed them, flapping his arms, kicking his feet, and hollering like he'd gone loco.

Just as he'd hoped, the bull reacted exactly as the escaped horse had. It froze in its tracks, wild-eyed and quivering.

The entire herd shuffled to a halt behind it.

"What the hell's going on there!" B.J. shouted.

One of the hands rode up, edging along the front row of now-stationary cattle, which pawed the ground, twitched dirty tails, and lowed in complaint but advanced no farther. "Damned if'n I know, boss. They just . . . quit walkin'."

"Well, get 'em moving again!"

"Sure thing." The hand prodded his horse in the direction of the lead animal. Joshua took a short sprint at the horse, and it reared, its front hooves desperately flailing the air.

"What the hell!" The horse came down with a bone-jarring thump, and the hand dug in his spurs, trying to force his mount forward. Joshua stepped nearer, and the horse backed nervously away, a clear circle of white showing around its brown eyes.

"Get goin'!" B.J. shouted.

"I'm tryin'! The horse won't go over there!"

"So get down and walk over there yourself, you dad-blamed fool."

The cowboy jumped from his mount. As soon as he released the reins, the horse turned tail and fled as if he'd just confronted a wolf. "Well, I'll be . . ."

Perplexed, he lifted his hat and scratched his head, watching his horse thunder away.

"Never mind that now. Get those cattle moving!" B.J. yelled.

"Yes, sir."

The hand roped the old bull around its neck, drawing the loop tight. He dug his feet in, getting a good hold, and yanked hard. "Come on now. Move!" The bull just bellowed in protest and took a step back.

"How'm I doin'?" Joshua shouted over his shoulder at Abigail, though his gaze never wavered from the terrified animal.

"Not bad." She wandered over to stand behind him, watching with interest as the bull tossed his massive head, making the hand stumble forward.

"What the hell's goin' on?" B.J. barreled up, looking like he was more than ready to start pushing the herd along with his bare hands.

"I dunno, boss. Somethin's spookin' 'em, but good."

"Must be me," Abigail said helpfully. "Us *strange* women, we sure are a scary sort, aren't we, B.J.?"

He shot her a killing glance. Two more of his hands rode up, and he gestured wildly at them. "You there! You get behind this damned animal, all of you, and push!" He roughly elbowed aside the man who still held the rope. "*I'll* pull, you damned weak greenbelly!"

When the men had arranged themselves to B.J.'s satisfaction behind the immobile bull, their sturdy shoulders firmly planted on its wide butt, B.J. hollered: "Now!"

He pulled, hard, throwing all his substantial bulk behind the effort, grunting with the strain. Cheeks bulging out like a swollen mushroom, his face purpled. Joshua waited until only the taut rope supported all of Hallenbeck's weight.

Joshua charged the bull.

It gave a pained shriek and jerked back, scrambling frantically away, backing the cowboys into the milling mass of cattle.

B.J. lost his footing and flew forward, the rope still clutched in his big mitts, and landed face down in a cloud of dust and curses.

Spitting dirt, he rolled over. He'd lost his hat, and the sun gleamed on the sweating bald spot thinly covered with damp blond strands.

"Never seen anything like it," the boss hand said with a touch of wonder.

A second man rolled to his feet, his arm held at a painfully awkward angle. "I've driven 'em through flooded rivers and 'cross plains filled with rattlers with less trouble'n this. What the hell's stopping 'em?"

"Spirits here," another suggested. "A curse."

"What?" B.J. roared. "Move those damn cows!"

"They ain't moving there, boss," the lead cowboy said. Sure enough, the bulk of the herd had already turned north, slowly circling back from where they'd come.

"But . . . But . . ." B.J. sputtered.

"Better give it up," Abigail advised him. "Or I'll put a hex on you, too."

B.J.'s jaw dropped as he stared at her. "You're crazy." He pushed himself to his feet and backed away. "Gone plumb insane, just like your father."

Abigail went still, her eyes narrowing. "What did you say?"

But B.J. didn't answer, just limped away, dragged himself up on his horse, and followed his herd home.

15

"*Well,*" *Abigail said,* when she'd had enough of watching several hundred bony rumps bob away across the plains. She turned to face Joshua, finding him close beside her, regarding her with open concern.

"I'm sorry," he said gently. "What B.J. said about your father. I'm sorry."

"It's all right." She cared little what B.J. Hallenbeck thought of her or her family. "It's just . . ."

"What?"

"How did he know?"

"No one knows?"

"I don't think so. I've been very careful. You know how proud Papa was. I knew how much it would hurt him, if people found out what was happening to him. And I was afraid that if everyone knew about his condition, they'd think it would be that much easier to take the ranch from us."

"You were probably right." He glanced after B.J. "Well, he found out somehow."

But how? No one at the Rolling G would have told B.J. intentionally. Someone must have let a hint slip. "I don't suppose it matters much." She dusted her hands together. "I guess it was silly of me to think we could keep it secret much longer, anyway."

"I'm sorry," Joshua said, and the sympathy in his voice was nearly too much for her. Understanding, concern . . . she hadn't had—or even *wanted*—those things for so long she'd forgotten what they felt like. But from Joshua, they felt as powerful and good as the first true, warm breeze of spring.

"You think he'll be back?" she asked, hooking her thumb in the direction of the departing cattle. "B.J., I mean."

"Eventually, I suppose. Not for a while, though. I worked for the man for six months, and if there's one thing I learned about B.J., it's that he don't take too well to being shown up. His pride's been bruised, but good, and he's not gonna take the chance that'll happen in front of his hands again any time soon."

He lifted his hand to his head, like he was going to push back his hat. His hand hovered for a moment at his temple before he chuckled and let it fall back to his side. "Don't have a hat anymore. I keep forgettin'."

"I like it," she said. Without the shadow cast by the brim, his eyes looked light, the blue-gray pure and clear. Like she'd be able to look right into them and read all his dreams, all his secret wishes, just the way he'd always seemed to be able to see right into her own soul. "I mean . . . you look good without the hat. Handsome."

He blinked in surprise. "Oh. Well." He cleared his throat. "Thank you."

It was so odd, this awkward, halting conversation between them. They were like strangers newly met, when before, even the first time, it had never been anything but easy between them.

"Thank *you*." Perhaps the strangeness was simply because he wasn't touching her. Before, they'd never been in each other's presence more than a few minutes without Joshua reaching for her in some way; linking his strong hands with hers, bumping shoulders or thighs, skating his fingertips along the back of her neck. This distance between them, the empty air, seemed alien and unbreachable. "For helping, I mean. For turning away the herd, and getting rid of Hallenbeck."

"Aw, shucks." He affected a gosh-darn grin. "'Tween't nuthin'."

"If today's any indication, you just might be useful come roundup time."

His smile vanished. "I . . . I don't know if I'll still be here then."

Abigail longed to snatch the words back. She didn't want to think about his eventual leaving. Their victory over B.J.—temporary as it might be—was exhilarating, and she wanted to ride the good feelings as long as she could. There hadn't been that many of them lately.

"I could have kicked you," she said, "when you were whispering all those things to me. Here I was, so scared my knees were wobbling like a new foal's, trying to show B.J. how tough and impressive I was, and instead you were making me laugh."

He brightened immediately. "It's a gift."

And it was.

Back when he'd first come to call, she'd tried hard to resist him. Abigail had no illusions about herself. She knew what she was, and knew well any man who came courting had not stars in his eyes but water and land.

But even then, as hard as she'd tried, Joshua had always been able to make her laugh. Always. No matter how angry she'd been, or unhappy, or how reluctant. How determined to remain immune to his charm.

And then he'd kissed her for the first time, and she'd learned there was one more thing he could always make her do.

He could always make her want him.

His gaze roamed her face, slowly, and settled on her mouth, a speculative smile playing about the corners of his own.

She knew that look, remembered it well. She'd seen it often enough on his face, and a thousand more times in her dreams. The look he always got, just before he reached for her.

This was not a good idea. Not a good idea at all.

"Oh no you don't." She took a quick step back.

"Sorry." His grin was unrepentant. "Old habits."

Unable to stop herself, she returned his smile. "You really are such a scoundrel."

"An improvement, then."

Puzzled, she wrinkled her brow.

"Better than a no-account, worthless scoundrel."

"Oh." She winced. "Sorry about that."

"It's all right." It shouldn't matter, Joshua thought. After everything that had happened to her recently, with all the trouble she had, his bruised pride should be the least of her concerns.

Except it did matter to him, and no amount of his trying to ignore it seemed to make it go away. It mattered what she thought of him, and always had.

"It's just . . ." Abigail's voice trailed off. How was she to explain it to him? Not without telling him things that she wasn't certain she wanted him to know.

But he was hurt. It was there, in the defensive hunch of his shoulders, in the way his gaze glanced off hers and roamed out over the land.

He'd helped her today when she'd needed it. She wanted to give something back.

"I was hurt, when you left me, Joshua. Hurt, and angry. And so maybe I called you a few names that I would take back if I could."

His attention snapped back. "What did you expect? That I'd hang around like a moon-eyed calf, begging you to change your mind? You told me no!"

"Well, I didn't think you'd just disappear," she said, stunned at how quickly her own anger rushed back, too. "For heaven's sake, Joshua, you thought I could just leave my family and my home and trail you all over the country? What kind of an example would that be for Marcus? My father would have had every right to come charging after us with a shotgun, if nothing else!"

"Aw, hell, Abbie, it's not like I wasn't gonna marry you."

She froze.

"You knew that." He took a double-take at her shocked face. "You . . . you didn't know that?"

"You never said anything," she said slowly.

"But . . . well, damn, of *course* we were gonna get married." He felt like the world had just tilted under his feet. How could she even have wondered? "Abbie, I sure as hell knew you weren't exactly the kind of woman who would run off with a man without taking vows first."

Abbie put a hand to her spinning head. Everything she'd believed for so long . . . what else had she gotten all wrong?

"You . . ." No more guessing, no more assumptions. She had to know for sure, exactly, what he'd meant. "You *wanted* to marry me?"

He was to her in two steps, staring down at her, so close that, if she took a deep breath, she was certain that they'd touch, her breasts settling right onto the hard

planes of his chest, and it was all she could do not to
gulp in as much air as she could grab.

"Yes. I wanted to marry you." Intensity filled his eyes,
his voice. "You had to have known that."

"No." He'd never said the words, and she'd never
found the courage to ask. It wasn't the sort of thing a
lady should ask, she'd always thought. Damn it, why
hadn't she asked?

"Well, hell." He shook his head, mystified. "I really
screwed that one up, huh?"

And just like that, all that anger and hurt she'd lived
with for eighteen months vanished as if they'd never
existed at all.

What now? With his words, everything she'd
believed had changed. Everything but the way he made
her feel, the way her heart lifted into her throat just from
looking at him. The way she thought that she'd need
nothing else in the world if she could wake up every
morning to Joshua's kiss.

All she'd have to do was raise up a bit. A tiny shift, a
little tilt, and her mouth would be on his. Exactly as she
wanted.

She swayed, and his eyes darkened. So simple, so
easy, just like she'd done a hundred times in her dreams.

But when then? Dear Lord, what then?

The anger had been so much easier.

The last time he'd left her, it had nearly destroyed
her, but she'd had the anger to stiffen her spine and
repair her heart. Without that, what would happen to
her? How much worse would it be this time?

For he was still dead. And if dead had turned out to
be considerably less absolute than she'd expected, it still
did not exactly make him a prime candidate for hanging
her dreams on. A future was impossible, no matter how
powerfully tempting it was.

"Abigail." He said her name as reverently as a prayer. If he only said her name like that, one more time, she'd forget there was no future for them and not even care. "If I'd said the words . . . when I asked you to leave with me, if I'd asked you to marry me, too, would the answer have been different?"

She wanted to say yes. *Yes*, it would have been different; *yes*, I'll marry you; *yes*, to whatever you ask me, even now.

But there was still her father. Still her brother, and the Rolling G, and every other responsibility she had. Nothing else in her life had changed, nothing but her heart.

"No," she said at last. "I still wouldn't have gone."

His eyes went cold, remote. It was the first time since he'd appeared to her again that he actually looked dead.

"I didn't think so." He wheeled away, starting off toward the horizon.

She stared after him for a moment, at his long, loose, graceful strides as he walked away from her. *No*, she thought suddenly. I will not let him disappear again.

"Wait!" she shouted.

He stopped walking but didn't turn. "What?"

"Will you stay and help me? Please?"

His head lifted and tilted as if to listen more closely.

"I need your help, Joshua," she added softly.

She'd asked for his help! Joshua could hardly believe it. He searched his memory, all those little remembrances of her that he'd replayed so many times when he was away, trying to think of one thing, anything, she'd ever asked of him.

There were none.

He spun. She stood proud, impassive, her face giving nothing of her thoughts away. But her hands were fisted around thick wads of her skirts.

"What do you want me to do, Abbie?"

She relaxed visibly. A hint of blush bloomed under her freckles. A trick of the sun? Or had his question lured that fresh color there? Had an answer sprung unbidden to her mind, a naked, sexy, familiar answer, before she'd been able to stop it?

God, he hoped so.

"What *do* you want me to do?" he repeated.

"Oh . . . Oh! You could put the iodine and tar on the calves for me, maybe."

He grimaced. The first thing she'd asked of him, and he wasn't sure he could do it.

To perform that physical action he'd have to focus his thoughts completely on it and nothing else. And there was no possible way that, right now, he was going to be able to think about anything but her.

"How about I'll catch and hold the calves for you?" It would probably require only his presence to keep the animals still. "Then, all you have to do is spread the stuff on? We'll do it together."

Her smile was quick, bright, and more beautiful than anything he'd seen in heaven or earth. "You're staying then?" she asked.

"Where else would I go? I'm staying right here with you."

16

Supper would be late. Even with Joshua's help, it had taken the better part of the day to doctor the rest of the calves. She'd enjoyed the whole process a great deal more than she probably should acknowledge, given the circumstances, but Joshua had been his usual charming, amusing, flattering self. And it had been funny as all get-out to watch the cows' reactions when he popped up right in front of them.

She couldn't help but compare it to the last time she'd done that particular job. She'd worked completely alone, swearing to herself the entire time, and came home with a beauty of a collection of assorted bruises and scrapes from the wriggling, kicking calves.

Still, despite the easier day, by the time she'd ridden all the way in from the western edge of their land, the light was fading. A slender, low ridge of clouds rimmed the horizon. Too far away to do any good, she thought, and it didn't look like they held more than a spit's worth of moisture in them, anyway.

Gaining the yard of the ranch, she swung down from Buttercup and reached beneath the mare to loosen the girth. "Hey, Joshua?" she said, loud as she dared. It wouldn't do for Sledge to hear her in the bunkhouse. "Did you get back yet?"

"Of course." He spoke from beside the porch. His rangy body propped comfortably against a post, he looked dark and tempting, like he'd been lounging there for hours, just waiting for her to ride up. It felt a whole lot better than it probably should.

"Just how much influence have you got up there, anyway?"

"Up where?"

"You know." It might be a tad rude to point, but she couldn't bring herself to say the word out loud. Seemed like it could be tempting fate, when she hadn't done much praying for so long, to ask a question like this. She straightened, giving Buttercup's sturdy shoulder a pat of appreciation for the hard work the horse had put in that afternoon, and briefly uncurled a finger toward the sky. "Up there."

"Oh, up *there*," Joshua repeated. He straightened and sauntered over to her, and her heartbeat skittered. Nobody walked like Joshua. He moved the same way he rode, with perfect, off-hand grace and a rhythmic roll of his hips that made her remember things she was trying very hard to forget. "You can say 'heaven', you know, Abbie. It's not a blasphemy."

"I know." She ducked her head, embarrassed. "It's just not a word I'm used to bandying about."

He cupped her chin, lifting her face to meet his gaze.

"Me, either," Joshua said, his voice peppered with amusement.

"Well, anyway . . . can't you put in a good word? Ask them to make it rain?"

He sobered immediately, his eyes going cold and sad. "I don't do miracles, Abigail."

But his hand was warm on her chin, feeling as real as anything in her life. A fragile flutter of hope sparked, grew. For the first time in months, she dared to believe that she just might make it through this summer with her family and her ranch intact.

Oh yes, she thought, *you do miracles very well indeed.*

Deep shadows filled the corners of the main room in the ranch house, hiding the scarred wood and rough edges. Abigail never found the time to care for the house as much as she would have liked—there was too much else to do—and she regretted it. It wasn't as neat as it should be, and lacked the gentler touches it held when her mother was alive.

She'd attempted to grow a few flowers in tomato cans on the kitchen window sill, hoping it would brighten up the place, but they'd long ago withered to brittle, skeletal remains. She must remember to toss them out. The floor needed a good shine, and one would think she'd have been able to at least stitch up a few colorful pillows to plop in the aged chairs. It hardly looked like a woman lived here.

But tonight, with the low, subtle light, and the room filled with the rich smell of frying beef, a steady hum of contentment seeped through Abigail. Marcus, despite shooting her disgruntled glances—he'd given up trying to talk her into letting him take a turn at watch—was working on his third helping. Her father, though he'd only downed a few bites of meat, happily soaked up the sop gravy with his fourth biscuit.

And Joshua was there—where she could see him, this time—draped into a chair in the corner of the sitting area, his lazily swinging leg looped over the chair's arm, and he watched her work with intensity and approval so clear in his eyes that she could feel it, tangible as a touch.

Contentment was not an emotion she had much experience with. That she would find it, now, with all the problems and potential disasters that still plagued the ranch, seemed almost ridiculous. She found it nonetheless, and, much as she'd like to attribute it to foiling B.J. that afternoon, she knew it was Joshua.

Her Joshua, the one thing in her life that had ever been hers alone, in a way even her own time and energy had never been. He was at the Rolling G for her, for no other reason, and the thought of it warmed her more thoroughly than a swallow of strong whiskey, even as she knew it would be dangerous and foolish to depend too much on that tenuous warmth.

Even Joshua didn't know how long he would be there. He'd been absolutely clear on that point. But she was no longer convinced that armoring herself against him was the only thing she could do. Perhaps it would be better to fill herself up with him, to enjoy this time to the fullest, to store up his presence and touch and voice.

Nothing would change his leaving.

All she could change were the memories she'd have once he was gone.

Sipping her coffee, she eyed Joshua over the rim of her cup, through the slender coil of steam that curled up from the hot liquid. How could he possibly look so much better dead than any other man she'd ever known did alive? He caught her close regard, rising half out of his chair as if he would come to her.

"Come outside with me?" he asked, inclining his head toward the door. "We could walk."

Before, their "walks" had never really included much walking. More like a very indelicate run for the nearest private place they could find. Still, she set her cup down with such speed that it thudded on the table.

"Yes."

"Yes, what?" Marcus mumbled, stuffing an entire gravy-soaked biscuit in his mouth.

"Oh . . . just thinking to myself. Planning for tomorrow."

Pecos pushed away his plate, which he'd scraped so clean it would seem almost a waste to wash it. "Find anythin' when you were out on the range today? Any more screwworms?"

"No, the cattle looked just fine." It was all she could do not to sigh in disappointment when Joshua dropped back down into his chair. Their stroll would have to wait; there was business to attend to first. "Saw a snake, though, that I had to run off our land."

"Run into B.J., did you?"

"Yes." She quickly filled them in on her encounter with B.J. Not all the details, but enough so they'd know what to watch for, just in case B.J. decided to make another attempt.

"I don't get how ya were able to run 'em off all by yourself." Lippy scratched at the lank, pale hair that fell over his shiny forehead.

She didn't dare look at Joshua; she'd knew she'd never be able to explain bursting out into laughter. "Just got lucky this time, I guess."

"Can't count on bein' lucky forever." Pecos tipped his chair back and worked at a strand of beef between his front teeth. "Want me to kill him for ya?"

"Ah . . ." He couldn't be serious, she thought. But Pecos' bland expression didn't change, his near-black eyes unreadable, and she decided she'd better not seem too tempted by his suggestion. No telling what he might do. "No, I don't think so, Pecos. But thank you kindly for the offer."

"If it don't rain soon, there ain't gonna be much else you can do."

"Well, I'm not quite that desperate yet."

"*You* ain't, maybe. But I'd bet my saddle that ol' B.J. is."

"Yeah," Lippy piped up, "if'n this drought goes on much longer, the bushes gonna be following the dogs around."

Marcus' snort of laughter ended in a fit of coughing. Pecos reached over and pounded him vigorously on the back. "You okay there?"

Marcus wheezed. "I will be soon as you stop bruisin' my back."

"Sorry."

"Cows need more water?" When Davis spoke, his voice rusty and cracked, they fell silent as quickly as a spark flared and died. He rarely seemed to pay any attention to the conversation that went on around him. It was far more rare that he attempted to enter it.

His eyes on his plate, he studied the designs he made in the sop as he swept the remnants of a biscuit across it. "I can get you more water."

"Sure you can, Papa," Abigail said softly. "You built the Rolling G right here, where there was plenty of water, didn't you?"

"If ya need more, I'll go down to the Gulf'n get it for you. Lotsa water there."

"Oh, well—" It was the most lucid speech Davis had given in several months. The others all looked at her expectantly, as if confident she would know how to handle this.

But she didn't know how to handle it, never had.

Whether to encourage him, to reason with him, to treat it as normal—all of those approaches had failed her, at one time or another. And every time she failed him, she was terrified that she'd just missed the last opportunity she would ever have to reach inside the muddled man he was now and find the one he'd once been.

"Well, you're right, Papa," she said, speaking with measured care, "there's plenty of water there."

"I'll just go on and get it, then. Ain't been to Galveston for a long time."

It felt overwhelmingly important to do it right. Every time, each time, a tiny, foolish part of her believed that, if she only could say the right things, lead his confused mind along the correct path, she would bring him closer to sanity.

And she and Marcus might finally have their father back.

The room was dead quiet, without even the clank of iron against the dishes, the swish of coffee in a cup. They all waited, to see if, this time, Davis would take a halting, precious step toward reality.

Logic. Calm logic, the kind he'd relied on when he was alive. Perhaps that would work. "Yes, lots of water, Papa. But it's all salt water. That wouldn't be good for the cows."

"Pah." He swirled the biscuit through the gravy, leaving wavering trails. "Fix that."

"You . . . can?"

He dropped the biscuit finally and raised his head, his bleary brown eyes holding a faint, forgotten spark of life. "Sure!" he said triumphantly. "Jes' tell that salt to get right outta there, then!"

Her small bubble of hope burst, leaving a hollow, echoing space inside her. Why had she even thought there had been a possibility? Surely she should have learned better by now. And the abrupt destruction of hope was always worse, a thousand times worse, than its absence had been.

A painful lump lodged high in her throat. Around her, the others quickly found other places to focus their eyes. Their plates, the ceiling, their toes; all were better than looking at her or her father.

All except Joshua. Though the moment he caught her glance, he tried to compose his face along sober lines, light danced in his pale eyes and humor lurked at the corner of his mouth.

Unwillingly, the picture lodged itself in her mind: her father, hip deep in the Gulf of Mexico, hollering for "that damned salt to get yourself on outta there, now!" And the water obeying him—just the way everyone had obeyed Davis most of his life—throwing out sparkling crystals, leaving the water fresh and sweet.

She bit on her tongue, trying to hold the laughter inside. She would not do it. Laughing at her poor father—what a horrible thing it would be. And how cruel they would all think her.

Still, as she saw Joshua's shoulders begin to shake, an absurd, awful, unstoppable roll of mirth welled within her. She pressed the heel of her hand hard to her mouth to block it.

"I— Excuse me." She jumped from the table and fled through the door, gaining the privacy of the porch before the strangled sounds escaped her.

"Abbie?" Marcus spoke from the doorway, his young voice cracking with concern. "You okay?"

"Just . . . Just leave me alone," she gasped.

"But—"

"I'm fine. Leave me alone!"

She heard the thud of the door behind her. Then it all

burst forth, deep, wrenching laughter as the tears rolled freely down her cheeks.

Joshua joined her, slipping through the wall to stand beside her on the porch as his own rich chuckle blended with her laugh-sobs.

"Oh!" she said when she could catch her breath. "How could you! How could you make me laugh!"

She quieted slowly, noisily, grabbing big gulps of harsh evening air, slapping the moisture from her cheeks.

"Oh God!" She was sick with the thought of what she'd done. "How horrid of me! I feel so awful."

"Aw, Abbie." He looped an arm around her to bring her near. She went, fitting close and easy against his chest, as if there were no other place in the world she belonged as well as right there.

Finally. It had been so long, so damn long.

His hands slid up and down her back, soothing, easy, warm. Her head rested comfortably right in the crook of his neck. For an instant, she imagined she caught a trace of his scent, skin and warmth and leather. Impossible . . . enticing.

"Abbie, way I figure it, you're either gonna laugh or you're gonna cry." His chin rubbed gently over the top of her head. "Ain't it better to laugh?"

"But it seems so . . . cruel."

"Crueler to be hurtin' all the time, seems to me."

They rocked together, back and forth, and her eyelids grew heavy, her body loose. Maybe, if she were very lucky, she wouldn't have to move until tomorrow morning. Surely she would sleep a whole lot better here than she had been in her bed.

"You know him better than anybody, Abbie. Which would your pa want?" he asked.

"He was so proud." She tried to think, to remember

what Davis had been like, long ago, before his mind had
started to fail him. And even longer ago, in those lost
golden days when her mother still lived and it seemed
the three of them had done little *but* laugh. What would
he have wanted?

"Do you remember, when I told you about learning to
swim?" she asked.

"Of course. It was only the day before yesterday." His
chest rumbled as he spoke, a tangible expression of his
voice. She almost asked him a question, any stupid question she could think of, just so she could feel that vibration again.

"Oh. Seems like a lot longer ago than that."

"Been a busy couple days."

"Sure has. Well, after I finally learned to swim, and I
was so tired and proud and relieved that I was almost
crying with it, Papa got himself bit by a turtle."

"A turtle?"

"So he said. I never saw it. He started bellowing like a
branded calf, went tearing out of the water and capering
around on shore like he was dancing on hot coals. He
looked so funny. His hair stuck out all over his head, and
he was swearing a blue streak, and I don't know that I
ever laughed so hard in my whole life. Him, either, once
he quit hollering. And you know what?"

"What?" He'd moved his hands up now, so he was
playing with the hair that escaped her braid, winding the
little wisps around his fingers.

"I was never sure if there really was a turtle. I think
he just faked the whole thing to cheer me up."

"He probably did."

She burrowed closer, and his arm tightened around
her, just as she'd wished. He'd always known exactly
how she wanted to be touched. "I think," she said tentatively, "I think he would want me to laugh."

With that, something broke free inside of her, the tight, cruel band that had twisted itself around her heart for so long.

What was happening to her father was horrible and tragic. She would do anything to change it if she could. But she couldn't, and he would not want her to suffer too, to live her life empty of any joy. That wasn't what Davis would want for her; she was certain of it.

Now that she felt better, she knew she should step out of Joshua's embrace and go back inside. But surely only a few more moments would not hurt. The solid wall of his chest was firm against her breasts, and his thighs pressed right along hers.

All the comfort that he'd been giving her suddenly flared to something else. Something darker, more tempting, sinful. Hardly realizing what she was doing, she rocked her hips against his, seeking heat, seeking sensation, seeking *him*.

"Abbie," he said, his breath escaping in a low hiss. He flexed in return, and, despite the layers of her skirts, she could feel the hard, familiar ridge of his erection.

She tilted her head up to look at him. He wasn't smiling now. His mouth was hard, his eyes dark, and she wanted him to kiss her.

Well, she wanted much, much more than that, but a kiss would be a decent start.

"Abbie," he said again, then angled his head down toward her.

She closed her eyes, waiting, lost to the anticipation, the memory, of what was to come. "You feel so . . . real."

He jerked as if she'd hit him. He put his hands on her shoulders and held her at arm's length. Did he think that short distance would blunt the want? He'd been a great deal farther away than that before, even in Colorado, and it had never diminished it.

"We can't do this," he said hoarsely.

"I thought that was usually my line."

"Yeah." His smile was wry and pained. "It's just— I don't know what will happen. This is not what they sent me here for."

"No, I suppose not." She pulled away and went to stand at the edge of the porch, leaning over the railing to look out at the dying evening. The sun retreated, leaving only a weak, narrow band of pink where earth met sky. All the rest was just flat, dull shades of gray, neither dark nor light; only empty.

"Abigail." His voice was rich with apology and regret.

"No, I understand." She did, damn it. That didn't mean she had to like it.

He hitched his hip up onto the railing, so he was half sitting as he faced her. The encroaching shadows hid him, his dark clothes fading into the murky twilight, making him appear the ghost she'd once accused him of being.

"Tell me what happened to your father."

17

She'd never talked to anyone about it, ever. Who did she have to talk to? Her brother was too young, and carried pain of his own. She would not burden him with hers.

The hands were, when all was said and done, hired help, whose livelihoods depended upon the owners of the ranch. She'd always thought it important to appear in control and confident to them.

And what good would it do to speak of it, really? Talking wouldn't change anything.

But she wanted to talk, she found. To Joshua, who deserved to know what had kept her on the Rolling G when he had offered her freedom and adventure, and who'd seen a bit of the world that existed beyond this physical one, a world that she sometimes thought Davis spent more time in than this one.

"All right," she agreed.

Joshua slid off the railing, hooking his thumb in his pocket. "Do you want to walk?"

"Yes. Let's walk."

Pushing her away, when her body had been close and warm and her lips had been parted and only inches from his—it had been one of the hardest things Joshua had ever done, after a lifetime of hard things. But he'd done it, because it had been even harder to risk that he would do something wrong, make a misstep, and they might end his assignment before he'd completed it.

If he managed nothing else in his afterlife, he was going to help Abigail through these troubles. He simply had to; there was no way he would be able to survive the rest of eternity knowing he'd failed her. That was a kind of cruel hell he could not even contemplate.

They moved away from the house, into the wide, empty spaces. In the distance, silhouetted against the feeble remnants of daylight, they saw Lippy riding out toward the waterhole, taking first watch over the cows. But here, they were far enough away that they couldn't even hear the pounding of his mount's hooves or the bellow of the milling herd.

There was only each other, and the wind and the grass and the sky. This was his version of heaven, Joshua thought, walking across the land as the night stole the day, Abigail by his side. If only he felt able to reach for her, to link her hand with his, it would be all he would ever ask, of this life or any other.

But he couldn't take the chance. Touching her was far too dangerous. He'd managed to stop once, and he could hardly believe he'd achieved that much, considering he'd spent the six months he'd known her before doing nothing *but* touching her—or trying his damnedest to figure out a way to do it again.

When the ranch faded into the distance, only a pinpoint of just-lit lantern light visible, Abigail was finally ready to talk.

"It started so slowly I didn't notice it for a long, long time," she said. "Little things. He'd forget to do something he promised. He couldn't find his bridle, when he'd always known precisely where everything was. And he put off making decisions—do we sell a few head now? Buy a new bull? Or wait for spring?"

She slowed her steps, the sound of the grass rustling as she passed and the sighing of the wind a low murmur under her halting voice. "I thought he was just . . . getting older, I guess. I really didn't think anything of it."

She'd blamed herself for that too, many times. If only she'd realized earlier what was happening to her father. But what would it have changed, really? There was nothing else to try, nothing different to do. Except perhaps prepare a bit better, and Abigail doubted that she would ever have been prepared enough for what had come no matter what she'd done.

"It was easy to take care of those things for him. To help here and there, to remind him."

Somehow Joshua's silence, his calm presence, was all the encouragement Abigail needed. Perhaps she'd been wanting to say this all along, and had only needed the opportunity. Joshua already knew of her father's condition—surely there was no betrayal in telling him all the details now.

"His temper kept getting worse, so much worse."

"He always did have a short fuse," Joshua said, remembering the loud and raging set-to B.J. and Davis had had over something that was so small that, afterwards, no one had been able to recall what had started the entire furor.

"But he never did, really. That was the odd thing about it." She shook her head. With the near absence of sunlight, it seemed the only thing that held color was her hair, becoming a deep, burnished red like hidden embers. "Before—long before you were here—he hardly ever got really riled. Papa always said a man should spend his energy fixing things, instead of wasting it complaining about them."

Her eyes were huge and dark in her pale face, glazed with a sheen of moisture. There was nothing he wanted more than to take her in his arms and soothe her, to tell her that he didn't need to know this—not now, not ever, not if the telling of it hurt her.

But he couldn't hold her, because he knew too well what almost happened the last time. And he thought that maybe, just once, she needed to voice it, even if it hurt. Though he thought it hurt him just as much to hear it, to listen to her story and be powerless to help. In truth, he hoped it did, because somehow it seemed fitting that he share her pain.

"His anger was unpredictable, unreasonable—I think, most of the time, he was as angry at himself as anyone else, at what he couldn't stop and couldn't understand, when he'd always been able to handle anything. But there was nothing he could do, so he raged at whatever—and whoever—he could find."

Davis had raged at Abigail, Joshua realized. He would have given all he was to have been here then, to be the one who'd taken the brunt of all that anger instead. For it must be a thousand times worse to be on the receiving end of all that wrath when it was coming from someone you loved, who was supposed to love and cherish and protect you back.

"Still, for a long time, we could all pretend everything was fine. It seemed like such . . . little things. Harmless. So what if he was a little confused? So what if he sometimes remembered what happened twenty years ago better than what happened last week? My mother was alive then, and he loved her;

why wouldn't he hang on to those memories so tightly?"

She fidgeted, smoothed her skirt, fussed with her hair, adjusted her collar, as if to delay what came next. Giving in to temptation, he captured her hands, pressing them to his mouth. As before, the muting of his other senses only multiplied his reaction to her, to the work-roughened texture of her fingers against his lips and the unforgettable, nearly overwhelming scent of her hands, flour and coffee and lilac water and the pure sweetness that was hers alone.

"You don't have to tell me anymore. Not if you don't want to," he said.

"But I do," she said, though she was surprised by it. She'd wanted to tell him even before he'd left Texas, but had never found the time or the way. And as long as she kept talking, perhaps he would stay here with her, hold her hands and brush them with the gentle heat of his mouth, and look at her as if she mattered more to him than anything else in the world.

It was a look she'd never been completely certain was real or practiced, some expression he'd learned to encourage a woman to fall at his feet. And she'd never been sure she cared if it was, no more than she cared right now. She only wanted him to keep looking at her just like that.

"But then, one day, he went out on the range. On foot, though he never did that. I saw him go, but didn't stop him." Her throat tightened. Another regret, one of too many. "I didn't want to get in another disagreement with him. But he never came back."

It had been the longest evening of her life. Waiting, wondering, disbelieving. Until she'd finally had to accept that he wasn't going to just stroll into the yard at any moment, a rope over one shoulder and full of a wild tale of the lost calf he'd rescued out of some bog.

"We went out after him, finally. Thank God we had a few more hands then. It took half the night as it was, until finally I heard the gunshot signaling he'd been found." She'd galloped back to the house, pushing her horse harder than she knew she should, her stomach in a burning knot, not knowing if he'd been found dead or alive.

"Was he . . . hurt?" Joshua asked.

"No. Not in any way that showed." Their hands were still linked together, and she curled her fingers, holding tight. "He'd simply got out there, and couldn't remember the way home. When he'd always known every inch of this land as well—better—than he knew the back of his own hand. And that's when I knew, for sure, that there was something horribly wrong with him."

"I'm sorry, Abigail. Very sorry."

Simple words, easily given, words a person said when they accidentally bumped your arm or interrupted a sentence. Such common words shouldn't have helped.

But they did, a great deal, because they came from Joshua, and were echoed in his voice and eyes and touch.

"He went downhill very quickly after that. It was like he didn't fight it anymore then. He mistook me for my mother a lot. Now, mostly, he doesn't even recognize any of us."

"And there's no chance he'll get better?"

"A chance? You would know that better than I."

"Me?" What did he know of this sort of thing? he wondered. He felt the lack, the harsh limits on his knowledge that his life had forced.

"It seems to me the only chance he has rests in God's hands now. You've got a lot more experience with that than I do."

He'd forgotten. He wouldn't have believed it, that he could forget about a detail such as his own death. But he'd looked at her, listened to her, touched her, and he'd not thought of anything else.

"When did it happen? How long ago?"

With his thumbs, he rubbed slow circles on the backs of her hands. They were meant to comfort, but did something else entirely. Something that had nothing at all to do with comfort.

"When he was lost, it was . . ." She frowned, trying to remember. "Two or three months after you left, I think. That's close, anyway."

Well over a year ago. It was a long time, Joshua thought, for her to have everything on her shoulders, strong though they might be. No wonder she'd grown thinner, strain etched around her eyes and mouth.

"The first signs," she was saying, "I don't really know. I didn't mark them at the time, they seemed so insignificant. Five years? Six?"

"Years?" Jesus, had she trusted him so little? "Why didn't you tell me?"

"Tell you what? It all seemed like it could have been nothing then. And the things he'd forgotten, the little problems he had—he'd forbidden everyone at the Rolling G to speak of them to anyone else. He couldn't have stood it if he'd thought that anyone knew his weakness. He'd rather be dead than pitied."

"But Abigail—" His grip tightened. "You couldn't tell *me*?"

"It wasn't mine to tell, Joshua."

"But maybe I could have helped."

"How? There was nothing you could do."

"I woulda liked the chance to try."

"It was my problem, Joshua, not yours. My father, my family, my ranch."

It always came back to that. It was the one thing he'd never been able to change in her. He could share her laughter, her body, her pleasure. But what Abigail saw as her responsibilities were always hers alone, no matter how much he longed to share them. In an odd way, it had come to seem more intimate to him than sex—his wish for her to let him shoulder some of her problems, if only for a little while.

"Joshua." She stepped closer to look up at him intently. "If I *had* told you, would you have stayed?"

"Of course I would have stayed! What else—" He stopped. He'd replied unthinkingly, a reflex. But would he have stayed?

In leaving Texas when he did he had, however unintentionally, added to her burdens. And, much as he longed to, there was so damned little he could do for her now. She deserved his honesty, at least. "I'm not sure."

"I see."

"If you had asked me to—"

"I wouldn't have asked." She jerked her hands free and turned away.

"Wait." He had to make her understand. He caught her chin, turned her head to face him.

What she'd said earlier had been the truth. What *could* she have told him? That her father was forgetful, cranky, a little confused? He would have chalked it up to Davis' age and her penchant for worrying. "If that's what you'd told me, just those little things . . . I wanted you to put me *first*, before your family, before your ranch. Just once, I wanted to be first."

She must have heard him wrong. *Just once, to be first?* Surely he'd been first many times, with many women. He was too handsome, too skilled at his job, too sure of himself, for it to be any other way.

But she could see it in his eyes, light and clear even in

the dusk—the regret, the yearning. Joshua, as unbelievable at it seemed, had thought he'd never come first with anyone. And, because it was something she understood, had felt herself a hundred times, she wanted to give it to him with a fierceness that she'd thought herself incapable of.

"I'm sorry," he said. "It was selfish, I know—"

"You were first with me, Joshua. Always, in every way I could."

"Abigail," he said hoarsely.

"But there was nothing else I could do. I couldn't leave them."

He stepped back, out of arm's reach, to keep himself from pulling her to him, to stop from bending her down into the long, parched grass and forgetting everything about why he'd been sent here. To think of nothing but the way her naked body felt against his. Instead, he did the next best thing.

"You were first with me, too. More than I even knew until I left."

Sadness washed her eyes, leaving them dark and lonely. "It doesn't change anything though, does it?"

"At least this time we know."

Knowing didn't help very much, she thought. It made it understandable, perhaps, but it didn't make it hurt any less.

"Look," he said, pointing up, and her gaze followed. The first star appeared, a tiny wink of silver against the deep blue sky. "Make a wish."

Abigail closed her eyes, and he was able to look his fill. The clean, sharp lines of her face always drew him. The angles intrigued him so much more than round, bland curves ever had. They etched interesting shadows across her pale skin, made her appear completely different depending on which way she tilted her head or how the light struck her.

Her lids fluttered open. He couldn't bring himself to look away, though, and she stared right back, until the rising heat in his blood made him blink and drop his gaze, lest he do something they would both regret.

"All done?" he asked briskly, trying to lighten the mood. Anything to keep from grabbing her and finding out just how much his body was capable of. "Aren't you going to tell me what you wished for?"

"Oh no." She tucked her hands behind her back and pursed her lips. Darned if she didn't look cute as a day-old foal. "If I tell someone, it might not come true."

"Well, I'm not exactly *someone*," he ventured. "I think it only counts if the person you tell is actually alive."

"Ah, yes." She rocked back on her heels. "Still, I'm not taking any chances."

"Come on." Curiosity pulled at him.

"How about, I'll tell you when it comes true?"

"All right." A definite glint of mischief sparked in her eyes, and something that looked like speculation when her gaze swept down his body. *Him?* he guessed hopefully. Was there anything he could do to make her wishes come true?

Because he sure as hell knew she held the fate of all of his.

"Well," she said reluctantly. "I should be getting back. If I don't bring Sledge his supper plate soon, he's going to start chewing on the blankets."

"I guess so." He didn't want her to go. He'd much rather have her stay and lean back against his chest so his arms looped securely around her as they counted the arriving stars.

"What about you?" she asked. "What are you going to do?"

He circled one finger in the air. "Go around the ranch

a few times, I guess. Check on things, keep an eye out. Usual stuff."

"Oh." But she made no move, just watched him with a smile trembling at the corners of her mouth.

"Walk you back?" he suggested, just to stretch it out a little while.

"Yes," she said, and the smile broke free. "Walk me back."

18

Juggling a steaming, overloaded plate and a mug of coffee in one hand, Abigail knocked on the door of the bunkhouse. Though the small building was only a few yards from the house, she rarely entered it. It was clearly the hands' domain, and still held the brand of forbidden territory to her.

"Come on, then," Sledge growled from inside.

She pushed the door open with her hip. The bunkhouse consisted of only one room, a modest rectangle centered by an old, soot-streaked black stove, its pipe running straight up through the roof. A coal-oil lantern sat on the stovetop, its light blotted by the haze of cigarette smoke filling the room.

There were a dozen metal bunks stuffed into the space, a few remaining flakes of paint hinting at the white they'd once been. Three sported bedrolls, the rest held only sagging mattresses no thicker than a rubbed dime.

The thin, rough walls were papered with pages torn

from saddle catalogs, for insulation and decoration.
Abigail wrinkled her nose at the smell; smoke, leather,
sweat, and liniment blended in an odor strong enough to
kill fleas—at least, she sure hoped so.

"Brought you your supper."

"Late tonight." Sledge's bunk was in the far corner.
He was propped up in it, smoking, a dog-eared Miles
City catalog unopened in his lap, his bulging war sack
slumped on the floor next to the bed.

"It was sort of a busy day."

He reached down and stubbed his cigarette out on
the packed dirt floor. She handed him the plate.

"How's your ankle?" she asked.

The dark look he shot her said clearly he didn't like
being reminded of his weakness. "Better, 'long as I don't
try and walk on it."

"Oh, well, maybe you'd like me to—" She made a
move to check his injury.

"No!" He jerked his leg out of her reach. "Jes' leave it
alone."

"All right, then."

"Be up tomorrow."

"I don't want you to try and rush it, Sledge. I know
you, and the last thing we need is for you to hurt it again
by using it before it's ready."

"Tomorrow." He stuffed half a slice of beef into his
mouth.

"Well, enjoy your supper. I'll be back in the morning
with breakfast."

"Stay."

"What?" She couldn't have heard him right. Sledge
preferred to be left alone to lick his wounds. She'd
learned that well enough over the years, and had the
blistered ears to prove it. "What did you say?"

"Ya said ya had a busy day." He jabbed his fork in the

direction of an empty bed. "You could tell me 'bout it, mebbe."

He was probably lonely, she decided. He certainly wasn't used to being cooped up all day, and probably wasn't much fond of the idea of the ranch running along without him.

After checking the bunk over carefully—no telling what the previous occupant might have left there—she decided it was probably safe enough, brushed aside the scattered piles of Lippy's patent medicine brochures, and sat down.

"You know we've been having trouble with screwworms," she said.

Sledge nodded, jaw working on a tough chunk of meat. "Lippy told me. An' told me, and told me, and told me."

"I'll bet he did."

"How many more did you find?"

"Not too many. I think we got them all doctored up all right."

"Good." He nodded and took a swig of coffee. A bit dribbled on his chin, and he backhanded it away.

"And I had a little bit of a run-in with B.J. and his herd," she said, casually as she could manage.

His fork clanked against his plate. "How bad is it? Any water left at all?"

"Water's fine," she said, hiding a smile. She couldn't share this victory with her father; sharing it with Sledge was going to be the next best thing. "He never got that far."

"What happened? The bastard's—sorry—heart give out and he keeled over right there?"

"Nope."

"What, then?"

"I stopped him." She did smile this time, enjoying his

obvious astonishment. "B.J. never made it within a mile of our border."

"But . . . how?"

She didn't think she'd ever before seen Sledge surprised enough to forget to eat.

"The lead cows took a dislike to the Rolling G, you might say."

"But—" He frowned, still confused, and contemplated his bandaged foot. "Best you should sell out, Abbie."

"What?" She wouldn't have been more surprised to see one of her old bulls suddenly take to the air in flight.

"I think you should sell out," he repeated.

"Why?" she asked carefully.

"It's too hard on you." He scratched his chin. "It's startin' ta show, Abigail. You can't say it ain't. I've seen what the land does to women. You'll be all skinny and worn before your time, then it'll be too late."

Unsure whether she should be insulted at his words or touched that he would put his concern for her before his love for the ranch, she smoothed her skirts over her knees. "Starting to show? Why, just tonight, Lippy complimented me, said I was looking as good as he'd seen me since he hired on."

"Really?" Sledge squinted at her, his eyes nearly disappearing into a network of fine lines. "Huh. Mebbe you are looking a bit better, at that. Must be the light in here."

"Besides, I can hardly afford to spend much time worrying about the effect on my looks."

"I know, but a young girl like you should be able to." He broke a biscuit in two, releasing a curl of steam, and stuck a slab of beef between the golden-brown halves. "And you ain't gonna be able to keep this up much longer, anyway. Then where will you be? If you sell out now, least you'll have somethin'."

It was almost more than she could bear, to hear all her fears coming from Sledge. Sledge, the one person in her entire life, since her father's deterioration, that she'd always been certain she could depend on to fight for the Rolling G as fiercely as she would.

"But where could I go? What could I do?"

"Wherever ya want." He waved the biscuit in the air, making a wide circle, before taking a big bite. "You'd have enough money for a while."

"And when it ran out? Then what?"

"Get a job."

"One that would let me bring Papa along?"

He stopped chewing and swallowed the bite whole. "That mightn't be a problem by then, Abigail," he said, his eyes already starting to grieve.

"No." She shook her head so hard her hair whipped across her cheek. She refused to even think of it.

He shrugged. "You could get married."

"To who?"

"You could find someone." He tucked the rest of the food in his mouth and mulled it over while he chewed. "Get you off the ranch, feed you up some, and let your hands soften a little. Who knows who ya could catch? Man'd be lucky. You ain't such a crockheaded filly as some, at least."

She couldn't help it. She laughed at what was clearly meant to be an encouraging compliment, and then wondered at her amusement. She doubted it was the reaction she would have had a few weeks ago, when she likely would have been deeply insulted. Maybe she'd been spending too much time with Joshua, but darned if it didn't feel wonderful, this new lightheartedness.

"I don't think so," she said. "What brought this on, anyway? I never you took you for the type to give up easy, Sledge."

"Ain't givin' up!" He scowled, indignant.

"I didn't think so."

"Gettin' a little stove up, is all." He wobbled his injured foot. "'Bout time to hang up my saddle."

She'd never thought much about Sledge getting old. He'd been a constant in her life, weather-beaten and grizzled from the time she could remember. Now that she took a good look, though, there was hardly any black left peppering his iron-gray whiskers, too long to be called stubble but not quite grown enough to be a beard.

If she'd ever considered it, she would have expected to bury Sledge with his boots on, on Rolling G land. Not far from her father, if it came to that. She tried to picture Sledge living out a quiet old age, in a musty rented room in the middle of a busy, closed-in town somewhere, but couldn't do it.

"I'm not giving up, Sledge. I can't."

He handed her his empty plate. "Suit yourself."

Halfway across the room to leave, she stopped and turned to face him again. "I'm gonna need help, Sledge. Everybody's. Yours most of all."

He scratched a match to life, the small flame hardly visible through the layers of blue smoke that hazed the room. He touched it to the end of a new cigarette and took a long draw. Finally he blew out a thick ribbon of smoke and nodded.

"You can count on me."

A day later, Abigail felt that she'd caught up enough on the work of the ranch to turn her attention to her long-neglected mending.

They'd finished supper more than an hour ago. Pecos was on first watch, and Lippy had engaged the surly, and surprisingly still-bedridden Sledge in a game of low-stakes poker.

Marcus had offered to take Davis for an evening walk, and the two shuffled off soon after they'd finished eating. She knew that Marcus had suggested it, in part, because he, still insulted that she wouldn't allow him to take his turn at night watch, didn't want to be in the same house with her any longer than necessary. All the same, she was thankful for the respite. She was rarely able to be home and work alone, without having to keep a fair part of her attention on her father.

She settled on the front porch in her mother's rocker, a pile of mending in a basket at her feet. The house still held the heat from the day's cooking, and it was only marginally better out here. The shade from the porch's roof helped a little, but the wind that fluttered the multi-colored scraps in her basket and blew in her face, bringing with it the scent of singed grass and baked dirt, was relentlessly hot and dry.

She dug through the pile of worn clothing, locating a pair of brown canvas pants. They belonged to Marcus, twice repaired already. She'd gotten halfway through the third fix three weeks ago when she'd been called away to check on a cow that Sledge worried might be showing signs of blackleg. The cow proved healthy, after all, but she'd never gotten back to the mending.

She inspected the half-finished patch, the large, clumsy stitches wandering zigzag along its ragged edge. With a sigh, she began to pick out the threads, admitting to herself that the sewing had been delayed so long not just because of more pressing work but because it was a task she really didn't like very much, too inactive and fussy for her tastes.

She'd only had a few quick glimpses of Joshua all day long. He'd stopped to chat with her briefly last night, when she'd taken her turn on watch. He'd quickly mentioned that he was out checking the herd and keeping an eye out for any signs of B.J., insisted he had no time to chat, and hurried right off again. Since then, there'd been no more contact with him than an occasional wave across a span of yards that were filled with a few dozen grazing cattle.

She appreciated his aid and diligence, she told herself. It was what he was here for. Not for keeping her company. Not for making her laugh, or for causing her to wish he'd have stayed a bit longer with her in the moonlight. She needed him to keep an eye on her land, and that was all.

Still, she couldn't help the reflexive catch in her breathing when she heard the muffled thud of a horse's hooves coming up behind the house.

Foolishness, she quickly berated herself. For one thing, Joshua had made it perfectly clear that he'd been sent to help her save her ranch and nothing else.

For another, she'd forgotten that Joshua no longer made any noise when he came up, and he certainly had no need for a horse.

The last faulty stitch pulled free as Horace cantered around the side of the house. His bright red face gleamed from the heat, and his lathered horse wasn't in much better shape.

What could he want? In the past, it hadn't been unusual for Horace to come over every couple of weeks, to pass an evening or a slow afternoon on the porch, talking with her. It had been a bit of a trick when her father had gotten so bad to discourage Horace from coming so frequently and guide him to times when he wasn't likely to encounter Davis. Even so, he'd been a regular visitor—until the drought hit, and the first time she'd turned down his request to let him water his stock at her pond.

He dismounted, leading his horse around the front and looping the reins around a post. With his thumb, he tipped back the brim of his hat. "Mind if I water my horse?"

"Of course," she said, stung that he'd thought he needed to ask, that she might deny him this common courtesy. "There are buckets near the well."

He cranked up a bucket of water, dipping a long drink for himself before bringing back a small, measured amount for his horse. The roan gelding eagerly stuck his nose in the pail and downed the water, looking expectantly around for more. But he'd been worked too hard to drink deeply until he cooled down.

The new step creaked beneath Horace's weight as he shuffled up the stairway, his head low, the brim of his hat shadowing his face. It appeared he could hardly bring himself to look at her. They'd been friends too long for Abigail not to regret the loss. People were a lot rarer than cattle in west Texas, and she didn't have that many friends to spare.

"Can I sit?" he asked, his voice as tired as his posture.

She nudged the nearest chair in his direction. "Sit."

It was straight-backed and rickety, the leather seat sagging and shiny with age, but he sank into it as gratefully as if it had been a pillow-stuffed armchair. He still didn't glance her way, just squinted out over the land like he was on watch himself.

"How's your family, Horace?" she asked. "I haven't seen your mother in a month of Sundays."

"She's all right." He was freshly shaved, his cheek scraped pink and raw. Abigail hoped that he hadn't duded up on her account. He never had before.

When it became clear he wasn't going to say anything else, she returned to her mending. There didn't seem to be anything to talk about but the ranches and the drought, and she didn't really want to know what bad shape he was in. She felt guilty enough, unable to help him, but she had a family to think of. The Rolling G was barely hanging on as it was.

If she lost her stock, she lost the land. It was that simple—and precarious.

She tucked her tongue in her cheek and closed one eye, trying to slip the thread through the needle. "Stupid thing," she muttered. There was no earthly reason why they had to make the holes so darn small.

Horace yanked his hat off with such force she jumped. Crushing it against his chest, he turned to face her. The waves of his light brown hair held the imprint of his hatband, and sweat curled the strands around his face and beaded his flushed skin.

"Two'a my heifers turned up blind today."

"Oh, Horace." She dropped the pants to her lap. "I'm so sorry."

The situation was clearly growing desperate, if the cattle had been without water long enough to start going blind. A few days at most, and they'd start dying.

"Don't be sorry." If he squeezed his hat any tighter, she thought, he was going to pinch right through the crown. "Marry me. Marry me, and let me have the water."

"What good would it do, really?" She placed her hands on her lap and leaned forward. The hidden needle jabbed her palm, piercing deep, but she ignored the pain, jerking her hand free. "There's not enough water for our combined herds. I can hold out for maybe three or four more weeks, as it is. With your stock, too, it'd be gone in a week, and then we'd likely lose them all."

"It could rain between now and then."

She glanced out at the sky, empty except for the brassy sun inching down in the west, looking strong enough to burn off any cloud that dared invade its territory.

"I don't think I can take that chance, Horace."

"With your water maybe I wouldn't have to lose all of *mine*, though!" His voice shook. "And then we could rebuild from what's left."

"You said you'd made some money last spring, from the drive north," she suggested. "If worst comes to worst, can't you buy new stock next year and start from there? It wouldn't be easy, Horace, but you could do it. I know you could."

"I spent ten years building *this* herd and I won't lose 'em! I won't!" He looked down at his knees and his hat trembled against his chest.

"I'm sorry, Horace." Pain throbbed from the point the needle had punctured.

Sorry wasn't enough, even though she was, deeply, more than Horace would ever know. If there was a way, *any* way . . . But if there had been, she surely would have thought of it by now. And she couldn't gamble her family's welfare. They had no reserves from last year to tide them over until the next.

"I could be good to you, Abigail." His ears reddened. "I promise."

"I know you would. But marrying just to survive one season seems to me like it would make it awful hard to get through the rest of them. You deserve better than that, Horace. And so do I."

She reached out to lay a comforting hand on his, but he jerked his arm away as if she burned him. Slowly, she drew her hand back to her own lap.

He had a right to his anger, she supposed. But it still hurt.

"I could help you with B.J. How long you think you're going to be able to stand against him alone?"

"B.J.?" she asked sharply. "What do you know about B.J.?"

"What's to know? I know Hallenbeck ain't the kind of man to stand around and watch his cows die." He looked up at her then and she sucked in a sharp breath at the expression in his eyes. Anger, raw and powerful, and something that looked very like hatred. "And neither am I."

"Horace, I—"

"Forget it." He blinked, and it was gone, his eyes now soft and sad and familiar. He shook himself slightly, then plopped his hat back on and headed for his horse. "Just forget it."

But, as she watched him spur his gelding away, she knew she wouldn't. And she had a very strong notion that Horace had no intention of forgetting, either.

19

Night watch just might have been the best duty she'd pulled all week.

Midnight was more than an hour gone, the world so hushed it seemed impossible that trouble might hover just over the horizon. The moon glowed yellow and bright. It almost seemed to be putting out heat of its own, but Abigail knew darn well it would have been a whole lot hotter out here in the daylight, so she was plenty happy it was only the moon.

Sleeping cows scattered in loose clumps over the uneven ground. Abigail rode Jojo, a very fine night horse that her father had trained himself more than five years ago. Jojo knew his job, and delicately picked his way in a large circle around the edge of the herd with scarcely a hint of guidance from her.

She could almost have pulled the rim of her hat down and, lulled by the sway of the slow-moving horse, drifted off to sleep. The cattle were quiet. Except the cattle really weren't the reason she needed to keep alert—her duty was to watch for someone creeping up on them, intent on mischief. She rubbed at her eyes, trying for the burn that would keep her awake.

And then warmth enveloped her. Not the harsh heat that still simmered up from the earth, but the kind that came from deep inside, each time Joshua touched her. Because he was suddenly there, mounted behind her on her horse, his chest solid against her back, his muscular thighs tucked snugly alongside hers.

This could keep her awake, all right.

"Hello, Joshua."

"Gee, how'd you know it was me?" He spoke against her ear, and she was certain she felt the gentle, tingling brush of his lips as he formed the words.

"Lucky guess."

"You know, this isn't always so bad, being dead." His arms slid around her middle, to hold her snug and close. As if she was going anywhere. "This saddle cantle would be in a *really* uncomfortable place, if I could feel it."

He had to do it just this one time, he promised himself. Just once, he had to hold her.

He'd spent the entire day trying to think of any other possibility. Trying to convince himself there was another solution for her. He hated even the idea of what he was about to do, even though he knew it was the right thing. But the only way he'd ever gather the strength to tell her what he knew he must was to allow himself this chance to hold her in his arms just one more time.

One brief time, that was somehow going to have to last the rest of eternity.

Good luck, buddy.

"Why is the horse not bothered by you on its back?" A silly, meaningless question, Abigail thought. But he was holding her, and felt good, so damn good, that she wasn't about to mention anything that was likely to bring either of them back to their senses and end this.

"Me and Jojo, we're old friends."

All those months alone, she'd been certain she'd remembered perfectly just what it felt like to have Joshua's arms around her. But this was more somehow, richer and deeper. Perhaps it was simply because, then, she'd always assumed there would be another time, another chance. She'd learned better now, and so she let the feeling sweep over her, stored every precious bit of it she could capture in her mind. If she'd known then that it wouldn't be forever, she never would have spent any time or energy or thought on any of the thousand inconsequential things that she'd rushed around doing, wasting the time she could have spent in his arms.

She wouldn't make that mistake again.

"Good thing the cattle are sleeping. You'd probably stampede 'em."

"No, take a whole lot more than me to stampede 'em on their home ground." Jesus, he didn't know if he could do this. He had to, he reminded himself. It was the only way to make sure she would always be safe and cared for, that she could have the kind of life she deserved. Still, it was easier to put it off a bit longer and talk about small things instead. "Besides, they're gettin' used to me, I think."

"It happens."

"Yeah." He swallowed, trying to get rid of the painful lump that had stuck itself right in the middle of his throat. No good; the lump stayed right where it was. "Sorry about that."

Jojo plodded on, hooves brushing a rasping sound through the sun-crisped grass, but Abigail stilled in his arms. "Why?"

"I don't know how much longer they're going to let

me stay." Whatever it was, it wasn't going to be nearly long enough. "It would probably be better if you didn't get to countin' on having me around."

He slipped her hat off her head, stuck it up between the saddle horn and Jojo's neck, where it would stay. Curls sprang free from the messy knot she'd jammed under her hat, and she made a move to try and tuck it all away.

"No, let me." Slowly, so it would last, knowing he'd never get to do it again, he slid the pins—he was getting much better at handling *things,* finally—from her hair, letting it all tumble loose. The wind caught it, blew it in his face and over his shoulder, springy and soft and infused with the scent of lilacs. "Jeez, I love your hair."

"It's red."

"I noticed."

"And it never behaves."

"Yeah," he said, and buried his face in the wild mass. What was so good about *behaving,* anyway? Where was the fun in that? "Thank God."

One of his hands, fingers spread wide, rested on her belly, his thumb angling up, just under her breasts. Abigail wondered if he even knew that his thumb was moving, whisking back and forth, the way he used to brush the pad of his fingers over her nipples. It was all she could do not to nudge his hand up farther, where it belonged.

Except that it was all so crazy. There was no place for this to go, nothing to hope for. He was dead, and a wild, lost part of her didn't even care, was quite certain that this little bit of Joshua was more than all of any other man could ever be for her.

She leaned back, closer to him. Around them, the cattle woke up. She'd spent a lifetime around cows and never discovered it, whatever mysterious signal they used that told them all to get up at the same time. Rump first, forelegs folded beneath them as if they were praying, they all got to their feet in a quick, peculiar motion that was somehow a lot more graceful that it should have been.

They milled around for a few minutes, bumping one another aside. The brown and red and white colors splotching their coats looked flat in the moonlight, just shades of black and gray, but sometimes light caught on a horn, sheered and reflected down a sharp curve. Finally, all selected a new spot and bedded down again on their other sides.

And Joshua had put it off long enough.

"I think you should marry Horace," he said in a rush, knowing if he didn't say it now, and fast, he might never manage to spew it out.

She stiffened. "What?"

Jesus, he had to say it again? He wondered if this was some new, cruel kind of punishment for him. They hadn't condemned him to hell, but they'd sent him here to help her, and the best way he could come up with to do that was to try to convince Abigail to marry another man. Had he really been *this* bad? "You should probably go ahead and marry Horace."

"You were there, this afternoon? When he asked me?"

"Only for a little while." Long enough. A whole, agonizing lot longer than he wanted to be.

"Why?" Of all the things she'd ever expected might come out of Joshua's mouth, this was the very last.

"Because you shouldn't have to do all this by yourself, damn it!" His voice was loud, razor-sharp. He sounded angry, though he hadn't meant to. He gentled his tone. "You've been managing everything all alone, for a long time. No one should have to do that."

"You think I can't do it?" She wished he wasn't behind her, wished she could look into his face and eyes and see what was there. See if he really meant to simply hand her off to another man.

"That's what I meant. I know you can do it. You've been doing it all along." He was glad she was in front of him, her face hidden from his view. He knew there was no way he could look at her, into her beautiful eyes, and still force himself to say these things. She would know that this was not what he wanted, that he'd rather be drowned again than let another man touch her. "You shouldn't have to."

"A drought is temporary, Joshua. Marriage isn't."

Oh God. She'd always known just where to hurt him the most. "There'll be more problems, Abigail. There always are. Don't you want somebody to help with them? Somebody to . . . " —he gulped, plunged on— "to share it all?"

"I never thought you liked Horace very much."

I hated him, Joshua thought. Hated him because she smiled at Horace, because she called him friend, because she talked to him, and Joshua had always wanted Abigail all to himself.

Jesus, no wonder he'd lost her. He was only surprised she hadn't kicked his sorry ass out of her life a long time before she had.

"He's not so bad." He cleared his throat, trying to sound normal. "You're friends, at least. And he's better than your other choice."

"Well, yes, he is better than B.J.," she agreed.

She sounded so reasonable, calm. Listening carefully to his reasons, weighing them, considering, preparing to make a decision based on clear-minded logic and practicality. Hell!

His hand flexed, tightening his hold on her, as if he

could fuse his skin with hers, as if he could make the bond permanent.

"You really think I should do this, Joshua?"

"Yeah." It sounded more like a croak than a word. "I think it would be the best thing."

"Well, then . . . "

Oh shit! He'd talked her into it after all. He'd tried to do the honorable thing here, but, down deep in his selfish soul, he really hadn't believed she'd take him up on it!

God, what had he done?

"I guess you just thought wrong, then." She shifted, settled more comfortably back against him, the saddle leather creaking beneath her. "Seems to happen every now and then, doesn't it?"

"But . . . But I thought you liked Horace?"

"I do."

"And it makes perfect sense."

"I suppose it does."

"Then why aren't you gonna marry him?"

"I was thirteen when my mother died." She tipped her head back, resting it on his shoulder, so she could look up at the sky. "But I remember, Joshua. I remember what it was like between my parents. They were *happy*. It didn't matter how hard the work was, how much they had to struggle. At the end of the day they'd look at each other and you could just see it, vibrating between them. They didn't care about the work or the worries. They did it together, and for each other, and that's all that mattered."

She'd rarely spoken of her mother. He'd never asked, thinking painful memories best left alone. But her voice was warm, full of affection and remembrance.

"That's what I want, Joshua. I decided a long time ago. I'd rather have nothing than have less. What if I settled for friendship and missed my chance to have it all?"

A chance. They'd had a chance, a wonderful, magic chance, and missed it. Well, not missed it exactly; something far worse. They hadn't realized what they'd had. Hadn't taken care of their chance, hadn't nurtured and protected it. They'd simply let it slip away, like a fading wisp of forgotten smoke.

"And so," she said, her hair tickling his neck and his cheek, "I'm not marrying Horace."

"Oh thank God," he said fervently. "I was trying, I swear, but I'd probably have ended up dumping lemonade all over your bridal bed."

She laughed, a little bubble of sound that got caught on the wind and lifted up toward the clear sky. "What was this all about, then, if you didn't really want me to do it?"

"I was trying to do the honorable thing."

"Well, just stop it, all right? You're really not very good at it."

He squeezed her lightly. "Hey!"

"We probably deserved the lemonade, anyway. What we said at B.J.'s party, when Horace called you a . . ." Her voice trailed off. "I'm sorry that you had to hear that, Joshua."

"A bastard?" He shrugged. "It's true, after all."

"What?" Stunned, she twisted around, to try and look at him, but they were too close, his face just inches from hers, and she couldn't focus on anything but his eyes, dense black pupils rimmed with pale, clear light.

"Here. If I'm going to tell you this story, we'd better get a bit more comfortable first." He lifted her out of the saddle and slid in himself. "Kick your leg over Jojo's neck."

She did, and he turned her so he held her sideways, snug against his torso.

"This isn't exactly the safest way to ride a horse."

"Good thing Jojo ain't the flighty sort then." He grinned down at her, daring her to complain. "Or don't you trust my ridin'?"

"I'll get too heavy for you."

"This is not a problem, Abigail." Her weight was perceptible, and her generous warmth, but there was no sensation of strain on his muscles, no tiring heaviness at all. "I can carry you like this forever."

"Oh." Her eyes began to sparkle, like a couple of the bright stars had decided to drop right on in and twinkle in the brown depths for a while. "And, since it's *you* we're talking about, I guess forever's a pretty long time, isn't it?"

"Durn right." But not long enough. No amount of time would ever be long enough, as long as she stayed right where she was.

"Now, about that story," she prompted.

"What story?" he asked innocently.

"Joshua . . ." She narrowed her eyes at him.

"That's how I got to Texas, in the first place. My mother, when she was young, worked for some rich guy back east. She and he . . . Well, when she found out she was expectin' without benefit of vows, it seemed like it was a mite easier all around just to become the 'Widow West' and come on out here. She got a job, keepin' house, at a spread down in the San Antonio Valley."

She should make him put her down, Abigail thought. But it was so comfortable, easy, to let the motion and his voice lull her. Here, there were no troublesome worries, no frustrating problems that couldn't be solved, as long as Joshua held her safe in his arms.

"Gave birth to me not two months after she got out here. Hardly slowed her down, I bet."

She laid her head against his chest. Perfect spot. She could nestle right there, and let his words wash over her, and hear his . . .

Heartbeat. He had no heartbeat.

She jerked up.

"What is it?" Instantly alert, Joshua scanned the horizon. "Trouble? Did you hear something?"

"Nothing." She blinked back the sting of tears, unwilling to explain them to him. She'd let herself forget that this was not real, had wanted to forget, that it was simply some trick of the Fates that allowed her to have this cherished bit of time with him.

But she didn't want to remind him, too, that this was all a temporary, if miraculous, illusion. She couldn't bear to spoil this night, didn't want to give him any reason to pull away.

"It's nothing," she repeated. "Please, go on."

His eyes searched her face. To distract him, and please herself, she snuggled in again, nestling comfortably into his embrace.

"It was a good enough place, I guess. Ma worked there the whole time I was growin' up. Nobody knew I was born out of wedlock, or, if they did, they didn't care. Then when I was thirteen, she took sick and was gone before I knew what hit her."

His arms, looped under her back and thighs, tensed, the muscles rounding and hardening, the sinewy strength she'd loved to test with the pressure of her fingers. She'd never been able to make a dent, but she'd had an awful lot of fun trying.

"Guess we have something in common, then," he said softly.

She wanted to hug him. To soothe him, to run her

hands over the hard lines of his face and arms. But the last time she'd tried to touch him, there'd been nothing there. If she could still reach out for him and grasp only air, she didn't want to know it.

"What then?"

"What do you mean, what then?"

"Who took care of you after she died?"

"I told you, I was thirteen."

She tried to imagine him at thirteen. Young, thin, and lanky, probably, and very alone. At least she'd had her father. And her brother, though he'd been only a baby. It had helped, somehow. Caring for him, holding him close, had eased the hollow grief. Who had Joshua had?

"But—"

"Nobody had to take care of me," he said flatly. "I'd been helpin' out, here and there, where I could. After Ma died, I just moved on down to the bunkhouse and they put me to work wranglin' the horses."

And there was her answer. He'd had nobody.

"I stayed for another two years. Then I just drifted on. Kept driftin', and then there was the war, and you pretty much know the rest."

"I didn't know any of this," she said wonderingly, and lifted her eyes, dark and wide with surprise, to his. "Joshua, I *loved* you, but I didn't know anything about you."

She'd loved him, she said. *Had.* Was it because her love was in the past, or his life was? He wasn't sure which one was worse.

"I guess we never really spent all that much time talkin'." He'd always been too busy kissing her, touching her, to spend enough time learning her. He regretted that now, even as he still felt the irresistible lure, to free one hand and close it over the slight curve of her breast.

"No, we didn't."

She'd loved him. He couldn't get the words out of his head, could feel them sinking deep into his soul. Why should the words matter so much? He'd thought she loved him, always assumed she had—but he found that thinking it and actually hearing the words were two different things.

The pale moonlight, clear and sweet as spring water, brushed over her face, kissing the sharp angles softened by a generous dusting of freckles and the wide curve of her mouth. What was it about her? He didn't look at her and see pretty or plain or any of the other list of things he usually saw when he looked at a woman. He looked at her and saw Abbie, and that was all his heart had ever needed to see.

"Abbie?"

"Hmm?"

There were a thousand good reasons why he shouldn't do this. He was going to do it anyway.

"I'm gonna stop talkin' now."

20

"*You think that's a good idea?*" She lifted her head, closing the space between them.

"Probably not. But it seems like it's probably gonna happen sooner or later, anyway."

"Might as well get it over with then."

"Yeah."

Neither dared to close their eyes. His mouth brushed hers briefly, there and gone as quickly as a streak of lightning.

He sat back and waited, without twitching so much as a muscle, for a full ten seconds before he finally accepted that he wasn't going anywhere. At least not yet.

"I'm still here."

"Looks that way to me." Her smile was flirty, teasing. "On the other hand, what would you call that? Hardly worthy of being called a kiss."

"Well, now that I know I'm not going to disappear in a puff of smoke, maybe I can do a better job of it."

"Maybe."

There was no testing this time. The sureness was born of familiarity; the swift, sharp rise of passion came from too many nights spent apart.

His mouth fit hers easily. Hers opened in welcome, his tongue tracing well-remembered paths along the edges of her lips, her teeth, stroking deep and slow.

He'd always loved her flavor. The way she looked and talked, one would have expected fiery spice. Instead, her mouth was pure sweetness, the kind a man could spend a lifetime tasting and never get enough.

She'd always thought that there was nothing more powerful than Joshua's kiss, power that seduced and lingered and imprinted itself on a woman's senses.

But after a year and a half of missing it, his kiss was even more. It was devastation, the kind she'd spent a lifetime avoiding but now welcomed with profound pleasure because it was impossible to do anything else.

He tilted his head, searching deeper. A thousand memories, a thousand dreams, spun together. Joshua's arms holding her safe and close, his mouth on hers as they moved across the night-drenched land.

He drew away slowly, and she nearly sobbed with the absence of his mouth. She opened eyelids gone heavy with hunger.

His smile was as warm as his voice. "That must not be against the rules, after all."

"Well, then." She cocked her head, considering. "Care to press your luck?"

Much to her disappointment, he hadn't.

Instead, he'd made some excuse about checking the

borders of her land, plopped her back in the saddle, and disappeared into the night.

It might have been insulting, if she hadn't seen the temptation shining clear and unmistakable in his eyes. And so, she'd occupied herself for the rest of her watch dreaming of just what he might do when he gave in to that temptation.

Abigail wondered if it was the first time he'd ever tried to restrain his . . . urges. She rather hoped so. If he hadn't had much practice at controlling himself, he'd never be able to hold out very long.

It was nearing noon now. She was certain he'd show up any moment.

She could sure use the distraction.

Inside the ranch house, it was dim and stifling. She'd closed the windows hours ago, hoping to keep out the blazing heat of full day, but it hadn't helped. It blocked out the light but was no barrier against the heat. She squinted through the deep shadows, trying to make out the numbers in her tally book.

She'd been working since shortly after breakfast. Ledgers and books and crumpled papers spilled across the table. No matter how many times she added it up, she couldn't seem to make the sums come out the way she needed them to.

The price of cattle was plummeting. Ranchers who could no longer water their stock sold them off cheap rather than have their deaths be a total loss. Though she could water hers, her empty pockets would force her to market some of hers sooner or later. Probably sooner, and she'd never be able to get a decent price for them under these circumstances.

She owed the hands nearly a hundred and twenty dollars in back wages. They couldn't be expected to work for future pay indefinitely. The food stores were dropping to meager levels; in perhaps two weeks she would be out of flour and sugar, with no money to buy more. They couldn't live on meat alone.

The truth was, she needed it to rain every bit as desperately as her neighbors did.

Frustrated, she scratched a thick, black line through the final sum, obliterating it so completely the point of her pen tore through the paper. She tossed the pen aside, listened to it roll off the table and clatter on the floor, and dropped her head to her hands.

The front door banged open, letting in a blast of harsh light and heat. Marcus stepped in and snapped it shut behind him.

"Nice and shady in here." He yanked off his hat and mopped his forehead with his sleeve.

"Everything going all right out there?"

"Yeah. Took Pa with me to water the horses, now he's gonna sit on the porch while I check over some of the tack. Wants a cup of coffee, though."

"I'll make some fresh." She hopped to her feet, grateful for the chance to do something other than wrestling with the ornery figures.

She opened a new bag of Arbunkle's—they only had two one-pound sacks left, she noted—and dug through the beans for the slender stick of peppermint always included.

"Want the candy?"

"Sure," Marcus said, brightening immediately.

She handed the sweet to him and reached for the grinder. Soon the rich, bitter smell of coffee filled the kitchen.

He flicked at one of the balls of paper she'd crumpled in her frustration, sending it scooting across the table until it bumped into a haphazard stack of ledgers.

"Having trouble?" he asked.

"Yes. I'd rather wrestle a wild steer than try and keep those books straight."

Sucking noisily on the stick of candy, he flipped through a ledger, quickly running his finger down the columns of numbers.

"Well, for starters, you're seven off on this sum right here."

"Where?" She came around the table and peered over his shoulder to see where he was pointing. "Darn it!"

It had taken her at least five minutes and three tries before she'd been satisfied with that figure, and he'd found a mistake in seconds. "Are you sure?"

"Yup." He bit off the brittle tip of the peppermint, releasing its cool scent, and crunched as he rapidly scanned the pages.

She leaned back and thought for a minute. It was a foolish idea. He was only twelve, after all. Still . . .

With the nearest school more than a hundred miles away, Abigail's mother had tutored her daughter, squeezing in reading and math between the household chores. In turn, Abigail had taught Marcus everything she knew. He'd always been a blindingly quick student, exhausting her store of knowledge more than two years ago.

Since then, he'd had to be satisfied by studying on his own, poring over the few books she'd managed to order for him when she could squeeze a bit extra out of the household budget. She'd been unable to buy him any new ones in more than year. She knew it had to be wildly frustrating for him, with so little to focus his fierce curiosity on.

"Marcus," she said, her decision made, "how would you like to take over the books for me?"

He immediately popped the peppermint stick out of his mouth and formed an O with his candy-sticky lips. "You mean it?"

"Yes."

"You'd . . . trust me with that?" His bright blue eyes lit up with hope.

"More so than myself, obviously, if I'm making mistakes. I could certainly make use of the extra time if you would take this off my hands. If you'd like to."

"Yeah! Yeah, I would." Eagerly, he retrieved the pen from the floor and plopped down on the nearest chair, attacking the mishmash of papers with an enthusiasm she hadn't seen in him since the last time she'd baked an apple pie.

The tension in her eased, just a bare notch. Perhaps she hadn't messed things up with Marcus so badly after all.

The water was coming to a boil; she could hear it bubbling in the big old pot. Time to dump in the ground coffee, one handful per cup. She turned to go back to the kitchen—and nearly ran right through Joshua.

"Oh! You—" She snapped her mouth shut, shooting a look over her shoulder at Marcus. Luckily, he was too engrossed in his new duties to notice her slip. His head bent over the books, he scribbled furiously away, mouthing numbers to himself.

"You're back," she whispered.

Lord, he looked good. The low, dusky light that leaked through the slats in the shutters carved deep shadows underneath the prominent bones of his cheek, made his hair look dark as glossy pitch. A wide, appealing grin stretched his mouth—except she could think of things she'd much, much rather he did with his mouth than smile.

"Yeah, I'm back." He still could hardly believe that he'd found the strength and restraint to leave her last night in the moonlight, when she so clearly wanted him to stay. There'd been a time that he would have gotten

176 SUSAN KAY LAW

on his knees and begged for the opportunity he'd had last night. He was only trying to do what was best for her, but, jeez, it was hard on a man.

He inclined his head toward Marcus. "You gave him a new job, huh?"

"Yes, I—" she began, until he brought his finger up to his lips to remind her she mustn't speak aloud. "Yes," she finished, barely mouthing the words, "he's taking over the books for me."

Damn, but he was proud of her. It swelled in his chest so strongly that he was going to pop a shirt button if it grew any more. He knew how hard it was for her to do this, to trust someone else with something that she considered her responsibility. Particularly to release one of her jobs to a boy that she'd raised practically from birth.

"That's good, Abigail."

"Oh, well . . ." She shrugged. "He'll probably be better at it than me, anyway. For sure he's going to enjoy it more."

"Now you just need to tell him that he can take one of the night watches."

She tensed immediately, twin lines furrowing between her brows. "It's too dangerous."

"He needs to do it, Abbie."

"No."

"I'll watch over him the entire time, make sure nothing happens to him. I would have suggested it right off, but I didn't think you'd trust me to do it."

"I wouldn't have."

It was one thing to put faith in her brother's ability to add a column of numbers correctly. It was quite another to let him risk his life out on the range.

"I promise." Joshua searched for the words to convince her. "I'll make sure he's safe, and he'll know that you believed he could handle it."

He could see her beginning to waver.

"But—"

"Trust me, Abigail."

And it all came down to that. He wanted her trust, needed it, longed for it. It mattered to him, more deeply than he'd ever realized.

"Marcus?" she called over her shoulder, never taking her gaze from Joshua's.

"Yeah, Abbie?"

"You're taking the four o'clock watch tonight."

21

"*I gotta ask you,*" Joshua said, pointing to the flattened, red-stitched pillow that slumped at the head of Abigail's bed, "*Life is duty?*"

She wrinkled her nose. "My mother made it."

"I should have known. The stitches are too neat to be yours."

Pulling a face, she tossed a pillow at his chest, which, to his dismay, simply sailed through him and thudded against the door. "You're awfully hard to pick a fight with these days."

After a long day, they'd somehow ended up back in Abigail's bedroom. Joshua still wasn't quite sure how it happened—this was probably a most unwise place for him to be, but here they were anyway.

Outside, the sun was gone, leaving the only light in the room the quavering golden glow from the coal-oil lantern. Abigail's shoes were off, her collar undone, and her hair curled loose and shiny around her shoulders. Seeing her like this, in her bedroom, relaxed and cozy, completely at ease with his presence, somehow seemed more intimate to him than times he'd touched her body in a dozen private, naked places.

Abigail wiggled back into the pillows and looked up at Joshua, who perched uneasily on the end of her bed, as far away from her as he could get without being too obvious.

"You know, Joshua," she said, "for a man who spent a fair amount of time and effort trying to get into this bed, you look awfully uncomfortable here."

"Yeah, well . . ." He glanced away and rubbed his palms on his thighs. "I guess maybe I'm out of practice at this, too."

"I'm sure it'll come back to you." She was probably enjoying this too much. But really, after all the times she'd nearly gone crazy, trying to resist his determined seduction, she found wicked satisfaction in seeing him battling so hard to keep his hands off of her now.

He was actually *nervous*, just from being closeted in her bedroom with her. He must be only a shade away from capitulation, if this could rattle him so much.

"You could come down here," she suggested, patting a clear spot beside her on the worn quilt.

His horrified gaze streaked to meet hers. "No!"

She tried not to laugh, she really did.

They'd been talking for at least an hour already. About everything and nothing, comparing days. The condition of the cattle, how to rid the waterhole of a bumper crop of turtles. Speculation as to who would win the contests at the fort this year. Possible ways to simplify some basic tasks, so her father could again perform them for himself.

Simple, everyday things.

Abigail understood passion; Joshua had taught her well of its wild, fierce power. But this warm companionship was new and wondrous, a gentle thing that snuggled close and deep in her heart. And she would miss it, she knew, every bit as much as she had mourned the passion.

But she refused to worry about that now. Tomorrow held no promises, no guarantees, and so she would simply enjoy.

His gaze traced her body, lingering, warming. Remembering.

Heaven had asked too much of him, Joshua thought. To ask him to come here and simply watch over this woman. She knew him too well, affected him too profoundly. Though he would try his damnedest to protect her, who would protect *them* from these dangerous, compelling feelings that had nearly destroyed them both once?

Still, he couldn't bring himself to turn tail and run from the room, seeking a safe distance from her. Because he'd learned darn well there was no such thing as a safe distance from Abigail; she called to him in a way that was undeterred by distance or time or even death.

Instead, he sought distraction. "I think you've got the biggest feet I've ever seen on a woman."

"Yep," Abigail said cheerfully. She tapped her bare feet together and flashed a cocky, flirty grin that blotted out every thought in Joshua's head but joining her on that saggy mattress. "And you just want to kiss my toes, don't you?"

"Yeah," he admitted reluctantly. "How come it doesn't bother you, when I said something like that?"

"Joshua." She scrambled up to kneel at his feet, tucking her skirts around her legs, baring her legs to the knee. "We might have messed up a few things between us, the first time, but there was one thing you always got very right."

Golden lamplight shadowed and shimmered around

his form, glowed in his eyes. Her Joshua. How colorless and lonely and dutiful her life had been without him. How would she ever survive that hollow emptiness again?

"I always knew, right from the first, no matter what anybody said," she went on, "it wasn't my land you wanted." Her smile flashed again. "You were after my body."

He bent down, pressed his lips against hers briefly. The kiss held nothing of passion; it spoke of long-held relationships, the kind of kiss one gave easily, without thought, knowing there would be thousands more, and so there was no need to imbue it with all sorts of deep flavors and layers and meanings. And, because of that, Abigail cherished it all the more, let it call forth those strong emotions, because a kiss like that was so rare, and it might never happen again.

"Now, *this* time—"

"Damn it!" Joshua swore, cutting her off. Bleak anger chilled his eyes, tightened his jaw. He left the bed and prowled the room, barely leashed frustration simmering around him like a heat mirage on the horizon. "Don't you understand? There *is* no 'this time.' I'm dead!"

She went to stand before him, stopping his pacing. Her hands shook with the need to touch him, to lay her palms along his cheek and test the rough rasp of stubble, to feel the muscles of his jaw work as he spoke. She didn't dare attempt it, terrified that she would not be able to touch him, not wanting to know what he was . . . and what he wasn't.

"You need more than a phantom, Abbie. I can't be what you need."

"I'm . . ." Words were thick and heavy in her throat, leaden as the weighty feel of regret and loss. "I'm not sure I care anymore."

Helpless before her admission, touched, overwhelmed, he wrapped his arms around her and pulled her close.

Damn it, he loved her. Always had. Loved the way she fit against him, the way her hair curled wild and bright. Loved the way she fought for her family, the fierce pride he'd often cursed. Loved the brown-sugar freckles that spangled her skin, and he bent his head to taste their sweetness, brushing his lips over her cheeks, her nose, her chin.

She deserved so many things. A husband who could stand beside her in front of the entire world, who could shoulder his share of the work and uphold his portion of the responsibilities. One who could love her well, with madness and tenderness, through the long nights. Children with blazing red curls and lanky bodies and tart mouths. A family, a home, a future.

All the things he couldn't give her.

He thought he'd had nothing left to lose. What more could a dead man surrender? But there was more, he found.

He could lose his soul.

"But I care," he whispered.

And then he left, vanishing through the wall and into the lonely night.

Abigail whisked the broom over the floor of the porch, sweeping away two days' accumulation of dust. She wasn't certain why she bothered; the relentless wind sifted more dirt over the porch almost as soon as she brushed it away. But she'd been too well trained by her devotedly tidy mother to neglect this duty.

It had grown still hotter, though she wondered that

that was even possible. The rising sun forced a wash of vibrant pink over half the sky and promised little relief from the soaring temperatures. A flock of carrion crows, black as death against the vivid shades behind them, winged their way east. Abigail hoped that they weren't heading for any of her stock, even as she knew that, if they were, it was too late for the unfortunate cow, anyway.

Tinged with just a hint of sourness, the rich, toasty smell of biscuits baking wafted through an open window from the kitchen. Abigail sniffed in appreciation and her stomach rumbled.

The bright, silvered ringing of the jinglebobs attached to Sledge's boots, his one vanity, alerted her to his approach. She quickly propped the broom against the nearest wall and whirled.

"Sledge! You're out of bed!"

"Yeah." His slow progress across the yard distinctly favored his injured ankle. Wincing in pain, he hitched awkwardly up the steps, keeping all his weight on his left leg. Abigail quickly dragged over a chair and waved him into it.

"Are you sure you should be up and about? Does it hurt much?"

"Couldn't stand to rot in that bed any longer. Thought I'd come for breakfast."

Sighing, he sank gratefully into the chair. Abigail lifted his foot and propped it carefully on the porch railing.

"Do you want me to fetch you some food out here?"

"That would be nice." When she moved to scurry into the house, he reached out a hand to stop her. "Wait. Gotta talk to you a bit."

"All right." Resting her hands on the arm of the chair, she crouched at his side. His mouth was pressed into a thin line; his face, grave. His eyes assessed her until Abigail grew uncomfortable with his close regard.

"Sledge? Does it pain you that much? What can I—"

His head snapped from side to side. "Ain't that."

She waited for him to continue, but he merely studied her with open concern.

What could it possibly be? Did he know something about all the problems on the Rolling G, something that was so difficult to tell her? It couldn't be that one of their hands was responsible. She refused to even consider it.

"Actually, I got up last night, too." His gaze skittered away.

"That's great," she said, now thoroughly confused.

"Thought I'd test out the ankle, wander up to the house and see if there was any of that raisin cake you made left over."

"Well, that's good, isn't it? If you can still walk this morning all right, after putting some weight on it last night?"

He rubbed his hands, gnarled and scarred from years of hard work, on his battered pants. "I heard you talkin'."

Talking? What was he getting at?

"In your room. All by yerself."

Oh Lord. He'd heard her talking to Joshua.

Frantically, she searched her memory, tried to recall exactly what she might have said. Had he heard her say Joshua's name? How could she explain it all to Sledge? The truth sounded more fantastical than any story she could possibly invent.

"I . . . talk to myself, now and again. Who doesn't? It's not such a big thing."

"Not like this." Worry scored deep lines around his frown. "It was like . . . you was carryin' on a whole, friendly conversation. 'Cept there weren't no other voice jawin' in there with you."

She straightened, squinting out over the yard, and fiddled with the rough fabric of her skirt where it gathered into the waistband. "Did you . . . hear anything of what I said?"

"You were talkin' too soft for me ta hear the words." He frowned. "But I heard you, goin' on and on, all right. And then you'd stop for a little while, like you was listen', before you started up again. It weren't like you was jes' mumblin' under your breath."

That was good, then. He'd heard nothing that would give them away. She blew out a long breath. "Really, Sledge—"

"I think mebbe whatever got Davis is gettin' you, too." Sledge's words spewed out in a fierce rush.

"What?" she asked, shocked. "You think I'm . . . going crazy?"

"I don't *want* to think it." He shook his head slowly. "But I don' know what else to think."

"Look at me." She squatted down beside his chair, resting her hands on the splintery wood of the arm, so she could look directly into Sledge's face. "Do I look like I'm losin' my mind?"

"No." He stared at her, his eyes searching hers.

Abigail had to force herself not to look away. Who knows what he might see there? Could confusion and worry and longing masquerade for madness?

"But Davis sure didn't look like he was, either, at first," he said with difficulty.

A slow, painful burn lodged itself in her belly. This was the last thing she wanted to deal with now, Sledge believing that her mind was failing her, just as her father's had deserted him. "Sledge, I don't know what to tell you to convince you of my sanity. It just helps me to talk out my worries to myself. That's all you heard."

"If you say so, Abigail," he said doubtfully.

She studied him for a moment, hoping he would read her sincerity in her eyes. Finally she sighed, patted his hand. There was nothing else she could do. Certainly he would be convinced of her insanity if she told him the truth, that she had been talking to a dead man.

"How about I get you that breakfast now, hmm?"

"Naw. I ain't too hungry this mornin'. I think I'll just haul my old carcass back to the bunkhouse." He struggled to his feet, and shuffled across the width of the porch, pausing at the top of the stairway.

"Let me help you down." Abigail looped his arm around her shoulder, taking his weight as he limped down the steps.

"I can manage it from here." Sledge dropped his arm, shoving his fists deep into his pockets. "There's something I gotta tell you, though, Abigail. It's only right to give you fair warnin'."

"I don't think I'm gonna like this."

"Probably not." The brim of his hat shadowed his eyes, making them look old and distant. A stranger's eyes, in a man she'd known for over twenty years. "If you get any worse—if I see any other symptoms—I'm gonna have to say somethin' to the other hands. And to Marcus."

And then what? She'd fail, completely, Abigail knew. Marcus would be terrified, and the hands would almost certainly leave—what other option would they have? They couldn't be expected to take orders from a woman who was losing her mind.

"Please don't, Sledge."

"I'm sorry. Ain't nothin' else I can do, Abigail."

He tugged his hat lower and turned away, his jinglebobs

ringing an awkward, uneven rhythm as he worked his way
back to the bunkhouse.

Abigail watched his progress, wondering if she
should call him back and try to explain . . . something.
But what could she say that wouldn't make her sound
even crazier than he already suspected she was?

Sledge was not the kind of man likely to have a whole
lot of patience for dead lovers and their heavenly assign-
ments.

"Well, shit," she murmured.

"Ain't it, though?" Joshua said from beside her.

"Oh!" She whirled, resisting the urge to clap her
hands over her mouth. "I didn't say that. You did not
hear that."

"I didn't? I coulda sworn you said 'well, shi—'"

"Stop!" she burst in, cutting him off abruptly. "Don't
remind me!"

"Why not? Cussin's good for you, sometimes. Takes
the strain off your liver."

"You would think so." She grimaced. "It's just so
unladylike, though."

"Abigail." He stepped close, laid his hand gently
along the slope of her cheek. "Who wants a lady? Ladies
are prim and fussy and pale, and they'd probably faint
dead away first time they had to pull a stuck calf."

He dropped his hand, but it scarcely mattered. His
touch was imprinted on her skin, branded into her heart.
His hair, nearly as dark as the fabric of his shirt, waved
low against his collar, and sun-lines fanned out from the
corners of his haze-and-sky-colored eyes.

"A man doesn't want a lady, Abigail. A man wants a
woman, a woman with enough grit and life in her to
stand by him and with him and up to him. And even to
stand without him, if she's gotta."

"Really?" she said, scarcely breathing. It ran counter

to what she'd spent years trying to achieve, what she'd worked to become. Despite that, she believed Joshua; no woman could see him now, hear the deep vibration of his voice and see the warmth in his eyes and doubt him.

"Oh yeah. What man wants to spend his time coddlin' and caterin' to somebody else's life instead of building one together?" His smile was full of love and sex and just a touch of awe.

"And you, Abigail Grier," he said, "are all the woman that any man could ever dream of havin'." His gaze slowly drifted over her face, marking each feature, and settled on her mouth.

"Joshua." She had no other words; just *Joshua*. No other words mattered a whit. Her eyelids fluttered shut. She lifted her chin, waiting for his mouth to make her feel all those things she'd just heard, make her know the truth of his words.

But nothing came, not the gentle brush of his lips or the urgent heat of his tongue. When she opened her eyes again, he was gone.

"Joshua!" She tipped her head back and shouted to the sky.

"I *hate* it when you do that!"

22

Joshua had been absolutely, completely determined to stay away from Abigail. He wouldn't see her, wouldn't touch her, wouldn't get anywhere near her.

He couldn't risk it. She was in too much danger, and did far too good a job of distracting him from his assignment. He couldn't take the chance that they might suddenly decide to yank him away for his lustful thoughts before he'd completed the task he'd been sent here for—making sure Abigail was safe.

Well, sure, if they were going to take him off the job for lustful thoughts, it probably would have happened the first day. It was lustful *actions* he had to worry about, and the only way he knew to make darn sure he wasn't guilty of any of those was to stay as far away from Abbie as possible.

He held firm to his resolve for all of—what was it?—fourteen hours or so. Amazing he'd even lasted that long.

It was just after sunset. Abigail worked at the well,

drawing up a bucket of water. In her, Joshua saw all the glory of the evening that had just collided with the night. Night glowed in the pale sheen of her skin, echoing the color of the rising moon; the brilliant color of her hair captured and reflected all the fiery red of the dying sun.

Okay, time for a new plan.

He could *look* at her. He just wouldn't *touch* her.

"Good evening," he said, for no other reason than that he hoped she'd look his way.

Abigail carefully balanced a full bucket on the edge of the well. Resting a hand on her hip, she glanced up at the rapidly darkening sky. "More like good night."

"Yeah, well . . ." He resisted the urge to clear his throat like an awkward, love-struck schoolboy. All it had taken was one glimpse of her strong hands working the well rope, one hint of her lilac-and-female scent, and every good intention he'd made flew right out of his head.

"Had a busy day, I take it." Her words were clipped and impersonal. Abigail had no intention of forgiving him for ignoring her all day long, just because he'd shown up at sunset with heat in his eyes.

"Was over at B.J.'s place, most of it."

"B.J.?" she asked, suddenly alert. "What were you doing there?"

Her white shirt looked startlingly bright against her dark blue slash of skirt, the sharp line between them luring his attention to her narrow waist as she walked toward him. Joshua tried to force his feet to move, to step back a little to a safer distance—out of arm's reach—but they refused to comply with the commands of his brain. The rest of him, it seemed, was much more inclined to listen to the demands of his heart.

And perhaps the desires of a few other body parts as well.

"Nothing much, really. Watching, listening. Hoping I'd overhear if he was planning somethin', so we could get ready for it. Or at least find some proof that Hallenbeck really is the one behind all the problems you've been having."

"Did you find out anything?" Her hair was swept back tightly, pinned and braided so only a few brave curls escaped around her temples. It exposed the delicate curve of her ear, tempting him. Jesus, did the woman have any idea what she did to him? Did she mean to torture him so much?

"Found out why he keeps that housekeeper around even though she's a lousy cook."

"Joshua! You didn't!"

"God, no." He shuddered. "Why do you think I'm here? Scooted home quicker'n you can spit'n holler howdy."

Home? He'd called the Rolling G "home." Abigail wondered why that made her feel so much like crying. "Aw, gee, and here I thought you rushed home just to see me."

"That, too," he said seriously, and that small slip was all that was needed to send Abigail's heart skittering in her chest.

Touch me. She wanted it so fiercely that Abigail was afraid she'd whispered the words aloud. What he'd been, what he was, all the things he could never be . . . none of that was the barest defense against the simple, powerful longing to have his hands on her body. How had she ever managed without it as long as she had?

"Do you . . . go over there much?" she asked with difficulty.

"I've been trotting over there regularly, listenin' in, soon as we started suspectin' him."

"You never told me."

He shrugged. "Not much to tell. Either he's a lot more clever'n I gave him credit for, or I'm unlucky. Never heard anything of any use yet."

"Or he's not the one behind it."

"Yeah, right."

The fact that he was actually managing to carry on an understandable conversation astonished him. How could he form words that made any sense, when there was no room in his mind for any thoughts but those of her?

Aw, hell.

Maybe touching wouldn't be so bad, wouldn't completely shatter the resolution he'd made. Long as he didn't actually kiss her.

He traced the curl of her ear, caught the lobe between his thumb and finger, and gently rubbed the tiny drop of tender flesh. There was only one place on Abigail's body that was softer, more delicate . . .

Oh no. Not a good idea to think about that. Not a good idea *at all.*

Her eyes soft and languorous, she tilted her head right into the open curve of his palm. The "no kissing" plan was starting to look a mite wobbly.

Abigail straightened so abruptly he could almost hear her spine snap. She stared over his shoulder.

"Joshua, is that—?"

The dread in her eyes should have warned him. Still, he was unprepared for the sight when he twisted to look, the thing every plains dweller hated above all—a far-off reflection of violent orange against the low, bruise-colored night sky.

"You warn everyone else!" he shouted. "I'll meet you there!"

And, even as he raced northeast, he heard Abigail's screams behind him, rousting the hands.

"Fire!"

*　　*　　*

Abigail galloped from the ranch and sped right into hell.

The glaring line of flames, perhaps two hundred yards long and slowly expanding, devoured its way east, prodded by a strong, relentless wind and fed by the tinder-dry grass. It left a broad band of charred, blackened earth behind it.

She leapt off Jojo and turned him free. There was nothing out here to tie him to, no way to force him to stay, and he squealed and fled the terrifying monster of fire.

Intense heat blasted from the flames and burned-over ground. Thick streamers of dense black smoke bubbled and churned, nearly choking her. She tied a dampened cloth around her lower face to filter out the worst of it, though the improvement was barely discernible. The blanket she'd snatched from the house and dunked in the well before riding off to meet the fire was heavy and sodden with water. It flapped loudly in the high wind when she shook it open.

"Joshua!" she shouted. "Are you here?"

"I'm here!" Though his voice sounded near, she couldn't locate him in the darkness. "Where's everyone else?"

"They're coming! Right behind me!" She attacked the greedy flames, beating the ground with her blanket, pitifully flimsy ammunition against the power of fire. Steamed hissed and coiled up.

The smoke lifted on an updraft of heated air, briefly revealing the bright, dancing inferno, and there was Joshua. Right in the middle of a twisting, brilliant ring of yellow fire, curling smoke wavering around his body, he was a dark, intense form cloaked in black, stamping at the relentless flames in a macabre dance.

This hell held the figure of the devil, but one who fought to destroy it.

"Joshua!" she shouted, certain he would burn away in the scorching heat.

"It's all right!" he hollered back. "It can't hurt me!"

He pounded the earth with his hands, got down and rolled madly among the blaze, trying to douse it, smother it, slow it, any way he could. But for every flame he snuffed, two more burst to malignant life.

The air currents shifted and dark smoke billowed back down, completely obscuring Joshua. Abigail's shoulders already ached from lashing the weighty blanket at the earth, but the pain was useless and so she ignored it.

They could not afford to lose a great deal of grass. Too much of her land had been already cropped, and, without rain, there'd be no new growth. This was one of the few remaining ungrazed sections of the ranch, and the fodder was absolutely necessary to the continued survival of the herd.

The thunder of the horses' hooves and the wooden clatter of wagon wheels accompanied the arrival of reinforcements.

"Thank God," she whispered, though He seemed a universe away.

The hands quickly tied their protesting mounts to the wagon, keeping the horses handy if they needed a fast escape later. They yanked slickers and blankets and gunnysacks from the back of the wagon, sloshing them through barrels of water, and sprinted to the advancing line of fire.

A *thwap, thwap* just to her left rang sharply in Abigail's ears. She turned her face away from the intense heat that seared her skin and met Marcus' eyes.

He fought the flames, wielding his soaked yellow

slicker like a weapon. She struggled with the urge to
order him home, out of danger, out of hell.

But this was his land and his battle as much as hers.

"You can take my right side!" she shouted over the
crackle of flames and deafening roar of the wind.
"There's no one over there yet!"

Pride lifted his chin and determination steeled his
young face. "Got it, Abbie!" He dashed around her to
take up his post.

Reality faded, then disappeared. Nothing else in the
world existed, nothing but the smoke and ashes that
made her lungs burn and eyes smart. No smells but the
stench of scorched grass and weeds, sagebrush and
cowchips.

Nothing but the painful, desperate work, the ache of
her shoulders from lifting and dropping the blankets, the
weakness of her wobbly legs as she dashed back and
forth to the dwindling barrels of water.

Bits of blackened grass and ash settled on her, coating her clothes, her hair, her face. The air churned with
dark cinders, like a vicious snowstorm formed not of
water but charred flakes.

Now and then the smoke rolled up, lifting here and
there to give glimpses of a flare of searing yellow and of
Joshua, a big, torn blanket that he'd taken from the
wagon flaring and flailing around his tall, lean form.

The thudding of wet cloth echoed in her ears,
resounded in her mind. Where she snuffed the advancing flames, streamers of smoke and ash and steam shuddered in the air. Sparks spiraled up, dancing in and out
of smoke rings, first glowing hot red, then fading to a
delicate rose before dying to black ash.

And through it all, the moon shone malevolent red
through the dense cloak of hot, deadly smoke.

The fire's progress slowed. But it didn't stop.

"Pecos!" Abigail beat her way over to the nearest hand, his face dark with ash and gleaming with sweat. "It's not gonna be enough! I need you to try and plow a firebreak."

"Got it." He hurled his gunnysack into the wagonbed and hauled out the old plow, hitching it quickly to the most reliable horse.

Water in a half-filled barrel shimmered with reflected firelight, as if it, too, had caught fire. Abigail dunked her blanket again, the feel of liquid against her wrist a stark, near-painful contrast to the torrid air, and went back to fight the greedy blaze.

Except she no longer tried to pound it into submission. Only to slow it long enough to give Pecos time to gouge out the wide strip of turned earth that was their only hope of stopping it.

23

Wary, hopeful, depleted, they stood in a watchful group on the far side of the strip of churned earth, clutching soggy, singed blankets, and awaited the greedy, advancing flames. The plowed belt seemed a dismally fragile barrier to halt the relentless destruction of fire.

"It's got to work. It's just got to," Abigail murmured to Joshua, who stood just behind her, his big palms on her shoulders.

His thumbs worked her aching muscles, rubbed along the tight ligaments that bounded her neck, trying to give her relief the only way he could. It seemed brutally unfair to him, that he could work all night without feeling so much as a twinge of protest from his muscles, while she must be aching right down to her bones.

"It'll be okay, Abigail. You'll survive, and so will the ranch."

He sounded so sure. Did he know something she didn't? Or did he simply have that much faith in her? Either way, it helped, bolstering her flagging energies.

The leading line of the fire hit the far edge of the break. With no fuel to feed it, the flames rolled back on themselves, spewing up a great, blotting cloud of ash and smoke.

The crackle and snap of the blaze diminished. A three-foot section burned itself out, leaving a black, gaping hole in the row of fire like a missing tooth.

"It's working!" Marcus shouted.

"Yes," Abigail whispered, her fists clenched tight. Only a little more . . .

With a harsh roar, the wind changed, strengthened, screaming from the west in a fierce, wild rush. The smoke blasted in their faces, temporarily blinding them.

Abigail blinked, trying to clear her vision. A cowchip, blown by the savage gusts, rolled across the strip of barren earth like a fiery wheel, throwing off bright sparks that curved through the darkness as it spun along. It reached the other side of the firebreak, and spawned dozens of small, potent fires.

"Hurry!" Abigail shouted, running to douse the nearest flame. "We have to get them out before they spread!"

But there were more cowchips, more voracious fires, and not nearly enough people for the battle. A loud *pop* shot a blazing sphere of tumbleweed high in the sky, a brilliant arch against the bleak, black sky like a dying comet.

The wind intensified. Showers of sparks flew across the sterile width intended to halt them, breeding fierce new flames as soon as they touched the arid grass.

"There's too many!" Abigail caught her breath on a harsh sob even as she flailed wildly at the small, rapidly multiplying fires. "We'll never get them all."

Joshua worked beside her, whipping a stinking gray blanket through the air, no longer caring if anyone saw him and noticed the unmanned cloth flailing away by itself. They'd explain later, if it came to that.

Sledge scuffled up, his stained yellow slicker slung over his shoulder. He yanked down the blue handkerchief that covered his mouth. "We're not going to stop it, Abigail."

"Yes we are!" Fueled by anger, she slashed her blanket at a hissing trail of sparks.

"Abigail, listen to me!" He gripped her upper arms and shook her, shouting into her face. "Give up! There's nothing else we can do!"

She jerked away from him. "Get back to work," she ordered him.

"It's useless!" he insisted.

She scowled, her eyes ablaze with determination as bright as the flames. "You work for *me*, Sledge."

His eyebrows, thick with dust and cinders, snapped down over his eyes and his mouth tightened. "Fine, boss." He spun on his heel, turning his rigid back to her, and limped to the wagon.

"Oh God!" She gulped, no longer able to tell if the ache in her nose and mouth and eyes was from the smoke, tears, or anger. "What are we going to do?"

"There's something I heard about once!" Joshua stood in the midst of a growing blaze that looked like it could swallow him whole and shouted over the roars of the flame and the screech of the wind. "It might work!"

"What?" she hollered, willing to clutch the shreds of any desperate idea. What more did they have to lose?

"You're not going to like it."

The brawny steer she sent Lippy after didn't like it, either. He dragged along behind Lippy's horse, fighting the rope, kicking his heels, bawling his protest at being hauled nearer the wicked flames.

Lippy halted his mount near Abigail. His hat had blown off and been sacrificed an hour ago, and his pale hair was lost under a thick coating of gray ash that also smudged his skin.

"This'un's the biggest I could find. What do you want me to do with him now?"

Despite the damp cloth bound around her mouth, acrid air burned Abigail's lungs. She felt the steady encouragement of Joshua's hand at the small of her back.

"Kill him."

The task was done quickly and efficiently, if not without some regret at the necessary waste. They bound the half-skinned steer between two sturdy horses, looping a rope securely from the dead cow's forelegs to the saddle horn of Pecos's mount, tying its rear legs to the horse Sledge had ridden out to the fire but which now carried Abigail.

"Ready?" she called.

Pecos simply nodded and touched his heels to his horse's flanks.

They straddled the line of flames, one rider on each side, dragging the heavy, lifeless carcass between them, snuffing out the blaze as they slowly worked their way down the row of fire.

Beneath her, Abigail's mount stepped gingerly over the burned-over ground, intense waves of heat rolling up from the scorched earth. His hooves kicked up spurts of soot that smudged her vision, covered his coat, and settled thickly over Abigail.

It was slow going. To protect their horses, Pecos and she were forced to climb down, retie the carcass, and alternate sides every few minutes, so that the horses' hooves would not be charred by the still-dangerous heat of the just-burned ground.

The smell of seared meat added to the acrid odor of burned grass and smoke. Before and after Abigail and Pecos, the others still worked, snuffing any stubborn flames, searching for stray sparks.

On and on they battled, as the night rolled by in a nightmare of heat and pain and destruction.

Abigail lost any sense of time. She felt as if she were functioning through a dense layer of scalding, unnatural fog, all sounds and sights—even her thoughts—slowed and blurred.

She was certain she would have tumbled from her horse and surrendered to the inevitable hours ago—if not for Joshua, who was there with a smile of comfort and encouragement every time she glanced his way. When she thought she could not ride any longer, he temporarily left his own fight and mounted up behind her, guiding the horse as he let her slump in his arms. And when she'd reached her limit and was convinced she had nothing left to give, he whispered of his faith in her and helped her rediscover it, too.

"That's it! We did it!"

At first, Marcus' jubilant shout barely registered through the cloud of endless night that clogged Abigail's mind. She blinked, slowly lifting her head to look around.

It was over.

The night and the fire had died. To the west lay miles of desecrated ground, churned by a hot wind, scattered with unrecognizable clumps of burned, black matter, trailing a few leftover wisps of smoke.

But to her right was rescued land, covered with a dense carpet of untouched grass. The sun had risen without her notice, the light barely penetrating the low, thick haze of dust and smoke, shining angry, vicious red, an echo of the battle they'd just fought—and won.

"It's over," she said numbly, yanking down the cloth tied over her lower face and taking a full breath for the first time in hours.

One more disaster, and they'd beaten it yet again. They'd survived another night.

"Yup." Pecos, standing on the ground beside her, met her gaze with a grin of pride. He reached up and quickly untied the ropes that still bound the dead steer to her horse. "Ready to go home?"

"Home." She looked at Joshua, yards away, alone, a tall figure cloaked in black and smoke, silhouetted against the scarlet ball of the rising sun. "In a moment, Pecos. Can you take Marcus back in the wagon, leave me this horse?"

"Sure. Think he's thrown himself down in the back of the wagon, anyway. He's plumb wrung out." Pecos hesitated, slid his broad hand down the horse's neck. "Tough night. You done good. Remind me some of my wife."

Embarrassed, he cleared his throat, turned away, and headed slowly for his mount.

"Thank you," Abigail whispered after him, knowing he wouldn't hear her. She'd never been quite so flattered.

Pecos and Lippy slouched into their saddles and turned their plodding horses for home. Sledge, his shoulders slumped, drove the wagon, with Marcus, already half asleep, out of sight in the back.

Abigail dismounted. Her horse, no longer spooked by the fire, would stay ground-tied where she left it.

By God, it was over! She'd stayed behind when everyone else headed home because she wanted to share the exhilaration and the triumph with Joshua first, just as they had when they'd chased B.J. from Rolling G land. But Joshua stood apart, his feet planted wide on a strip of still-smoking earth, staring at the destruction, and he seemed as remote from her as he ever had when he was hundreds of miles away.

She walked over to him, stopping only a few feet away, but still he didn't look at her. Tentatively, she reached out to touch his arm, but when her hand reached the place where his arm looked to be and found nothing solid, she curled a fist and let it drop at her side.

"Joshua?"

He turned to her then, his eyes starkly bleak.

"God, Abbie, I'm so damn sorry." How could she look at him like that, he wondered, welcome in her eyes instead of the accusation and recrimination she should be confronting him with? Didn't she know how badly he'd failed her last night?

"It's not so bad, Joshua. We got it stopped in time, I think, there'll be enough grass—"

"No!" He cut her off, his hand slashing the air. "Not that!"

She frowned, puzzled. "What, then?"

"I should have stopped it." His jaw went tight, his features sharp and angry. "I should have found out what B.J. was up to before it started! I should have caught it more quickly! And I should have been able to put it out for you!"

"Lord, Joshua, is there anything else you want to blame yourself for while you're at it? You want to tell me you started it yourself? Or maybe the entire drought is your fault."

"Abbie, you don't understand—"

"No, it's my turn now." She stepped closer, forcing him to look at her, to listen to what she had to say. "You're just one man—"

"I'm not a man. Not anymore." She should know that better than anyone.

"Yes you are." Lord, she wanted to touch him, to have his arms around her out here, on the land they'd saved together. But, for some reason, it didn't work that way; she couldn't be the one to reach out first. She could only feel him if Joshua touched *her*. And, right now, his body vibrating with tension and barely controlled anger, it didn't seem like he was going to be reaching for her any time soon.

"Maybe not quite in the same form you were before, and maybe you got a few extra . . . talents . . . but you're still just one man."

He laughed, a hollow sound with no amusement in it. "Lot of good those extra talents are doing you."

"It's taken me a long time, Joshua, to stop blaming myself. To learn that I can't do everything alone. And you're part of what taught me that. Can't you do the same thing?"

"I should have helped more, Abigail."

"You did help me. More than you realize, I guess. I never, *never* would have made it through last night without you."

"Yes, you would have. You're the strongest woman I've ever known." He tried to hang on to the guilt he knew he clearly deserved. But her care was stronger, and the regret that churned in his belly eased. "But I'm glad you didn't have to."

"Me too." Her face felt tight and itchy, and she swiped at it. Her palms came away streaked with soot and grime and she started to laugh.

"What?"

"Look at us." She spread her arms and spun, showing him the mess she'd become. "I look like I've been rolling in ashes, and you're as clean as if you were going to a church social!"

Abigail was right. Gray cinders dusted her hair, and it

was impossible to tell what the original colors of her clothes had been. The whites of her eyes glowed brightly against the dirt coating her skin, and, when she smiled, her mouth was a brilliant slash like a sliver of bright moon against a dark, clotted sky.

This time his smile was genuine. "You look beautiful."

"Of course." She bobbed a quick curtsy.

"You do." He cupped her cheek, his thumb stroking down her cheekbone. "You blistered here, from the heat. Does it hurt?"

"Only a little." Hardly at all, she amended, when there were so many more interesting things to feel, the simple pleasure of his touch and gentle warmth of his hand.

"Here. Let me try." He closed his eyes, thinking only of the smooth, unmarred texture of her skin, conjuring up images of early spring breezes and mountain air, willing his body to draw the raw heat and soreness into itself. His fingers burned, pain spreading down his arm before slowly fading away.

Coolness flowed from his hand into Abigail's skin, like the soft purling of fresh spring water. Pure, clean, healing. The burning on her cheek faded, slipped away until nothing remained but the sweetness. Joshua's eyes opened, their color cool and rich as a deep lake.

"Better?" he asked.

"Much."

God, what a woman she was. So many others would have collapsed hours ago. Hell, anyone else probably would have given up months ago. What had he ever done to earn even this bit of time with her? "You are something else, you know that? Come here."

And he tugged her into his arms.

Abigail sighed and settled in. This was so much better,

Joshua taking her weight so her legs no longer had the burden of holding her up, his arms giving her his strength, his presence giving her joy. It was as if his embrace drew the experiences of the night from her, washed away her tiredness and resentment.

"Abigail?" His chin rubbed over the top of her head. "Maybe . . . you should think about taking Pecos up on his offer."

"Pecos?" Why were they talking about Pecos now? Now, when there were better things to do than talk? She would have lived the night over again to have been given the luxury of touching him, of wrapping her arms around his back and sliding her palms over the firm muscle of his shoulders. But, since she could not, she simply let her arms dangle at her sides and surrendered to the old wonder of having Joshua hold her.

"His offer . . . about B.J." He would probably be damned for even suggesting it. But frustration gnawed at him, his inability to solve her problems, once and for all.

"You can't mean that."

"I'm not so certain I don't."

She didn't pull away, just leaned back a little and tipped her head up. "I couldn't do that, Joshua. I can't . . . I can't hurt someone because of what he *might* have done, or because of his potential. We don't *know*, Joshua. It's not enough."

Joshua sighed deeply. "Yeah, I figured that was what you'd say. But it was worth a shot."

She flashed an impish smile. "What's the matter? Want to be relieved of duty so quickly?"

"God, no," he said fervently and dropped a brief kiss on her ash-covered forehead. "Never that. Who knows what they might want me to do next?" He shuddered. "I could end up counting nuns or herding sheep or learning to play the harp."

"How horrible." She feigned abject sympathy. "Well, I've got a duty for you now."

"I don't know," he said as doubtfully as he could. "What is it?"

She cocked her head at the horse they'd left her. "Escort me home?"

"What? The independent Abigail Grier isn't insisting on riding home alone? Every man in Barrens would be shocked out of their boots."

"Does that mean no?"

He clicked his heels together and gave her a respectful bow. "At your service, ma'am."

"I do believe I could get used to this."

24

"What are you doing?"

"Oh, you're awake." Joshua grinned down at Abigail as he carried her up the front stairs of the ranch house. "What's it seem like I'm doing? I'm giving you a ride inside, of course. Gonna tuck you right into bed."

"For heaven's sake, Joshua, put me down. What if someone sees us?"

"Hmm." He stopped on the porch. The roof blocked the light of harsh morning sun, casting him in dusky shade, so his eyes seemed to glow at her from the shadows. "You probably look pretty funny, I suppose, floating along three feet in the air with your butt pointed at the ground."

"Joshua!"

"Abigail!" he mimicked. His grin was unrepentant, and completely irresistible. "They'd probably think they'd been sucking in too much smoke and it was making 'em see things, that's all. Besides, I bet they all got their lids glued together by now."

"Oh." She plopped her head back on his sturdy shoulder. "You're probably right," she agreed.

Not that there weren't several good reasons to have Joshua put her down. Someone *might* see them. Not to mention she was perfectly capable of walking herself. And she was getting far too accustomed to the feel of his arms around her.

But all those fine, true reasons didn't seem to hold much weight against the absolute comfort he offered.

Through a veil of contentment, she vaguely remembered Joshua lifting her to the back of the horse amidst the smoldering ruins of acres and acres of Rolling G land, and him mounting up behind her. He'd insisted on handling the reins, though it had taken a couple of tries before he got the horse going in the right direction. Odd how doing things like that seemed more difficult for him some times than others.

She remembered the feeling of complete safety, of his long body curved protectively around hers, and then she didn't remember anything more.

"How far did we get before I feel asleep?"

"Oh, maybe two steps." He'd loved it. Abbie had been dirt-streaked and reeking of smoke, and she'd curled right up against his chest, gave a soft little sigh, and gone straight to sleep.

Trusting him to keep her safe and get her home.

He'd briefly considered taking a really long route back to the ranch, just to prolong the trip. Giving him more time to watch the slow rise and fall of her chest in slumber, and feel her warm breath flutter in the hollow of his throat. Sense had won out, unfortunately, and he'd decided she'd be better off in her own bed.

"Can you nudge the door open with your foot? My hands are kind of full," he said.

"You could put me down."

"Not on your life. I finally got you right where I want you."

"Good." Her eyes, reddened from smoke and irritation, still twinkled.

They awkwardly pushed open the door and he swept her inside, making a beeline straight for her bedroom.

"Where are we going?"

"I told you. I'm taking you right to bed."

"Joshua!"

"Why, Miss Abigail! Certainly you didn't think I was suggestin' anything improper, did you?"

"You weren't?" She frowned, but humor twitched the corners of her mouth. "I'm so disappointed."

Jesus, how had he ever lived without her? Those six months wandering through New Mexico and Colorado, trying to pretend that he'd get over her someday—just to get over her was all he'd asked. Even then, he knew he'd never forget her. Empty, long, pale months, scraped bare of all laughter and joy.

He felt a hundred times more alive now, dead, than he'd ever felt while he still breathed but tried to live without Abigail.

"Don't I wish." He kissed the very tip of her black-tipped nose. "But you're tired. You need sleep, and I'm going to make darn sure you get it."

"But I need to clean up a little first. And I need to check on everyone and make sure they all got back okay."

He almost ignored her, inclined to hustle her into her bedroom and toss her on the mattress before she had anything to say about it. But he knew Abigail better than that, and knew she'd never truly rest until she made certain everything and everyone was as they should be.

He sighed and dropped the arm beneath her knees, letting her slide slowly down the length of his body, and he heard the catch of her breath.

It was foolish of him, to tempt them both like this. To play with desire and want and *almosts*. Someday it was going to get the better of him, and he'd lose control and be buried deep within her before he had time to think.

But he couldn't seem to stop, either. He knew painfully well what they couldn't have, and he couldn't find the strength to deny them this little that they could.

She stayed full against him, his arm wrapped around her lower back, while her eyes darkened and the memories simmered in them both. Joshua thought he could detect the change of her heartbeat, hear the seductive rhythm speed up as her blood heated and thickened.

"Abigail, I . . ." He let the words trail off, because there were really none worth saying. No words would ever change what was between them. No mere words could fix the fact that she was alive and he was dead and neither one wanted to hurt the other anymore.

"It's allright, Joshua. I understand."

She stepped away, scraping ash-coated curls away from her forehead. "I think I'll just go ahead and wash up, and—oh!" She peered over his shoulder, into the seating area, and smiled. "Look at that."

Marcus had made it into the house, but he hadn't gotten much farther. He slumped in an upholstered armchair in the far corner of the room, hazy morning light beating in the window and casting a bright rectangle across his lap. One boot was off, dropped on its side on the floor. His right foot still carried its worn, caked boot, and it propped on his knee at an awkward angle. His head rested on the back of the chair, his chin pointing at the ceiling, and his mouth was wide and slack.

He was fast asleep.

"Do you think we should move him?" Abigail asked.

"Naw, he looks comfortable enough. He'll wake up and shuffle off to bed soon, I'm sure."

"Could you close the shutters, please, so the light doesn't hit him? I'm going to go check on Papa."

Joshua tugged the shutters closed, sealing out the sun that showed every promise of strengthening long before noon to an intensity that would rival last night's fire.

"Joshua!" Abigail bolted out of the bedroom, her voice edged with cold fear. "He's gone!"

Joshua dropped the latch he was in the process of fastening. "What?"

"Papa! His bed is empty!" Her skin blanched white beneath the soot that streaked her face, her eyes pinched with worry.

Marcus stirred, snorted, and his head lolled to the other side, rolling across the chair back before he quieted back into deep sleep.

"Maybe he just went out to take a piss, or—"

"You don't understand!" Abigail pressed a hand to her stomach. "He . . . wanders. He can't find his way back. So, whenever we're gone, we tie up the door so he can't get out alone. He *has* to be here!"

Aw, shit. What else could go wrong? How much more could she survive? It was grossly unfair that his Abbie had to go through all this. When he got back up to heaven, him and the Big Boss were going to have a bit of a talk about treating ladies like her right.

"Okay." He crossed to her quickly, folding both her hands in his, trying to sound unconcerned. It would do no good to encourage the worry, to let it feed on itself until it burgeoned into dark fear. "He's probably around here somewhere. We'll look through the house, first. Maybe he just rambled over into your room and fell asleep in there."

Abigail sucked in a deep, steadying breath. "Yes, maybe."

And they both wished they were more convinced.

"I'll take my bedroom. You check in the kitchen first."

Abigail was down on her knees, peeking under her bed in foolish desperation—perhaps the fire had scared Davis into hiding—when Joshua appeared at the door.

"Abigail," he said in a calm voice that somehow froze the blood in her veins despite its studied quietness. "I think you'd better take a look at this."

He led her back into her father's bedroom, where before she'd glanced around only quickly, just enough time to see the mussed, empty bed.

She couldn't believe she'd missed it the first time. For it was so obvious how her father had escaped.

The single, uncurtained window still held remnants of shattered glass, razor-sharp triangles that jutted from the frame like broken teeth.

"No!" Abigail rushed to the window. Outside, crushed glass scattered over the barren ground, a wicked glitter in the hot sunlight. Dark droplets spattered the earth, a shiny red trail leading away from the house. "Oh God, it's blood. He's hurt, Joshua, maybe he's—"

She buried her face in her hands, unable to even say the word. She'd worried about it; perhaps, sometimes, in a guilty part of her she rarely acknowledged existed, wondered even if it would be for the best. But she had never truly felt the cruel horror of it.

"You don't know that. Let's not assume the worst." Joshua gripped her upper arms. "Do you have any idea where he might go?"

"No, he just . . . walks." Forcing herself to shove away the fear and focus on action instead, she tried to pull away from Joshua. "Let me go, Joshua, I have to wake everyone up and tell them what to do, we have to—"

"No."

"But—"

"You're tired, Abigail, and so is everybody else, and there's a lot of land out there."

"I have to try!" Her voice cracked, as if it were old and fragile. "Oh God, I should have left someone to watch him! But I thought we needed everyone out to fight the fire, and I didn't think he— He hasn't tried to escape for such a long time." She closed her eyes, as if by doing so she could blot out the guilt as well as her vision. "What if he was drawn by the light and came to the fire? What if we didn't see him?"

"Abbie," Joshua said, his voice sharp as the crack of a whip. "It's not your fault."

"But—"

"I won't let you do this to yourself. I won't let you blame yourself for doing the best you can."

"Don't you understand?" she whispered. "He's my father, and he's hurt and he's lost and—"

"I do understand." Though his hands still held her tight, his thumbs stroked gentle circles on the caps of her shoulders. "But I also understand that I can cover this ground faster than all of you put together."

She hesitated, demands and thoughts and responsibilities whirling through her head until she couldn't grasp and recognize a single one.

"Let me do this for you, Abigail." His throat burned. Why was there so much hurt in a body that was supposed to be beyond suffering, no longer susceptible to the physical concern of discomfort? Perhaps he felt some of Abigail's pain; if it would lessen hers, he would gladly accept it as his own. "I'll find him for you."

He *could* inspect all of the Rolling G faster than they could. Abbie knew it. But it went against everything she'd ever been taught, ever believed. Davis was *her* father, and she should be the one searching for him.

"Please, Abbie." God, he wanted to be able to do this for her. To let her stay here safe and sound and rested while he hunted for a lost, confused old man. "I'll bring him home to you. I promise."

She bit her lower lip to stop its trembling. "How will you get him home?"

"I'll manage."

Battered by exhaustion, sapped by months of worry and years of responsibility, Abigail had reached the limits of her strength. Joshua could see it in her dark eyes, the way she tried to marshal some reserves that had been depleted long ago.

"I promise," he said again, wishing he could give her more, unable to offer anything else.

She closed her eyes and nodded. "Find my father, Joshua."

25

He'd ordered her to rest. She couldn't do it.

Joshua had headed out immediately, following the trail of blood. She'd watched him until he'd disappeared into the empty stretches of grasslands, and stared a little longer than that. And then she'd shuddered and gone to work.

Just on the remote chance that they'd overlooked something and her father hadn't gone far, she hunted every square inch of the old shed and the lean-to, the corral and the well, and—twice more—every dusty corner of the house.

She broke the remaining, dangerous shards of glass from the bedroom window and collected all the crushed bits she could gather from the ground outside, trying to ignore the sparse line of dark droplets and the disturbing images they conjured. Though she hadn't prevented her father's injuries, at least she could make certain no one else got hurt on the broken glass.

Marcus roused briefly, and she hurried him into his

own bed before he'd even managed to crack his eyelids open more than a bare sliver. She'd wake him up and tell him when she had something to tell.

Smoke still clogged her nostrils. Her skin itched from sweat and dirt. For lack of anything more useful to do, unwilling to simply sit and give in to the despair, she fetched endless buckets of water from the well, scrubbing and scouring her body and hair until her skin felt raw and tender.

The first few buckets quickly turned black; the next three, deep gray. When it finally got to the point where dunking her head in the water produced only a fine film of ash on the water, she called it good enough and moved on.

She left her clothes soaking in a basin of soap and cloudy water. It seemed very unlikely that her blouse would ever again achieve a color that approximated white.

She wasn't used to having nothing to *do*. Especially when there was something that needed doing—finding her father—but there was someone else so much better suited to do that task than she. She didn't need to cook; everyone else was fast asleep and wouldn't appreciate being awakened for a belated breakfast. She couldn't ride out to check on the herd; what if Joshua brought Davis back and she wasn't here?

Nervous and unsettled, plagued by thoughts of what might have happened to her father, she aimlessly wandered the house, fidgeting with the stacks of plates in the kitchen and refolding the thick red-and-black blanket that lay draped over the back of the rocking chair.

The room seemed to shrink, narrow. It closed in, squeezing the hot air against her until she thought her lungs would burst with it. The walls swam in front of her eyes, blurring and buckling as if the heat was softening their rigid support.

Gasping, she ran out to the porch. The door banged shut behind her. She leaned her forehead against the rough, weathered wood of a post, taking great gulps of air until her breathing finally calmed and it no longer seemed like her heart's violent pounding would bruise her chest from the inside out. She lifted her head.

The air held the tang of smoke beneath the stronger scents of animals and grass and earth. The sky pulsed blue, and waves of heat shimmered where it met the brown-brushed land.

She could not imagine the Rolling G without her father's presence. This land had formed him. Honed his body, weathered his skin, shaped his thoughts.

The tight knot in her stomach abruptly eased.

Davis had loved the land, had nurtured it even as it had nurtured him. Surely it would not take him from her.

She slipped into her father's chair, the one he'd spent hundreds of hours in as he stared out at his piece of the world, just as she did now.

It would be all right, she thought.

Joshua would find him. He'd promised her.

"Abigail." A hand shook her shoulder. "Abigail, wake up."

"Hmm?" She sleepily blinked her eyes open to find Joshua's bright ones looking directly into hers. She'd imagined this so many times, awakening to Joshua calling her name and his face bare inches from hers, that for a moment she remembered nothing else. Her mouth curved up. "Good morning."

"Your father, Abigail—"

"Oh my God!" She snapped up, fear and guilt lancing

through her like a hot needle. She must have fallen asleep waiting for them. How could she possibly have forgotten that her father was missing? "Did you find him? Is he—"

The word would not come.

"Shh." He cupped her cheek in his palm, his thumb resting near the corner of her mouth. He almost hadn't awakened her. She'd looked so peaceful in sleep, her hair fluttering around her face and her lips parted on her deep, steady breaths. But he knew she'd never forgive him if he didn't alert her the moment he'd returned. "I found him. He's all right."

"Thank God." Her breath expelled in a rush and she sagged.

Joshua moved aside, so she could see her father sitting in the nearest chair, his bleary, blank eyes staring at nothing. His nightshirt was torn and splotched with dark stains. Dust coated his bare feet, thick, dark crescents of dirt beneath his broken toenails.

But he was home, and he was alive.

Abigail flew to his side.

"Papa! Papa, are you okay? It's Abigail. Do you hurt somewhere? Can you tell me?"

His eyes, expressionless and glazed with weariness, rolled her way only briefly. His head drooped, his chin bumping his chest.

"Joshua, is he all right?"

"I think so." Joshua knelt beside her, carefully inspecting Davis' thin, desiccated figure. "He's had a long night, and he's plumb tuckered out, I'm sure. And I think he's probably in hard need of something to drink. But he didn't seem to be seriously hurt."

"Oh, please, I hope so." Her hands wouldn't stay still. They fluttered over him, checking his forehead, probing his limbs for broken bones, pressing her fingers to his neck to feel the thready but real beat of his pulse. "The blood?"

"He just cut his hand up some. I couldn't find any other injuries."

Cautiously, Abigail turned his hand over, gently forcing open the tight-curled fingers. The cut bit across his entire palm, a ragged dark-red streak that was clotted with dirt and grit. "I've got to get this cleaned up, okay, Papa? You wait right here and—"

She stopped, still holding his open hand in hers, unwilling to leave him even for a moment.

Joshua touched her briefly on the shoulder. "If you tell me where everything is, I'll get it for you."

Abigail looked up at Joshua's familiar, handsome face, his features tender with concern. Not to have to face this all alone this time . . . The difference was extraordinary, heart-wrenching. She had no idea how she would ever thank him for being here when she'd needed him.

While he followed her quick instructions, she examined her father more closely, seeking any injuries that weren't immediately apparent. His physical condition seemed not much worse than it was before.

As to his mind . . . She had no way to gauge his condition. He ignored her questions, let her poke and prod where she would without any protest. But his unresponsiveness was no different than it had been a dozen other times.

While Joshua fed Davis sips of water from a thick mug, Abigail attended to his hand, carefully dabbing the cut with soapy water. The gash slashed fairly deep, but hadn't sliced anything crucial as far as she could tell. There'd be a scar, of course, but what did that matter?

"Where did you find him?" she asked.

"Southeast corner of the ranch." Joshua refilled the

mug from the pitcher he'd found on a high shelf in the kitchen and held it to Davis' lips. "You know where all those strange rocks are?"

"Of course. There's nothing else like it anywhere else around here."

"That's where he was, curled up right next to the biggest one, just rocking back and forth."

How many hours had he been there? She could hardly bear to think of it, to picture her father alone and terrified, huddling next to a boulder for comfort and protection.

She consciously set aside the image of her father curled up next to the rock, alone. She would not think of it. It was over now, and it was impossible for her to go back and change it. And it was unlikely Davis remembered any of his adventure, anyway. She wasn't even certain he had the capacity to feel frightened any longer.

"How did you get him back here?"

"I carried him."

Abigail dipped her forefinger in kerosene and spread it over the cut, the potent, oily fumes strong in her nostrils, and slanted a glance at Joshua. "Really? How did you manage that? I thought the only person you could touch was me."

"Finally figuring out how to do this 'spirit' job." But it was too little, Joshua added to himself. And far too late.

Too late, because he hadn't learned in time to head off all of Abigail's troubles in the first place. And too little, because the skills he'd gained hadn't been enough to solve her problems, either.

Frustration clawed hard at him. What he could do, what he *did* do, was such a pitiful offering against what he wanted to be able to give her.

"Joshua," she began hesitantly, "could you . . . fix his hand, the way you healed my blisters?"

"No." He shook his head, wondering what kind of beings they were that they did not allow him to perform even this small service for her. He knew it was not supposed to be for him to wonder why, but it angered him just the same.

He felt disconnected, lost, as if there were some great truth they intended him to discover from this whole thing and it kept eluding him, twisting so far beyond his grasp that he was not even able to attempt to capture it.

"I tried it, right after I found him. I thought maybe I could give him some . . . strength, some energy. Nothing. I think that I just don't have the same kind of . . . connection with him that I have with you."

"Don't worry about it," she said lightly, trying to brush it off as if it were insignificant, wishing she had never made the suggestion. The regret in Joshua's eyes was almost more than she could bear. "His hand will heal just fine on its own."

She wrapped Davis' palm in a long strip of torn, threadbare sheets, knotting the bandage securely. "There. That should do it."

Joshua helped her guide Davis to his room. Marcus snored heartily from his own bed, unaffected by the bright light that streamed through the broken window.

Davis climbed into bed without a murmur. Abigail bent over him, her just-washed curls falling softly over her shoulder as she bent to drop a kiss on his forehead—a kiss her father ignored. The strong sunlight washed her with color, bringing out all the fiery spice in her hair, drawing out the gold that hid deep in her brown eyes.

Why were they given only one chance at life? If only he could do it again, have just one more opportunity, he would surely do it right this time. He would make absolutely certain that Abigail Grier got every single thing she deserved, every wonder and joy and gift that life had to offer.

God, if only he had just one more chance.

She watched her father sleep, her sharp features softening with relief and love.

"Come on," he said, slipping an arm around her shoulders, wishing with all he was that he could give her more than this small support, knowing this was all he had to offer her now. "I promised you this hours ago. It's your turn. Let's go tuck you into bed."

26

He guided her into her bedroom, where a slice
of light burst through the window, bringing with it the
faint blurring of smoke, and, he figured, probably the
harsh scent of it, though he couldn't tell. Joshua wondered how long it would take for the smell to fade, and if
they would catch the person who'd set the fire first.

The bastard.

No, he decided, that wasn't nearly strong enough a
term. Bastards were born to that label, had no choice in
it and no part of earning it. The person who was bent on
stealing Abigail's water and destroying her ranch had
done so with deliberate determination.

Her head sagged against his shoulder, as if even the
effort of holding it up was too much for her. Her lean
body brushed along his side, nudging and retreating and
back again as they walked. In different times, under different circumstances, it was something he certainly
would have relished and quite probably tried to take full
advantage of.

Beneath his arm her shoulders shuddered, quaking as wildly as buffalo grass faced with a strong gale wind. Harsh noises escaped her, brief explosions of emotion translated to sound that were cut off abruptly as Abigail tried to gulp them back in.

"Abbie? Abbie, what's the matter?"

She shook her head and her hair, smelling of soap and lilacs and a hint of smoke, brushed against his cheek.

"Are you . . . crying?"

"No!"

With his free hand, he cradled her chin, urging her to look at him. She ducked her head away, but he was as insistent as he was gentle, and finally she scraped back the curtain of hair that hung down, screening his vision, and lifted her face.

"All right, fine. I'm crying. See?" She glared at him. "Are you satisfied?"

"But . . ." He was at a complete loss. Anger and tears warred in her eyes, and he hadn't the faintest idea which to address first.

"Ah, I hate this. This always happens. I'm just fine while something's happening, and then when it's all over and I know everything's going to be okay and I should be happy I can't hold it in anymore and I fall apart! And my nose turns red and my eyes swell and my head aches and, damn it, I *hate* it!"

"I really think your father is not all that much worse for the wear," Joshua ventured.

"I know that!" she snapped. "That's what makes it all so stupid!"

"It's . . . stupid to cry?" he asked, feeling his way slowly. Women were complicated creatures. And Abigail was a complicated woman.

"Have you ever seen me cry before?" Her question sounded more like an accusation.

"Ah . . . no."

"See? That's because I don't! Because it's a waste of time and energy and—" A sob shook her body like a strong hiccup. "Oh God, why can't I stop?"

"Abbie." His fingertips brushed her cheeks, slick and glistening with spilling tears. "If you *feel* like crying, maybe you should just go ahead and—"

"I don't feel like crying!" Tears brimmed her eyes, stuck her short brown lashes together in spiky clumps.

Comfort had never been an element in his life. He knew nothing of it, receiving or giving, and was completely ignorant of its soothing words and supportive gestures.

His tongue felt like it was stuck to the roof of his mouth. Nothing he said so far had seemed to help, but he refused to do nothing, stand here like a helpless idiot, and simply watch her weep.

If he did not have the words to comfort her, perhaps he had the touch.

He bent down, smoothing his lips over her wet cheeks, her nose, the tang of her tears salting his tongue.

"Abbie," he whispered, "My Abbie."

She stood unmoving, silent, letting him touch his mouth where he would. Warmth swept the length of her jaw, following the path of his mouth; her heart fluttered as he kissed each eyelid. The ache in her chest eased. Her breathing evened, deepened, as she surrendered to Joshua, to his hands and his mouth. To having all the little twinges of worry and fear replaced in her, one by one, by the feelings he drew forth.

She angled her head, to find his mouth with her own. He stilled, not responding, but not yet pulling away. She could almost hear his doubts, sense his thoughts: *Can we? Should we? Dare we?*

Please, she thought, *don't leave me this time*. She needed this, needed him. It seemed impossible that she would find it in her to survive another day without it. She craved the strength of it, the pure, physical joy and the raw power.

And, as if he'd read her thoughts as she'd understood his, Joshua gave himself over to her and the wonder of what they made together. With a groan, he looped an arm around her waist and dragged her body tight against him. He tilted his head, the pressure of his mouth going deep and strong, and his tongue swept in to seek hers. He cupped her neck in one hand, his thumb stroking delicate shivers beneath her ear.

Joshua had always wanted Abigail's passion, had craved it, gloried in it, enjoyed it as thoroughly as his own. He'd nurtured it and encouraged it and done all he could to draw it forth.

But he'd never focused on it to the exclusion of his own. Never ignored the demands of his own body in trying only to read hers.

This is for her.

The command beat in his brain even as the taste of her sweetened his mouth, as the softness of her skin heated his palms.

Only for Abigail.

Abbie, he thought, as he pressed his mouth to where her pulse trembled in her neck and was rewarded by her soft sigh. *Abbie*. He circled her ribs with his hands and she arched into his touch. *Abbie*. He lifted her from her feet and laid her carefully on her bed.

But he'd lied to himself, he found. How could he say he did this only for her, when the pleasure beat within him so strongly? How could he not respond, when he bared her breasts for his hand and they were small and pretty and waiting for him?

"Abbie," he whispered again, and he didn't know if the words came from his throat or his heart.

Abigail threw her arms wide, her shoulders making shallow impressions in the old mattress, and let Joshua do as he would. The warm room was hazy with sunlight, the sounds of her ragged breathing filling the air.

How had she ever lived without this? Without the feel of Joshua's warm mouth, tugging gently at her nipple? Without the feel of his hands on her skin, the deepening weight of his body as he settled on her?

She needed this so much, a time when the world narrowed down to nothing but man and woman, to the slow threads of sensation that spun webs of rich emotion, binding them together. Worry and anger and fear vanished beneath the steady demands of her body.

After stripping off the clothing soiled by the fire, she'd thrown on only the barest minimum of covering, a shift and a ragged, button-front dress. It was the work of only a moment for Joshua to free her from them, leaving her naked to the light of the sun and heat in his eyes.

"Wait," she said when he reached for her again. "You too."

After so many times in darkened sheds and on blankets spread beneath dark skies, when impatience, haste, and caution kept most of their clothes on, she wanted one time like this. In her own bed, with the light strong and unflinching and not a single thread to form a barrier between his skin and hers.

He stood beside the bed, his dark figure limned by sunlight, fingers working rapidly down his buttons. He ripped off the shirt and discarded it as if it were worthless before bending to attack the fastenings of his pants.

Abigail took one look at his naked body and wondered if she still breathed. She'd imagined him, imagined *this*, so many times. How could she still have been so completely unprepared for the power of it? Lean muscle roped his arms and shoulders, the drifts of hair on his chest shades darker than that on his head. Faint lines of demarcation separated the sun-marked skin of his face and hands from the paler areas of his torso.

"I want to touch you."

He stood tall, hands on narrow hips, and stared at her, his expression hardening. Abigail cursed the words that had slipped out, for reminding them both of what they couldn't have, of the impossibility of it all.

And then he joined her on the bed, drew up her hands, and wrapped them tight around the warm iron bars of her headboard.

"Don't let go," he said, his jaw tight and his voice urgent. "Promise me."

"I promise."

He laid himself down on her, fitting his arms, his legs, his body to hers, covering her completely, pressing her down into the mattress with his welcome weight, meeting every exposed inch of her skin with his.

"Can you feel me now?"

"Yes," she gasped.

The kiss he gave her so full of sweetness, it seemed impossible that it could also hold such pure sensuality. She sighed into his mouth.

Slow hands, warm mouth, overwhelming heat. His hands stroked and molded the swells of her hips. His tongue teased the tips of her breasts, laid down damp trails across her ribcage.

He reared up, allowing a wash of hot air to flow over her skin. She preferred his weight, and stretched out a hand to him to urge him back.

"You promised," he said, his features sharp and intent.

She wrapped her hand back around the metal rod, but it was too smooth, too clearly formed of iron instead of flesh, to satisfy her.

For Abbie. It beat over and over in his head like a prayer. He knelt between her legs and spread his palm over her stomach, his thumb and little finger stretched wide enough to span from hipbone to hipbone. His hand contrasted sharply, dark and male against the pale, speckled skin of her belly.

A bar of unrelenting sunlight fell across the bed, fading the jumbled colors of the quilt. But it only brightened her, turned her hair to fire and made her skin glow.

He bent, slipping his hands beneath her hips, lifting, and placed his mouth flat against her. He tasted salt and sweet, sex and *her*, tasted of the deep pleasure that grew from giving pleasure to another.

She arched against his mouth, the shifting of her hips a counterpoint to the stroking rhythm of his tongue. A keening cry broke from her lips.

Abigail fisted her hands harder around the headboard, fighting the need to reach down and run her fingers in his hair, to hold him, to share with him something of what he was giving her. Wanting to urge him on, to guide his body deep and fill the empty spaces within her.

"Joshua!"

A man would give his soul to hear his woman cry his name like that. Her legs shifted restlessly; her hips rose, seeking, needing more.

And then he slid his tongue inside her and she broke apart, shuddering against his mouth. Joshua was certain that it had been worth his death, to share this with her just one more time.

When she calmed, he pulled away, lightly pressing the heel of his hand against her slick flesh to soothe and encourage the last, sweet aftershocks of pleasure.

He moved up to lie beside her, smiling into her eyes that were soft and smudged with passion. Bright color bloomed under her freckles. Curls clung to her damp cheeks and neck.

She blinked, her smile spreading slow and satisfied, a hint of mischief sparking into her eyes.

"Can I let go now?"

His bark of laughter was a little strained. He may have convinced his mind that this was all just for Abigail, but certain parts of his body were protesting most emphatically.

She released the headboard, and he pulled her close, tucking her up against his chest, letting the soft feathering of her breath against his skin cool his body even as it warmed his heart.

"Joshua?"

"Hmm?" Her back was long, narrow, firm with muscle, and he allowed himself the luxury of sweeping his hand over it, his fingers whisking over the small bumps of her vertebrae.

She tilted her head back so she could look at him.

"Is that it?"

"Whaddya mean, is that it?" he said, pretending indignation. "I thought you—"

"I did," she said quickly, crimson flushing her skin from chin to forehead. "But aren't you going to . . ."

He sighed and dropped a chaste kiss on the tip of her nose. A chaste kiss was about all he figured he could risk at the moment. "No."

"But what about you?" Her lip tucked beneath her teeth, her eyes searching his, Abigail reached down between their bodies and stroked her hand over the thick, hard curve of his erection.

"Abbie." He shuddered at the sensation; her palms weren't smooth and soft; they carried the mark of her work, and their slight abrasion made her touch all the more erotic. Covering her hand with his, a low, hissing sound escaped him as he, just for a moment, surrendered to the strong pleasure of pressing her palm harder around him. And then he linked their fingers and tugged her hand up to rest between their chests.

"What we just did . . . I was sent here to help you. Those were my instructions. If I really stretch it, I could say that what we just did was helping you."

He gave in to the urge to brush a quick kiss across her lips, still damp and parted from loving. "But what you're talking about— Abbie, no matter how much I want to, no matter how hard I try, there's no way I can make it out to be anythin' but helpin' *me*."

"But—just stopping like that, isn't it hard?"

He simply lifted an eyebrow at that. "You should know that better then anyone."

"Oh you!" She stifled an exasperated bubble of laughter. "I meant *difficult*, and you know it."

"Yeah, I do." With their clasped hands between them, temptation was too near, easily within his reach. He forced his gaze to her face—as if that were a safer place to look. But this was Abbie, and there nowhere safe to look, no place that didn't make him want her. "But it would be a whole lot harder to make a mistake now, and have them take me away before this is finished. I have to make certain you're safe, Abbie. I *have* to."

"All right." She thrust out her lower lip, pouting, and he leaned down to run his tongue over it. It was madness, teasing himself like this, but the pleasure was too sweet for him to deny himself this, as well. He was already forfeiting more than he would ever have believed.

"But, if you look at this the right way," she went on, "we could say that you'd be doing that for me, too."

"Really?" he asked, amused by the light of battle in her eyes. "How do you figure that?"

"After you . . . left . . ." she paused, her expression softening, "that was the one thing I always regretted, that we'd never . . . That we hadn't . . . "

"Had sex?" he supplied helpfully.

She colored, delightful pink blooming under her freckles. "I was going to say had *relations*."

"Relations, huh? I could have sworn we had relations." He slid one hand up to frame her collarbone, and he could feel the subtle, frantic flutter of her pulse under his fingertips. "Let me see if I can remember back then . . . were you naked?"

The color intensified, deepening to a shade nearly as vivid as her hair. "Pretty much."

"Was I naked?"

Did he have to keep saying that word, *naked*? Abigail thought frantically. She remembered it too well, Joshua in the dim, mote-filled light of the old shed, his unbuttoned shirt barely hanging on at the shoulders, his pants unfastened and shoved down around his hips—where *she*, in a fit of hussy-dom, had pushed them—with his . . . his . . . Oh Lord. She gulped.

"All the important parts," she said quickly.

"They were at that."

He was having far too much fun with this.

"Now then." His forehead puckered, as if in intense concentration. "Did you have pleasure?"

"I . . . ah . . ." The words stuck in her throat. "Yes," she croaked.

"Thought so," he said smugly. "The screamin's usually a dead giveaway."

"I didn't scream!" she protested, but he was blithely continuing.

"And *I* sure as heck had pleasure." He grinned at her. "That woulda been kinda hard to hide. It can get a little messy."

Her face was on fire. She didn't know why she'd ever brought up the subject. If he would just release her hands, she'd at least be able to cover her face and then he'd have to stop looking at her with that irritatingly *male* expression on his.

"Considerin' all that, then, Abbie, I'd say we pretty much *had relations*."

If he laughed at her, she was going to hit him. She didn't care if he was made up of air and dreams; she'd find a way, she swore.

"Joshua West, how much of a fool do you think I am? I know good and well that wasn't everything!"

In a flash, his eyes went serious and intent. His thumb stroked up her throat, rubbed softly under her chin.

"Yes we did, Abbie. We had everything."

Her heart skittered. "I just— I didn't want you to have more with *them* than you had with me."

"Them?"

"You know. Other women." He opened his mouth to speak, but she charged in fiercely. "And don't you tell me there weren't any other women, Joshua, because I know you better than that!"

"Okay, I won't." He sighed, trailed his thumb over the deep curve of her lower lip. How could he explain something like this to her? It had been so long ago, and meant so little, and she meant so damn much.

"You know what it's like, Abbie. All the hands, you get a little coin and a free night and you run on in to town together. Go to the barber, then to the saloon."

"And then upstairs," she said softly.

"Sometimes." He touched her face, the tip of her nose, the curve of her eyebrow, like he couldn't get enough of her, like he had to test each feature and see if it were real. "I started going when I was . . . oh, fourteen or so. *Everybody* went. Woulda seemed weird if I didn't."

"I suppose it would have."

"I didn't know any different. But there wasn't . . . there just wasn't much *there*. It didn't take me all that long to figure out that what I could do with those women weren't all that different than I could do by myself, just a helluva lot more expensive."

"So then . . . you stopped going?"

"Well . . . no," he said honestly. "It was just what we all did."

Her eyes lowered. "I understand," she said to his chest.

"No, I don't think you do." He tipped her chin up, hoping she would see the truth in his eyes. "'Cause then I met you, you see. And it didn't take me two shakes to figure out what I'd been missing all along."

He drew her up close, holding her against his dead heart. Except his heart didn't feel dead. It ached, hurt with knowing Abbie, wanting Abbie, loving Abbie. "What you and I did together . . . incomplete as it might seem to you, Abbie, it was still a thousand times more than I ever had with any of them."

It was a stupid question to ask, Abigail knew. She found herself asking it anyway, and caught a painful breath waiting for his answer.

"And after . . . after you left me?"

He chuckled, the sweet sound a deep vibration beneath her ear. "Well, I can't say I didn't try, a couple of times. I was kinda annoyed at you, after all. But I never even got my britches off. The woman would talk, or I'd look at her, and my body would go "that ain't Abbie" and that was the end of that. Got my butt out of there so fast they prob'ly thought I was a ghost then, too."

The air expelled from her lungs in a relieved whoosh.

"Oh thank goodness. I really didn't want to have to kill you again."

"Jealous, Abbie?"

"Absolutely," she said firmly. "Joshua, if it didn't really matter to you—my . . . virginity, I mean—why'd you try so hard to get me to give it to you?"

He sighed, dropping his head back against the pillow, cursing himself for the man he'd been. "I've been a cowhand too long, I guess."

"What?" Her head popped up, her eyes alight with interest.

"I'm used to brandin' things." He slid his fingers through her hair, catching the curls, combing out a tangle. "For some reason I got it into my head that, if you gave your virginity to me, then you'd be *mine*, once and for all."

His.

She wondered what he'd ever had to call his own. A gun, a saddle, a meager war sack holding only a razor and an extra pair of socks? Natural for him to want something of his own, she supposed.

And, damn it, she wished she'd been the one to give it to him.

"God, what a stupid ass I was," he said, voice harsh with self-recrimination.

"Yeah," she agreed lightly. "But you sure were a *sexy* stupid ass."

That surprised him; he gawked at her for a moment, as if he wasn't sure he'd heard her right, and then a wry smile quirked his mouth. "How did I ever manage without you?"

"God knows." She dropped her head back to his shoulder. His fingers played up her arm, polished her shoulders. She wondered if he was even aware he was doing it, it seemed so automatic and natural.

"Abbie?"

"Hmm?" She yawned and snuggled deeper into his embrace.

"I do love you."

"I know," she said, and drifted off to sleep, safe in Joshua's arms.

27

Abigail slept straight through until four o'clock. She hadn't dreamed, and doubted she'd even moved, making it by far the best sleep she'd had in months. Perhaps relief, after a horrendous night, was a good sedative.

Or, she thought with a secret smile, all those wicked things Joshua had done to her were the key to a particularly good night's—day's—sleep. She'd be more than willing to test out that theory.

Luckily, even so late in the afternoon, she woke up, refreshed and bursting with renewed energy, sooner than anyone else on the ranch except Pecos. While he rode out to check on all the animals, she started supper. The rich, long-simmering stew of chopped sweetbreads, and organ meats, and tinned vegetables was the hands' favorite dinner, though she'd often wondered if they loved the dish for its taste or the profane name she'd never been able to bring herself to say. She figured they'd earned it last night.

She set the table with a new checked oilcloth, and centered it with a pretty blue pitcher. Too bad there weren't any wildflowers around to stick in it, but the drought had killed them off long ago. Still, she was pleased with the effect, and with the rich, dark, meaty aroma that wafted from the stew pot. There were plenty of leftover biscuits, and she sprinkled them with water and slipped them into the oven to heat. Not as good as fresh, but they'd do.

Apparently, from the grins on everyone's faces when they filed in to supper, they'd more than do. Marcus took a deep sniff as he came in the door, and his stomach growled so loudly she could hear it clear across the room.

"All right," Pecos said gruffly, "who let that wildcat in here? I can hear 'im growling."

"It wasn't me!" Marcus put in quickly. "It was Lippy, sure shootin'."

Abigail laughed, amazed they all seemed so lighthearted after having to fight the fire all night. Or perhaps that was why; they battled, and they'd won, and it made everything seem just a little sweeter.

"Since you're all not hungry at all—"

A hubbub of protests drowned out the rest of her sentence. She laughed. "All right, all right. Why don't you go ahead and start eating? I'm going to get Papa up to the table."

After he'd awakened, her father hadn't left his rocking chair the entire rest of the day. Perhaps his experiences of the night before made him all the more unwilling to leave something that represented familiarity and safety.

He'd picked at the bandage on his hand, removing it three times before Abigail gave up and left it off. She'd smeared the wound with thick, greasy salve and hoped that would be enough.

She bent next to his chair. "Papa? Are you ready to come to supper?"

He pushed the chair harder, so that, at the end of each arc of motion, it teetered on the tips of its rails before rocking back in the other direction.

"I'm just going to check your hand first, okay?" She peeled his hand off the chair arm and turned it over.

Good. So far, there were no angry red streaks marking an infection. "It looks pretty good, Papa. Are you ready to eat?"

To her surprise, he looked directly at her for a moment and nodded his agreement. Only rarely did he seem to acknowledge her questions. Thank the Lord, she thought. He'd evidently sustained no real injuries, physical or mental, in his trek across the plains last night after all.

He allowed her to guide him to his chair. She filled two plates and placed one in front of Davis as she slid into her own chair.

"I have to tell you, Miss Abigail, you make the best son-of-a-bi—"

Pecos' emphatic throat-clearing stopped Lippy in mid-sentence. His ears reddened and he shot her an apologetic glance before continuing. "Ah, I mean, you make the best son-of-a-*gun* stew I ever tasted."

"Why, thank you Lippy," she said, hiding a smile. "Even if I do say so myself, this really is a very good batch of son-of-a-bitch stew, isn't it?"

Spoons clattered against the table. She took one look at the shocked expressions on their faces and burst out laughing. Marcus was the first to recover, and he joined in.

Enthusiastic applause came from beside the door. *Joshua.*

He'd been gone when she awoke, so this was the first

time she'd seen him since she'd fallen asleep in his arms. He leaned against the wall, his arms folded, one booted foot crossed over the other at the ankle.

"Good evening," she mouthed.

His response was a slow smile, one filled with memories and promise and simmering heat. She quickly lowered her gaze to her plate. The chunks of meat and potatoes were a much safer place to look. If she kept looking at Joshua, she was likely to jump from the table, drag him off to her bedroom, and force him to deliver on all those things his smile pledged, and then wouldn't the hands *really* be shocked.

She speared a piece of onion, sneaking peeks at Joshua out of the corner of her eye. She wondered if this was hard for him, to stand there and watch them eat and not be able to do so himself. Could he smell the food? Could he remember the rich tastes?

"So why you hidin' over there in the shadows?"

Abigail looked up at her father's question, to find Davis' gaze fixed on Joshua.

"What?" She wrinkled her brow at Joshua, but he merely shrugged, surprise written clear on his handsome features.

"Come eat," Davis ordered.

Around the table, the hands stopped shoveling food into their mouths and shot uneasy glances at each other. As accustomed as they all were to Davis' unpredictable behavior, they were still far from comfortable with it.

"Papa?" she asked tentatively. "What is it?"

"It's that young man of yours. Can't you tell?" Davis scowled. "Ain't seen him around for a while."

Lippy shifted in his chair. "Do you think he's talking about Joshua West?" he whispered, as if it would make it better not to say the words out loud.

"I don't know." She'd never considered that anyone

else might be able to see Joshua. Why her father? And why now?

"I'm done." Abruptly, Davis shoved away his half-eaten supper. "Tired."

"I'll take him," Marcus offered, worry pulling down his mouth. Abigail couldn't tell if her brother was more concerned about her father's hallucination or whether Abigail was going to fall apart at the mention of Joshua's name. From the anxious looks he kept shooting her way, she suspected it might be the latter.

Sledge tipped back his chair and frowned. "What do you suppose that was about?"

"I don't know." No longer hungry, Abigail poked at a bit of liver, chasing it around her plate.

"Well, it ain't as if he hasn't talked to dead people before," Lippy put in.

"Yeah." Sledge absently tapped his spoon on the edge of the table. "But why the hell would he start talkin' to West all of a sudden, after all this time? He never liked him all that much, anyways."

Davis's outburst put a damper on the rest of the meal. Especially after a downcast Marcus returned and reported that Davis, apparently exhausted, had already fallen back to sleep. They quickly gobbled their food without any further conversation. But still not fast enough to suit Abigail, who wanted to shove them out the door so she could talk to Joshua alone.

Finally, she herded them all out, assigning Marcus early watch to get him out of the way, and slammed the door behind the last man so fast she nearly caught him on the rump with it as he left.

She whirled on Joshua. "What was that all about?"

"I wish I knew."

"But he—he *saw* you Joshua, I'm certain of it."

"Yeah, I think so, too." He took her hand and led her over to the sitting area. "Here, sit down. This might take a while." He sat down beside her, hitching his foot up on his knee and sprawling his arms along the back of the sofa.

Abigail had more trouble settling in. She went through three different positions, trying to find a comfortable one, before tucking one foot beneath her, and drummed her fingers on her thigh.

"But *how*, Joshua? And why?"

"I'm not sure." Possibilities sifted through his brain. Once again he mentally cursed them for sending him here without preparing him fully. Shouldn't there be some sort of School for New Spirits or something? A guidebook? An apprenticeship? Something.

"I think," he said slowly, testing the idea as he spoke, "maybe Davis is caught between here and there, just as much as I am. Maybe that's why he can see me, when nobody else can."

Abigail nodded. That made sense. "And, he's probably not bound by the same preconceptions everybody else is, either."

"Yeah."

The idea hit her with all the force of a sudden storm. "Joshua? If you're between both worlds, and you're not all the way there yet, maybe you can—"

"No," he said, cutting her off. "Don't even start thinking it."

Disappointment and hurt welled in her eyes, setting his heart to aching. But he refused to give her false hope, to let her start to believe there might be a way for him to find his way back to her.

For he simply was not the kind of guy that heaven was going to waste its miracles on. Who was he, anyway, to even think of such a thing? He was just an old cowboy, like a thousand others, an ordinary man who'd loved a woman and lived his life and made a whole lot of mistakes.

Her frown softened, and a gleam sparked in her eyes.

"Joshua," she said. "I've been thinking about last night—well, this morning, I guess it was—and—"

Joshua brightened immediately. "Yeah, me too." He waggled his eyebrows at her.

"Not that—"

"Not that? I must have done something really wrong if you're not thinking about that. You better let me try again. I promise I'll do better this time."

"Joshua!" Caught between exasperation and laughter, she finally gave in and grinned at him, unable to resist him in this roguish mood.

"Now then." He reached for her, obviously intending to make good on his promises.

"It's not that!"

"It's not? Darn." His gaze, full of speculation and anticipation, raked her from head to toe. "Well, still, that doesn't mean we can't—"

"Would you stop!"

"Sorry." He sighed and sat back on the sofa. "Go ahead."

"Good." She smoothed her skirts over her knee. "I touched you last night."

"You sure did, darlin'." He slid closer. "As I recall, I touched you, too."

"That's not what I meant! Could you just be serious for a little while?"

"Yes." His playful mood vanished. He touched her face, his fingers drifting down her cheek before coming to rest at the side of her neck. "Go ahead."

"Ah—" She tried to gather her scattered thoughts. How was she supposed to make any sense when he was touching her like that? "Last night, after you . . ." Her cheeks heated. "After . . . *that*, I touched you."

His thumb stroked the length of her neck, up beneath her chin, and back again. "Go on."

"Since you came back, I've never been able to touch *you*. Before last night, whenever I tried, there was nothing there. I've always been able to feel it when you touched me, but I couldn't do the same."

His hand stilled. "Try it."

"Okay." Oh Lord. She wanted this to work so badly. Needed it to, needed to be able to feel him so much that her hands shook. In slow, halting inches, she reached for his chest.

"Please," she whispered.

But her hand just kept going on, moving right through the air and the place where his chest should be as if Joshua had no more substance than a daydream.

"No!" She swallowed hard against the sob that welled in her chest. She'd allowed herself to hope. She should have known better.

Joshua's eyes were unwavering, the gray-blue intense and unreadable. "I'll just have to be the one to touch you, then."

With deliberate care, he laid his palm over her breast, his hand strikingly dark against the bleached white of her shirt.

"Joshua," she said on a breath. "Do you see it?"

For, even as she watched, his hand changed. Solidified. The bit of translucence that always marked him transformed and coalesced into something that looked very, very real.

"I see it." The rest of him was unchanged, still the same faintly insubstantial form that he'd owned since he'd returned to her. But his hand—his hand now the hand of a man.

"What does it mean?"

He didn't know, any more than he knew what to expect next. Every time he thought he began to understand, began to learn his tasks and new abilities, something altered. And not just in his body—in *him*.

"It means that I will simply have to keep touching you," he murmured, just before he lowered his mouth to hers.

28

It should have been a cause for celebration.
The ranchers in the vicinity of Barrens, Texas were separated by both vast distances and the incessant demands of their work. These conditions made the opportunities for gathering in one place rare, which in turn usually made any chance to do so a festive occasion.

The grounds for the Fourth of July contests were set up right outside the entrance to Fort Barrens. Officers' wives ran refreshment booths along the fort walls. Bright streamers on long poles snapped above the hastily rigged canvas roofs that shaded the booths. Young soldiers in crisp uniforms, their bright buttons shining in the sun, flirted with ranchers' daughters, who were thrilled with the opportunity to have a slightly wider selection of eligible men.

There were those who'd suffered losses in the War who still harbored carefully nurtured resentment against the Union soldiers. These individuals had no intention of celebrating the birth of a country that they were none too fond of.

But this part of Texas had always seemed a country of its own to most of them. Most were too busy struggling to eke out a living to spend much time bemoaning what people thousands of miles away were arguing over. The fort's commander had instigated this celebration three years ago in an attempt to improve relations between his men and the area settlers, and for the most part everyone had always been able to put their differences aside for this one afternoon. After all, a party was a party.

This year was different.

Temporary benches, hurriedly hammered together, ringed the cleared, roped-off space where the competitions took place. As Abigail perched on one end of a bench and watched the lead cowhand from the Bar B try to cling to the back of a twisting horse, the difference in atmosphere from the year before was palpable. Thick tension simmered in the air, as relentless and oppressive as the vicious heat.

Unwilling to leave either her father or the ranch for so long, she hadn't planned on coming this year. She also hadn't much relished the idea of spending a whole day avoiding B.J., and watching Horace avoid her.

But Lippy had puffed up his courage and announced his intention of trying his hand at bustin' broncs. He had been obviously disappointed that she might not be there to cheer him on while he tried to "uphold the honor of the Rolling G." So Sledge had offered to stay with Davis, and had practically pushed her out the door to send her on her way.

Abigail looked around the sparse crowds, nodding greetings at acquaintances. B.J. held court across the way, surrounded by his hands and a few hopeful widows.

He'd not so much as acknowledged her presence. Abigail was vastly relieved.

The horse finally rid himself of his rider, who hit the ground with a thud and a yelp of pain. It had been a decent ride and scattered applause broke out among the spectators.

"It sure is quiet around here today." Joshua slid onto the bench beside her.

"Yes, I noticed." Though there were occasional shouts of encouragement from the thin crowd, there was none of the steady hum of laughter and swell of excited conversation that usually accompanied the contests. "Did you find Marcus?" Abigail uttered the words softly out of the side of her mouth. She'd chosen a seat far enough away from everyone that she could speak quietly without anyone being the wiser, as long as she didn't turn to him and start to carry on a loud, animated conversation.

"Yeah. He's with Billy, huddled up by one of the candy booths, eyeing Hezkiah Wilson's daughter."

"Ah." The next competitor lasted only a few seconds, drawing hoots of derision from the Bar B contingent. "He seemed okay, then? He acted so strangely on the way over here, I was worried about him."

"Seemed as well as could be expected, to me."

"As well as could be expected?"

"It's an unsettlin' thing for a man, the first time a woman gets her clutches in deep." Joshua grinned. "I was sick to my stomach for a week, myself."

"Serves you right."

"Yeah, but it's got to be easier when you're twelve than when you're on the far side of twenty-five."

Twenty-five. When he'd met her. Abigail slanted a glance at him out of the corner of her eye, undecided as to whether to laugh out loud at his teasing or throw herself in his arms, she was so deeply touched.

But this was hardly the place to do either without drawing attention to herself. "So you think that's all it is then? I was afraid, maybe, that he was worried that he'd get teased about not entering anything, and — Oh! Hush up. It's Lippy's turn."

On the far side of the enclosure, Lippy was mounting up on an good-sized buckskin. Even from here, Abigail could see the horse had a nasty look in his eyes.

"Why is he insisting on doing this?" she fretted. "He might get hurt! And, even if it's not much, I need him healthy and working."

"He's showing off for you, of course."

"What?" she said, amazed.

"He'll do fine. Watch now, here he goes."

The handlers backed away from the horse, and, soon as he was free, the buckskin burst into motion. Bucking, twisting, kicking his rear feet high as if he could batter up against the bottom of the sky.

"Oh, look at that! He's doing good!"

Lippy's good fortune continued, and he managed to stay on a full count of five longer than anyone else had. When he finally tumbled off, Abigail held her breath until he jumped to his feet, clearly unhurt. He located his hat, which he'd lost early on, plopped it on his head, and craned his neck, obviously searching for someone. When his gaze lit on Abigail, he gave a huge grin and tipped his hat at her.

She clapped so hard her palms burned.

"I bet I could have stayed at least twenty seconds more," Joshua grumbled.

"I'm sure you could have." She tried not to look too amused. Though he was probably right; two summers ago, he'd swept the prizes in almost every single event. Their relationship had been tremblingly new then, and she'd almost burst with pride with the astounding knowledge that a man such as him favored her.

"You should have donated Buttercup. The whole thing would have been over in no time."

Joshua finally shifted in his seat, turning his back on the ring. It was too hard to watch the competition, wishing he was out there, knowing he'd never be able to do it again. Joshua'd always liked the challenge and excitement of the contests, not to mention the way Abbie had congratulated him on his victories.

Besides, he'd rather look at Abbie than at a bunch of old cowhands and some mangy horses any day.

She'd taken extra care today, coiling her hair into a tight twist. Tiny wisps of curls fluttered at her temples, and Joshua longed to search out all the pins and let the rest tumble down as well. Her pale blue dress had a slender flutter of pale ivory lace at her throat, and tiny buttons marched down the front of the bodice. His fingers itched to start undoing them.

Too much temptation. He'd probably do well to get out of here before he couldn't help himself and embarrassed her completely in public. Joshua doubted she'd much appreciate glancing down and finding most of her buttons unfastened.

"I'm gonna go on back to the ranch now," he said. "Best I keep an eye on things over there —"

"Can I sit down?" Horace stepped up and started to lower his rump to the bench — right in Joshua's lap.

"Ah . . ." Abigail's eyes went wide, and she raised a hand as if to stop him.

"Please?"

Joshua scooted out of the way just before Horace plopped down and she let out a sigh of relief.

"I . . . didn't know you were here. I didn't see you around earlier," Abigail offered, conscious of how upset

Horace had been the last time she'd seen him, unsure of just what shape their friendship was in.

"I just arrived. Had a few things to attend to, first." Bracing one hand on his knee, he leaned toward her. "I owe you an apology, Abigail. I'm sorry about what I said the other day. I really didn't mean to . . . I'm sorry."

Joshua took up a post behind them and glared down at their bent heads. Horace was tilted Abbie's way, like a tree that was gonna tip over in the first strong wind and fall right into her lap.

"It's all right, Horace."

"I was just frustrated, I guess, that my stock was doing so poorly. But I never should have taken it out on you."

"It's forgotten."

Darn it, Joshua thought, why was Abbie forgiving him so easily? Horace had *hollered* at her, for heaven's sake, and Joshua knew full well that Knicker had upset her. She shouldn't be giving Horace Knicker the time of day.

"Thank you." Horace bobbed his head. "How about you? How are things going? I don't see Davis anywhere around."

"He's not here." Abigail pressed a hand to her belly, trying to figure out what excuse to use this time. She was so tired of making up lies.

But why should she, really? She no longer hoped that her father would recover. No longer believed she needed to guard a pride that he'd lost with his sanity.

Much of what had kept her from telling anyone of her father's condition was her own reluctance, she realized. If she never said the words out loud, never told anyone outside the family, then maybe, somehow, it wouldn't be true.

With acceptance came a measure of peace. "He — he

won't be coming to events anymore, Horace. He's really not . . . he's really not very well."

"Oh, no." Horace's voice dripped with sympathy. "What happened? Is there any hope?"

"I . . . don't believe so."

"My dear Abigail. This must be so difficult for you."

Horace grabbed one of Abigail's hands and clutched it to his chest. A weak, almost concave chest, Joshua consoled himself.

It was all Joshua could do not snatch her hand back. At this rate, Knicker was going to start drooling over her fingers at any minute.

"If I can be of help to you in any way," he said solicitously, "I want you to feel free to call on me immediately."

Aw, hell. If Horace could touch her, well, so could Joshua.

He bent down and placed his mouth on her, right at the nape of her neck. She jumped, and he smiled against her skin.

Abigail swatted at the air behind her neck. "Stop that!"

"Stop what?" Horace sounded puzzled.

"There was . . . a fly buzzing around back there, bothering me."

Abigail's scent, lilacs and sun-warmed woman, invaded Joshua's senses. Soft little wisps of hair tickled his lips. He opened his mouth, sweeping his tongue along the edge of her collar.

"Ah . . . Horace?" Her voice went high. "Are things going better for you?"

"Well, no, actually, three more cows died just last night," he said, a distinct quiver in his voice.

"Oh, I'm so sorry."

Horace sighed deeply. "There's nothing anyone can

do, I suppose," he said mournfully. "I'll just have to pray that I'll be able to save one or two of them."

Even as he busied himself nuzzling the side of Abigail's neck, Joshua rolled his eyes. That was as blatant a play for sympathy as he'd ever heard. He only hoped she didn't fall for it.

"Abigail, are you all right? You seem to be a bit flushed," Horace asked with theatrical concern.

"I'm . . . fine. I just feel so badly about what's happening to you. I wish there was some way —"

Damn it! She was falling for Horace's sob story.

With calculated deliberation, he reached around her body and cupped his palm over her breast.

Abigail shrieked and sprang to her feet. "I'm really sorry, Horace, please forgive me, but I just remembered I have . . . to do something, and I really have to go *right now*."

Not looking back at what she was sure was Horace's bewildered, and probably hurt, expression, Abigail put her head down and charged through the crowds.

Four wagons clumped together in the shade near one wall of the fort. She ducked behind the nearest one and whirled on Joshua, who'd been unwise enough to follow her.

"What in the *world* did you think you were doing? How *could* you have—"

"Heck, Abbie, I would have thought you'd have figured out what I was doing by now."

This was the most frustrating part of Joshua's present condition, she decided. She could beat him over the head until she collapsed from exhaustion and he wouldn't feel a thing.

"My Lord, Joshua, I was never so embarrassed in all my—"

"He was making you feel guilty," Joshua put in.

"What?" Abigail jammed her arms over her chest and glowered at him, determined that Joshua was *not* going to talk and smile his way out of this one.

"Truth now, Abigail. You were falling for it, weren't you? I could see it. He was whimpering about his cows, giving you abused puppy eyes, and you started feeling all upset and guilty that you hadn't been able to help him, like it was all your fault in the first place, weren't you?"

"Well . . ." All right, maybe she *had* been feeling a tad guilty. Horace had looked so sad.

"Every single person you know is *not* your responsibility, Abigail. Horace Knicker is a grown man, and ranchin's a risky business, for you as much as anybody else. He can take his lumps just like everybody else."

"Hmm." Horace had been awfully apologetic, come to think of it. Especially after he'd been so angry with her the other day. Perhaps he really had just been trying another tactic to wheedle her out of some of her water.

Which did not, however, let Joshua off the hook. "Whatever the case with Horace, Joshua, I still cannot believe you did that! My Lord, you touched my—my—in *public*! With people around and everything!"

"Oh yeah." His eyes lit up, and he was all too clearly relishing the memory. "Wasn't it great? I can't believe I didn't think of it before. No one'd ever know. You could be sitting at the table, chatting with the hands, and I could just slide right underneath your skirts, and— Hey, wait a minute! Where are you going?"

Abigail rushed through the small crowds of spectators, looking for a clutch of people to bury herself in. Preferably *big* people, ones who would hide her for a little while. Not that Joshua wouldn't find her eventually, but perhaps she'd have enough time to get her temper and body under control first. A body that had responded to Joshua's words all too readily, in a way that was probably improper in her own bedroom in the middle of the night and which was surely blatantly sinful at midday in the midst of a gathering of her friends and neighbors.

She slipped into a small group of soldiers, briefly acknowledging their greetings before pretending to be absorbed in the activities in the center of the competition enclosure.

They were setting up the calf scramble now. Three calves—the most belligerent ones to be found—would be released into the area, to be chased madly around by all the young people who wished to join in. The three who managed to rope a calf and drag it into the large circle marked in the center would be the declared the winners.

Three burly hands dragged the calves to widely spaced starting points, awaiting the signal to release them. The contestants were herded into the center in one big clump, a group of perhaps two dozen children ranging in age from five to fifteen.

"They're just about ready to start, huh?" Joshua said from her left.

She refused to look at him. She was still annoyed at him, and, besides, she was terribly afraid that, if Joshua got a good look in her eyes, he'd see the residual passion and go ahead with exactly what he'd suggested behind the wagon. Or worse.

She occupied herself searching out the children she knew. There was Billy Mallery, Marcus' friend, a head taller than the rest, who'd been the first to capture a calf last year. And, next to him, someone with a blaze of red hair . . .

"Oh dear," she whispered. "Marcus is out there!"

"Is that so bad?"

"You know it is."

"That was two years ago, Abbie." Two years ago, the

last time Marcus had entered, when he'd been thoroughly embarrassed by his performance, painfully teased by some hands from the Bar B, and had sworn never to enter another competition as long as he lived, so help him God. "He's grown a lot since then."

"Yes, but has he *improved*?"

Marcus's face looked glum. He shifted from foot to foot, all the while shooting hopeful glances in the direction of the Wilson girl, who stood in a group of her friends, obviously attentive to the upcoming event.

Tension curled in Abigail's stomach. *Oh please*, she prayed, *let him have just this one thing. It's not such a big thing, and it would mean so much to him.*

A shout from the fort commander signaled the start. The hands released their calves and scrambled out of the way as quickly as possible. The children took off at a dead run.

The calves, already confused by the unfamiliar surroundings and unhappy at being hauled around by the hands, got one glimpse at the mob of shrieking children charging their way, kicked up their heels, and fled.

Following the action was difficult. Contestants pelted after bawling calves, kicking up choking clouds of dust. They zigzagged around, staggering behind their prey, tossing ropes that missed the calves and instead snared the heels of other children.

"You know," Joshua suggested, "I could—"

"Don't you dare."

"You don't even know what I was going to say."

"Yes I do." She shot him a glance meant to drive that idea right out of his head.

"He'd never know."

And Joshua would never know just how tempted she was to allow him to help Marcus win. Marcus would be so thrilled. But how could an accomplishment mean anything if it was achieved through interference instead of one's own skill? "No."

The contestants tended to move as a group, chasing after the nearest, and, with luck, slowest, calf together, hoping the other children might accidentally drive an animal their way.

Except Marcus, who was a good twenty yards away from the rest, walking slowly, his head down as if deep in thought. A limp sack draped over his shoulder.

Billy Mallery efficiently roped the largest calf and slowly towed it toward the center circle. The children dashed after the remaining two, which ran together just in front of them, tantalizingly out of reach.

One of the animals suddenly broke off in a burst of extra speed, putting some distance between it and the hollering crowd of his pursuers. The children apparently decided the other calf was an easier target, because they all turned to try and chase it down.

The faster one, dark brown with a white face, shot for the nearest clear space he could find. Except between him and that space stood Marcus.

The calf planted its feet and bellowed, clearly unwilling to get any nearer to the human in its path. Except this one wasn't screaming and chasing him. Marcus stood quietly, his eyes on the calf's.

"Go Marcus!" Abigail shouted, knowing this was the best chance he'd ever have. "Joshua, where's his rope, for heaven's sake?"

Slowly, making no move that might startle the skittish animal, Marcus lowered the sack to the ground and dug into it. He pulled out a shallow dish, which he set on the ground and filled with something from a small jug.

"What's he doing?" Abigail hissed at Joshua. "Why isn't he roping it?"

"Well, I'll be." Joshua smiled broadly. "Just wait."

The calf took a cautious step forward, eyeing the human in front of it with suspicion. It bawled a protest, but it been on short rations for weeks and the sweet smell of water was just too much for it.

The calf stepped forward and dipped its head to the dish. Marcus sidled carefully up beside it, hiding his rope behind his back.

"Oh!" Abigail shouted. "Did you see that? He got him, he got him, he got him!"

It was not the neatest job of roping anyone had ever seen. Marcus simply dropped the noose over the calf's head, snagging one ear on the way down. Still, it worked, and Marcus quickly tightened the rope and put his shoulder into dragging the unhappy calf to the center ring. It was slow going, until Marcus thought to fetch the water and lead the calf along with that.

When Marcus achieved the winner's circle, Billy clapped him on the back so hard that Marcus nearly ended up face down in the dirt. Flushed with victory, Marcus waved at Lizzie Wilson before he caught sight of Abigail cheering madly.

And Abigail knew that, if she could bring her father back to reality for just one moment, it would be this one, and the sight of Marcus's beaming, triumphant smile.

29

"You're back."

Joshua smiled down at Abigail as he climbed into bed next to her. "And you're awake."

"Maybe I missed you." She rolled to her side, scooted over to give him room. She rested her elbow on the mattress and propped her head in her hand.

It must be far past midnight, an unusually dark night. Only a little pale light spilled through the window.

"I wanted to look things over, make sure everything was all right after this evening."

"And was it?" Abigail held her breath, waiting for the answer.

"Yes."

"Good." He'd found no more dead cows, then. They'd come across three, on the way back from the fort, all clearly marked with the Rolling G brand. Freshly slaughtered animals, right on the route they'd take home, as if someone wanted to make absolutely certain they found them.

He sprawled out beside her, mimicking her pose, except turned on the other side to face her. He touched her jaw. "About the cows . . . I'm sorry about that, Abbie. That I couldn't prevent it."

"Joshua, you have nothing to apologize for." She rushed on before he could argue. "And I'm tired of you trying to apologize for things that aren't your fault. You're doing every single thing you can—we all are. I know it, and so do you. I'm incredibly thankful to have you here, and that's that."

He smiled at her fierceness. "All right."

"All right? Just like that? I'll have to remember this. I don't think I've ever won an argument with you quite so quickly before."

"I'll try not to make a habit of it."

He tugged her close, settled her with her head on his shoulder and her legs tangled with his, his arm draped around her waist, and contentment sighed through her.

It was exactly the position she'd fallen asleep in that evening. Like two long-married people, she thought, too tired from their day to give a physical expression of their love the attention it demanded, and so they turned to a softer way, sharing emotion with warmth and closeness instead of sex. Not as exciting, perhaps, but somehow deeply touching all the same.

He combed through her hair, and fingered small circles on her shoulder blades.

"Joshua? Aren't you sleepy?"

His answer was slow in coming. "I . . . don't sleep."

Surprised, she twisted, looking up into his guarded expression. "You don't sleep?"

"No." He shrugged, pretending it didn't matter, this symptom of his inhumanity, just another reminder of the barriers that separated them.

"What do you do all the time, then, while I sleep?"

"I keep an eye on the ranch. And I watch you." He'd spent hours watching her. Drinking in her scent, listening to the subtle sounds of her breathing, watching her pulse beat in her throat. Storing up images, memories, feelings. Remembrances that would have to last him forever.

"You watched me all that time? Weren't you bored?"

"No."

At his simple answer, so obviously true, Abigail's heart squeezed. She'd been so certain that she was madly in love with Joshua before, but that emotion, strong and turbulent as it had been, paled next to the feelings that bound her to him now.

"I don't know if I can go back to sleep," she said, "knowing that you're watching me. What if I drool?"

"Not too much."

"Joshua!"

"I can leave, if it bothers you."

"No! Stay."

"What then?" One corner of his mouth lifted. "We could just stare at each other for the rest of the night, I suppose."

"That doesn't sound so bad to me." His face blurred in the darkness, shadows carved beneath his cheekbones and jaw. But his eyes gleamed light, beautiful. "Or you could tell me what in heaven's name you were doing in Colorado for that flood to get you in the first place."

"It's not so much of a story." His hands were warm, rubbing tension out of the small of her back. "I couldn't stay in Texas, after you turned me down." His eyes shimmered with the memories, with regrets. "I'd had more than enough of the South, during the war, so west seemed the obvious choice."

"You never talked about it. The war, I mean."

He filled his fist with her hair, relished the silken feel

of it against his rough fingers. "It's not pretty. Not the kind of thing a lady wants to hear." He smiled. "Even one who's more of a *woman* than a lady."

"It couldn't have been any worse than I've imagined."

"You . . . imagined it?"

"Of course. I knew you'd been there."

They were memories he'd kept well buried. Memories that had deserved that burial. It felt strange to dig them up, to pull them out and look at them and tell her about them. Unexpectedly freeing.

"It was— Aw, damn, I'm not even sure what the hell I was fighting about. I was young, and everyone I knew was going, and so I went, too."

It wasn't an unusual story, Abigail knew. But this was Joshua, and that made all the difference, made her have to fight against the lump that rose in her throat.

"I was just a plain ol' foot soldier. Expendable. Belly-deep in the muck with shots flying right over my head." With no family, no one to even care whether he lived or died. He hadn't even had an address to put on the forms he'd filled out when he'd first joined the army, in the space that asked where to send his remains to.

He tightened his arms around her, squeezing so tight that it almost forced the air from Abigail's lungs. But she said nothing. If it helped him to hold her that tight, she'd gladly welcome the discomfort.

"I guess it doesn't really matter why I went in the first place. Don't take long before you're mostly just fightin' for your life and the one of the guy next to you, anyway."

He buried his face in her neck, letting the smell of lilacs and sleep-warmed woman overwhelm him, using it to wash away the remembered odor of battle, of sulfur and smoke and blood.

"That's pretty much it," he mumbled, once the images receded again. "Got any more questions for me?"

"Of course."

He lifted his head, looking into her smiling eyes. "You do?"

"It's too late to back out now, Joshua. I've got you at my mercy. Maybe I'll interrogate you until dawn."

He could think of worse ways to spend the night.

"Go ahead."

"When you asked me to go away with you— Why were you so insistent we *go* someplace? What was so wrong with staying here?"

He sighed. How did she always, unerringly, find her way to the times and places that he'd behaved the worst, said the most stupid things? She was going to expose all his flaws before she was finished.

"I knew what everybody was sayin'."

"I'm not sure I understand."

He shook his head. "I knew what I was. A poor, kick-around cowboy, with nothing to offer you but a hitch in his step. I knew people were sayin' that I was just chasin' after you 'cause I wanted a share of the Rollin' G."

Her eyes went wide, beautiful, deep and dark as the night.

"I wanted to show everyone that I was the kind of man who could look after his own, without havin' to take handouts from his father-in-law. I figured, after we went somewhere and got a little more established, after I proved I could make it on my own, we could come back if you wanted to." How many other foolish things had he done, in the name of pride? he wondered. "I wanted everybody to know that I wasn't courtin' you for the ranch."

"But Joshua,"—her smile went straight to his heart— "*I* always knew that."

"I know that—now."

And suddenly all the guilt, all the regrets and frustrations and *didn't*s that were all twisted up together in his guts, let go.

He was tired of kicking himself for all the things he'd done wrong, everything he'd been unable to prevent. He had not chosen this situation, hadn't picked the limitations on him, the things he could and couldn't do. He'd done his best. Made the best choices he knew how at the time.

Because Abigail was in his arms, smiling at him, and he knew that somewhere, somehow, he must have done something very right to earn this.

30

Abigail swiped at her forehead with the back of her hand, scowling at the steer in front of her, who refused to stand still for its treatment. Ungrateful ox.

It was just another hot, miserable day in west Texas. And more of her cows had come down with screw-worms.

She was working on the southeastern corner of the ranch, not far from where Joshua had located her father. Because the areas of ungrazed land were getting smaller and farther apart, they'd decided to divide the herd. Abigail was with a small group, and she knew Sledge had driven the bulk of the rest of the herd to an untouched patch of grass just to her northwest.

She wasn't certain where Lippy and Pecos were; they'd scattered to other corners of the ranch right after breakfast. Marcus had promised to stay home and keep a sharp eye on Davis. Abigail wasn't taking any chances that her father might wander off again.

Joshua was off on one of his tours of their borders.

He'd been reluctant to leave her. It was obvious that their discovery of the slaughtered cattle the previous night had worried him and he was convinced that whoever was behind it—though Joshua was certain it was Hallenbeck—would make another, probably more decisive, move soon.

Truthfully, seeing the carcasses arranged along the wagon path had spooked Abigail a bit, too. But if someone was going to run around killing off her cows, she wanted Joshua wafting around checking on them instead of worrying over her, and she'd finally convinced him that she'd be all right by herself for a little while. After all, she had her gun, strapped comfortingly at her waist, and he really wouldn't be gone very long.

She slapped the doctored steer on its rump, sending it on its way. Around her, other cows slobbered over the grass and crunched contentedly, flicking their tails at the swarm of flies that hovered over them.

Pressing a hand to the small of her back, Abigail arched, working out the stiffness from a morning of bending and turning. She picked up her jar of salve and walked through the herd, carefully checking for any more infected animals.

Simultaneously, all the cattle stopped eating and lifted their heads.

Perhaps someone was coming. Shading her eyes, Abigail squinted into the distance.

In the flick of a tail, they were off.

"What the—?" She looked around, wondering what had startled them all. She hadn't heard a thing.

The deep rumbling started beneath her feet, growing stronger and stronger until it quivered in her belly.

"Damn it!" Sledge's herd must have spooked, too. And they were all coming her way.

There was no time, nothing she could do. No place to

hide, no escape fast enough. The cattle were quicker than she was.

Around her, the running herd thickened, then surged into a teeming mass of cattle packed so tightly that she couldn't distinguish individual animals, just a roiling torrent of tails and long, sharp horns.

Don't move, she ordered herself. Abigail fought the panic that told her to run, escape, to try and fight her way out. Her heart thundered in her throat.

And then Joshua was there, wrapping his body protectively around her as if he could shield her from the crushing herd.

"Don't move!" he shouted in her ear.

"I know!" A herd in full stampede would generally split around anything—and anyone—in its path. The real danger came when they slowed down. More than one cowhand who'd survived a stampede had been killed once the confused, exhausted cows began to mill.

Strange as it seemed, Abigail was safest right where she was—as long as she didn't move.

Easier said than done. Every nerve in Abigail's body screamed *run*. Her vision blurred into a moving patchwork quilt of brown and black and white hides.

Joshua debated whether he should attempt to simply lift Abigail right out of the mess. He was fairly sure he could do it. But *fairly* wasn't a chance he was willing to take with her life. The alternative was too brutal, the possibility of Abigail caught beneath the trampling hooves.

He knew he had to try to head off the cows, to force them into circling before they broke for Horace's land. But not yet; not until they'd all safely run past Abbie.

No, there wasn't anything he could do yet, except hold her while she trembled in his arms.

The cows didn't bawl in fear. But other deafening

sounds made up for what they didn't voice, the roaring thunder of their hooves and the crash of horns slamming together.

Intense body heat blasted off the animals, feeling to Abigail like it would sear her skin. She turned her face against Joshua's chest and wished she could block out the noise of the stampede as well as the sight of it.

She lost all sense of time; it no longer had any relevance beyond the endless waiting for the herd to run itself out.

The Rolling G had a small herd. How could there be so many of them? she wondered. It seemed like there were thousands more, as it went on and on.

Gradually, the intensity of heat and sound lessened. Abigail raised her head, to find only a few stragglers galloping past her.

"God, Abbie!" Joshua grabbed her upper arms and held her a bit away from him, where he could check her over any signs of injury. "Abbie, are you all right?"

"I think so," she said slowly, mentally cataloging all her parts. They seemed in working order. "Yes, I'm fine."

"Oh, thank God." He kissed her hard, a kiss that mingled terror and shock and sweet relief.

"Do you think you can go and head them off?" she said when he'd raised his head. "I can't. Lord only knows where my horse might've run off to."

"Yes, but—" He stared over her shoulder and his face hardened, his eyes going sharp and cold. "Not just yet."

Abigail turned to find Sledge madly galloping toward them.

He yanked his horse to a stop and nearly flew off it. "Abigail! Are you all right? I don't know what set 'em off, and I couldn't stop 'em!"

"I'm all right, Sledge."

"Abbie," Joshua said, his voice soft and very dangerous. "Get out your gun."

"My gun?" she asked, so confused she forgot to worry about whether Sledge might hear her.

"Get out your gun and ask him why he stampeded the herd."

Wide-eyed with shock, Abigail stared at him. Joshua would have given much if he could have spared her this, but the truth was the truth.

"I saw him, Abbie. I was heading back to you after looking over the west border, and I saw him start them off."

Slowly, as if she were moving through water, she turned to Sledge. "Dear God, Sledge, why?"

"Why, what? I don't know, they just—"

"*Sledge.*"

He must have heard the overwhelming hurt in her voice, seen the accusation in her eyes, for suddenly he sagged, turning into an old man in the space of a few seconds.

The sound of galloping horses rolled to them.

"Might as well wait 'til they get here for the explanations," Sledge said, without a flicker of expression shading his words. "That way I don't gotta do 'em twice."

Pecos and Lippy streaked toward them, jumping off and gaining Abigail's side before their horses had even skidded to a full stop.

"What's goin' on?" Lippy panted, puffing from his mad ride across the plain. "We felt the rumblin', and came quick as we could."

"We found out who's behind all the problems we've been having, that's what's been going on," Abigail said quietly.

"Who?" Lippy craned his neck, searching for the villain.

"Right here." She nodded at Sledge.

"But . . . But . . ." Lippy was struck dumb, motionless, stunned as a poleaxed steer for a good ten seconds. Then his face flushed bright red, a vein throbbing in the side of his neck.

If Pecos was equally surprised, he didn't show it. His only reaction was the narrowing of his eyes to thin, dangerous slits.

"All right, Sledge. Go ahead," she ordered.

"I tol' you you shoulda sold out."

"So?"

"So this place is no good for you. It drove Davis crazy, and it's turning you into a withered old maid, and Marcus sure as hell don't want it."

"What?" Obviously the stampede had damaged her ears, for he certainly could not have said what she just heard. "Are you trying to tell me you sabotaged my ranch *for my own good*?"

Sledge compressed his lips together into a thin line.

"Ask him how much B.J. paid him," Joshua suggested, playing a hunch.

Abigail folded her arms against her chest and lowered a glare on Sledge. "How much is B.J. paying you?"

"That's ain't really the point—"

"*How much*?"

"Well, hell." His voice grew petulant. "I been a hand—a good one—all my life, and what have I got to show for it 'cept a pair a worn-out boots and a nasty case of rheumatism? Ain't I earned a little bit of retirement money?"

Anger burst in her brain, throbbing behind her temples. "And that's a good enough reason to try and kill me?"

"Kill you!" If Sledge's shock was feigned, he was the best actor she'd ever seen. "I knew you got enough sense not to go flapping around in the middle of the stampede. You weren't gonna get hurt."

"And what about dumping me into the well? I wasn't going to get hurt then, either?"

"The *well*? What the hell are you talk—"

The *crack* of sound barely registered through her haze of fury. Neither did the geyser of dirt that kicked up near her feet.

But Lippy's shout sure did.

"Oh gawd! Someone's shootin' at us!"

31

Something slammed her from behind and drove her painfully down to the ground.

She squirmed beneath the dead weight, trying to lift her head enough to see what was going on.

"Stay down!" Sledge hissed in her ear. "He's behind those rocks, shootin' at us."

"Who is?"

"Hell if I know."

She heard the sharp report of a gun, then, very near her, the bark of returning fire.

Sledge eased up just enough so she could lift her head a fraction.

The buffalo grass provided poor protection against an ambush. A few yards to her right, Lippy lay on his stomach, firing his pistol at measured intervals at the nearest of the weathered boulders that marked this corner of the Rolling G.

Beyond Lippy, Pecos, his own gun clenched in his hand, crawled slowly through the grass beneath the cover of Lippy's shots, making his way to the rock and the gunman behind it.

And Joshua— Where the hell was Joshua?

And just what the *hell* was going on? First there'd been the stampede, and then Sledge was the one who was trying to run her off the Rolling G, and now someone *else* was shooting at her, and Sledge was trying to save her?

No wonder her head hurt.

An unholy screech echoed through the air, the sound of rock grinding on rock. Ever so slowly, the boulders began to shift, grating on one another.

The rocks let go, tumbling over and crashing down in a cloud of gray dust, exposing a very shocked Horace Knicker, who immediately raised his hands—and his gun—in surrender.

If the rest of the day was somewhat less exciting, it was still much busier than Abigail would have liked.

It took most of the day to haul Sledge and Horace off to the fort. A young captain locked them up in an otherwise empty block of cells and promised that, very soon, they'd be issuing B.J. Hallenbeck a similar invitation to enjoy their "hospitality."

To Abigail's relief, he'd also promised her that Sledge's sentence was likely to be light. For, though much of the problems at the Rolling G were his responsibility, the truly dangerous ones had been engineered by Horace. And, when it had come down to it, Sledge had tried to protect her life.

Abigail had a hard time believing it was all over. After so many weeks of tension and worry, the absence of it left her stunned. She remembered little of the long ride home, too busy trying to make sense of the bits of thoughts that flew through her mind, seemingly without regard to logic or any connection to one another.

Now, an hour past sunset, she stood in her night-shadowed room, staring at Joshua, and wondered: *how long?*

A minute? An hour? A day? How long before God snatched him from her? Would he disappear in the flash of an instant, without even the chance for a word of good-bye? Or would he fade away slowly, like morning fog burning off, while she desperately tried to clutch at the shreds to try to hold him here?

"When?" she whispered.

"I'm not certain." Joshua blinked, a film of moisture sheening his eyes. "Soon, I think. They sent me here to keep you safe, and now you are. My assignment is finished."

She wanted to rage, to batter at the walls of heaven until she *made* them allow him to stay. But this was beyond her control, beyond her world, leaving her with nothing to do but cry.

Only she had years left to cry. She would not spend one precious remaining moment with Joshua so foolishly.

She walked to Joshua, her footfalls echoing in the still room; lonely, empty. "If this is all we have," she said, "let's not waste it."

He cradled her face in hands that trembled. "Oh, Abbie."

"I don't want to regret anything this time. I don't want to leave anything undone."

He lowered his head slowly, inch by inch. She wanted to cry to him to hurry, to remind him they didn't know how much time they had. But she was powerless to do anything but wait for him and pray that they'd have enough time.

Enough! What a foolish prayer. There would never be enough.

Their mouths met, a kiss encompassing a thousand memories, a thousand promises that could never be fulfilled. Her breath rushed out of her parted lips, poured into him, filling him with Abbie.

Not enough time. The thought burned in his brain, in his soul. He tried to push it away, tried to focus on the woman in his arms and the love in his heart, and not what he was about to lose. But it hovered over his shoulder, whispered in the hollow spaces inside him, and flavored their kiss with tears.

Without lifting his head, lips clinging to hers, he slid his hands down, over the long slope of her neck and sturdy curves of her shoulders, and found the buttons that held together her dress. He dealt with the buttons easily—too easily; they slid through the holes as quickly as the minutes were slipping away from them.

When she was naked, he broke away with a sigh of regret, stepping back so he could look at her once more and brand the vision of her in his mind. He needed to remember her like this, faint moonlight shadowing her form, her eyes languorous with the passion he'd called forth.

He stripped for her, without eagerness or impatience, unwilling to let the uncertainty goad him into speed. Into rushing through this night. He meant to take his time, to draw it out, to savor it, to—as Abbie had said—leave nothing undone, nothing unsaid.

He took her by the hand and led her to the bed she thought of as her bridal bed, the one she wished with all her heart was a beginning instead of a bittersweet end.

"Joshua," she said as he laid her out on the soft sheets, "I love you."

His smile was as fleeting as it was sad. "I know."

Unwilling to close her eyes for even a moment, needing to capture everything of this night she could, every sight and sound and smell and feeling, she kept her eyes open, watching as he bent over her body.

He touched her. His hands skated down her arms, floated over her thighs. His thumbs circled her nipples, drawing soft sighs of pleasure that began deep inside her. His fingers rippled over her ribs and danced over her belly, slipping down to stroke shallow and deep, to make her arch against his hand and call his name.

He tasted her. His mouth roamed, teased. The inside of her elbow, the hollow of her throat, the swell of her breast were all places that drew him. Ever so gently, his teeth closed over her nipple, and she lifted her hips against his.

In so many ways, Joshua was disconnected from this world—denied taste and smell and texture. But with Abbie, it was all there, in acute, near-painful clarity. Her, he could taste . . . smell . . . feel.

With her, he was whole and alive and *real*.

It was as if, when she breathed, he breathed again, too.

He wanted to sate himself in her, to drown so deeply in Abbie that he would never find his way out. To absorb her through his skin.

He moved up to kiss her again, laying himself between her legs. His erection nudged the opening to her softness, making him grit his teeth with the need to bury himself deeply within her, but he found himself unwilling to take that last final step that would take them toward completion.

Take them toward the end.

"Joshua." Abigail could see him over her in the dark, the harsh planes of his face and the soft warmth of his eyes. She'd thought he'd taught her of passion, that they'd explored together the many shades of pleasure they could make between them.

But this was something more. Something that blended heat and warmth, coupled passion and friendship and companionship, condensed a lifetime of loving into one single night.

She tilted her hips to nudge him closer, bringing a bare inch of the tip inside, stretching her, giving her a hint of what there could be.

Joshua shuddered, a groan ripping from him, and slid in, entering her completely.

It was as much as she'd dreamed, and a hundred times more.

Unthinkingly, she threw her arms around him to hold him close.

Her heart stopped.

Oh God. She could touch him!

She could feel the broad, hard muscles of his back beneath her palms, the mist of sweat that slicked him and made it easy to slide her hands over his skin.

She bit his shoulder to stifle her sobs, the trickle of tears slipping down her temples and dampening her hair. Her hands grew greedy. She streaked them over his body, seeking the contours she remembered, the swells of muscle and the angles of joints. She skimmed her palms over his back, pressing them flat against the hollows on the side of his buttocks, letting them ride with the flex of his hips.

The smell of him seeped through her, and the heat of his skin. She could feel him stroking deep inside, the sweet-achy slide of flesh on flesh, hard on soft.

"Joshua!" And then she lost all thought, released all grasp on the earth and herself, bursting into a place where there was nothing else but him.

*   *   *

Hours later, Abigail awoke to an empty bed, an empty heart, and the sound of rain.

32

Joshua had given her one last gift.

She ran across her room, dashing through the house, stumbling down the stairs in her haste, and fled out into the rain.

It soaked her immediately, warm torrents of water that poured over her, as if heaven had simply opened a dam and let the water rush through.

The sky was low, thickly covered with a sheet of bruise-gray clouds. So dark, it was impossible to tell even whether it was day or night.

She ran away from the ranch and into the open plains, where the fierce wind blew the rain in sheets against her face. Mud spattered her bare feet. Long blades of grass slapped at her shins.

Her thin nightdress grew as soaked as if she'd jumped into the pond, and it clung to her body. Her hair plastered to her head, streamed down her back.

When she could run no farther, when the ache in her side made her bend at the waist to ease it, she threw her arms wide and lifted her head to the sky, slowly spinning, letting the warm rain mingle with the tears on her cheeks. She opened her mouth, let the sweet, pure water pour in. It tasted new, fresh.

In the distance, where the dense, black clouds were most impenetrable, a brief, intense light flashed. Lightning? But she heard no thunder.

The water blurred her vision, and she blinked to clear it. The sheets of water undulated, like curtains stirred by a breeze. Her heart rose into her throat.

There was something there.

She blinked again, and her vision cleared, revealing a black shape steadily walking to her from out of the storm.

A form that was solid, alive, and lovingly familiar.

"Joshua." She broke into a run, the stitch in her side forgotten. His pace picked up, faster and faster until he, too, ran madly through the furious rain.

Three feet apart, they stopped, stared at each other.

She was afraid to go to him, afraid to try to touch him and find that he wasn't there, that he was only a wish and a dream given form by her loneliness and heartache.

He wore only a black pair of pants that sagged low on his hips. Water poured over his chest, slicked his shoulders. With both hands, he wiped the rain from his face and slicked his hair back, throwing the bones of his face into bold relief, dark and wet and beautiful.

"Abbie," he said softly, yet she could hear him perfectly over the pounding rain, "it's really me."

Slowly, he stretched a hand to her . . . a hand missing the first joint of the middle finger. Just as it had been when he was alive.

"Oh God!" The emotion burst forth within her, wild, free, and powerful as the storm. She hurled herself in his arms, and they closed around her. Strong. Safe. *Real*.

"It's you, you're really here, how can this be?" The words came out in short bursts, between the sounds of her sobs and her laughter. "Wait a minute, let me see."

She bent and pressed her ear to his chest. His steady heartbeat thundered in her ear, echoed in her soul.

"My God, you're really alive!" She was a whirlwind of motion, unable to touch him quickly enough, everywhere, to run her hands over every inch of his body and make certain that it was really him. "I thought you said you didn't do miracles."

"The rain? I had a little help."

"Not the rain." She flashed a smile, one that felt wonderful and free. Happy. "You."

"I had a little help with that, too."

She didn't want to ask. Better to revel in the moment, to drown herself in joy. But she had to know. "How long?"

His eyes were dark, intense as the storm. "Forever."

Their kiss was flavored with rain and tears and miracles.

"Joshua," she said against his mouth, unwilling to draw back any farther, even to speak, "what about my father?"

He cupped her face in his big hands. Scarred hands, with one damaged finger. A man's hands. His thumbs slid easily over her wet cheeks, a soothing stroke.

"I'm sorry," he said, the words stark with regret.

Abigail swallowed hard. "How long?"

For a while she thought he wasn't going to answer her. "I can't tell you that."

He wrapped his arms around her, pulled her close, tucked her head beneath his chin. The heat of him soaked through her clothes, warmed her deep inside.

"But I can tell you this," he said. "When it's all over, all the pain that happened here won't matter anymore.

And there'll be someone waiting for him on the other side."

So many questions. But there was plenty of time to ask them. A lifetime. Now, she simply hugged her arms around his waist and thought perhaps she'd never let go.

"I can promise you, though," he went on, his voice vibrating in her ear, "that there'll be blessings along the way, too. And that, no matter what, you won't have to do it alone anymore."

It was more than enough.

They rocked together, as the sweet rain poured down and washed the land clean. As the parched, sterile earth soaked in the water, and new life burst deep and green within it.

"Joshua?" she said at last.

"Hmm?"

"I guess it's a good thing they never found your body in Colorado, huh? This would have been awfully difficult to explain."

The laughter swelled, filled his heart and his life, and lifted up through the clouds.

Joshua still thought that letting him die was an awfully strange way for the Big Boss to matchmake, but who was he to complain?

He'd found his own heaven in West Texas.

Author's Notes

Alzheimer's, the disease from which Abigail's father suffered, was identified in 1912. Today there are still few effective treatments. Those seeking more information may wish to contact the Alzheimer's Association at 919 N. Michigan Ave., Suite 1000, Chicago, IL 60611–1676, or call (800) 272–3900.

Fort Barrens, Texas, and the immediate vicinity are entirely products of my imagination. However, west-central Texas is a mighty big place, and I'm certain many a cowboy and his lady have found their own heavens there.

Let HarperMonogram
Sweep You Away

❧❧❧

A KNIGHT TO REMEMBER by Christina Dodd
RITA Award-winning Author
A gifted healer, Lady Edlyn saves Hugh de Florisoun's life, only
to have the knight claim her as his own. Iit will take all Edlyn's
will not to surrender to the man determined to win her heart.

HEAVEN IN WEST TEXAS by Susan Kay Law
Golden Heart Award-winning Author
Joshua West is sent back from heaven to protect Abigail Grier,
the Texas beauty who once refused his love. As the passion
between them ignites, Joshua and Abigail get a second chance
to find their own piece of paradise.

THE PERFECT BODY by Amanda Matetsky
Annie March has no idea how a dead body ended up in the
trunk of her car, no less a perfect body! When someone tries to
pin the murder on her, sexy police detective Eddie Lincoln may
be Annie's ticket to justice—and romance.
*"Smart and sassy...a charming combination of mystery,
romance, and fun."* —Faye Kellerman

CANDLE IN THE WINDOW by Christina Dodd
A HarperMonogram Classic
Lady Saura of Roget is summoned to the castle of a magnificent
knight whose world has exploded into agonizing darkness.
Saura becomes the light of Sir William of Miraval's life, until a
deadly enemy threatens their newfound love.

And in case you missed last month's selections...
A ROYAL VISIT by Rebecca Baldwin
An affair of state becomes an affair of the heart when Prince
Theodoric of Batavia travels to England to find a bride. He
is looking for a titled lady, but a resourceful and charming
merchant's daughter shows him that love can be found where
one least expects it.

SIREN'S SONG by Constance O'Banyon
Over Seven Million Copies of Her Books Are in Print!
Beautiful Dominique Charbonneau is determined to free her
brother, even if it means becoming a stowaway aboard Judah
Gallant's pirate ship. But Gallant is not the rogue he appears,
and Dominique is torn between duty and a love she might
never know again.

THE AUTUMN LORD by Susan Sizemore
Time Travel Romance
Truth is stranger than fiction when '90s woman Diane Teal is
transported back to medieval France and must rely on the
protection of Baron Simon de Argent. She finds herself unable
to communicate except when telling stories. Fortunately she
and Simone both speak the language of love.

GHOST OF MY DREAMS by Angie Ray
RITA and Golden Heart Award-winning Author
Miss Mary Goodwin refuses to believe her fiancé's warnings that
Helsbury House is haunted—until the deceased Earl appears.
Will the passion of two young lovers overcome the ghost, or is he
actually a bit of a romantic himself?

Let Your Imagination Run Wild

DREAMCATCHER by Dinah McCall

"A gripping, emotional story that satisfies on every level."
—Debbie Macomber

Amanda Potter escapes her obsessive husband through the warm embrace of a dream that draws her through time. Detective Jefferson Dupree knows his destiny is intertwined with Amanda's and he must convince her that her dream lover is only a heartbeat away.

CHRISTMAS ANGELS: Three Heavenly Romances by Debbie Macomber

Over Twelve Million Copies of Her Books in Print
The angelic antics of Shirley, Goodness, and Mercy are featured in this collection that promises plenty of romance and dreams that come true.

DESTINY'S EMBRACE by Suzanne Elizabeth

Award-winning Time Travel Series
Winsome criminal Lacey Garder faces imprisonment until her guardian angel sends her back in time to 1879. Rugged Marshal Matthew Brady is the law in Tranquility, Washington Territory, and he soon finds Lacey guilty of love in the first degree.